An evil from beyond...and a traitor in their midst...

time of treason

THE TYON COLLECTIVE BOOK TWO

Susan M. MacDonald

WWW.BREAKWATERBOOKS.COM

LIBRARY AND ARCHIVES CANADA CATALOGUING IN PUBLICATION
MacDonald, Susan M., 1962-, author
Time of treason / Susan M. MacDonald.
(The Tyon Collective ; book 2)
ISBN 978-1-55081-471-2 (pbk.)
I. Title.
PS8625.D7725T54 2014   jC813'.6   C2014-900564-4

 Canada Council **Conseil des Arts**
for the Arts   du Canada   Canada   Newfoundland Labrador

We acknowledge the support of the Canada Council for the Arts,
which last year invested $157 million to bring the arts to Canadians
throughout the country. We acknowledge the Government of
Canada through the Canada Book Fund and the Government
of Newfoundland and Labrador through the Department of Tourism,
Culture and Recreation for our publishing activities.

PRINTED IN CANADA

Breakwater Books is committed to choosing papers and
materials for our books that help to protect our environment.
To this end, this book is printed on a recycled paper that is
Forest Stewardship Council® certified.

MIX
Paper from
responsible sources
FSC® C004071

For Christopher, Caileigh and Jamieson.

This book is dedicated to my mum, Margot.

Riley Cohen stood with her back to the door and waited for the axe to fall. Her heart was pounding hard enough to rattle her teeth. Her legs felt like jelly and a sick weight settled in the pit of her stomach. Any minute, the apartment would be crawling with Tyon operatives. *Don't panic*, she repeated silently, over and over. *Keep still. Don't make a sound. And* don't *touch your orb*. She clenched both her fists to keep from gripping the powerful crystal in her pocket but it was nearly impossible. Every fibre of her being was programed to answer the orb's Tyon call. Which she was *not* going to do.

What on Earth had she done to deserve this?

The answer, of course, was nothing. It was her special abilities that created this disaster. The Tyons had inserted a gene in her DNA that granted her the skill to read minds and heal physical injuries just by concentrating her thoughts, which made her a potential weapon for the Tyon forces as well as their enemies. The same genetic aberration had made Alec Anderson, the boy shivering with fear and exhaustion next to her, more powerful than any other human alive. One of his powers, to open and move through rifts in time, had helped them escape the most formidable evil force in the galaxy, and brought them back here to where it all began. But that ability was a double-edged sword. Moving in time was something so rare and so dangerous that it wasn't permitted. The Tyon scans had apparently noted the time rift he'd created to escape and had

1

tracked the shift, and consequently her, Alec and their Guardian, Darius, to this apartment. Which meant the Tyons were baying for Alec's blood. And it would be up to Darius to bring them to safety.

"Get us out of here," she whispered through clenched teeth. "We're toast if they find us."

Darius Finn leaned over. "Shut up. I'm working on it." He grunted in pain. He was holding tightly to Alec's kicking older brother; one arm around his chest like a steel band, pinning Peter's arms to his sides, and the other tightly clamped over Peter's mouth. "They'll search this room any minute. Use the window."

"Are you crazy? We're on the second story. There's no fire escape," Riley hissed back. But it was no use. Darius was right. Any second now Darius's former commander, Logan, and his goons were going to barrel through the one-inch plywood door she was leaning against, slap them all in the alien equivalent of handcuffs and march them off.

"Open it. Climb out." Darius gave the order but it was unnecessary. Already Alec was climbing onto his desk and reaching for the screen.

Riley groaned. That might be fine for Mr. Super-Ninja-Tyon-Operative Finn or Alec-the-mega-athlete but she was an ordinary seventeen year old girl who was *not* flinging herself anywhere without a safety net and tranquilizers. The window over the desk was wide enough for any of them to climb through. That wouldn't be the problem. The broken legs when they landed would.

"Alec is dead if they get him," Darius mouthed the words. "Move."

Suddenly, the sound of footsteps on the other side of the door broke the silence. Riley shot Darius an agonized glance. It was too late. They were here. Any second they'd find Alec's parents, both unconscious from a combination of the fight that had broken out when the three of them winked into existence from the future and Darius's necessary modification of their memories. The instant Logan woke them up…

Heart in her mouth, she zipped over to the desk and clambered onto the chair. Alec had pulled the screen off with practiced ease. He gingerly put the screen on the floor and gripped the upper sill.

"No sign of an Operative, sir," a man's accent-less voice cut through the silence from the apartment hallway.

Riley flapped her hands at Alec to hurry him.

Alec leaned back to whisper, "Roll when you land," before he ducked through and disappeared from sight. Riley nipped into his vacated spot and gripped the sides of the window. Without looking down, she shimmied her legs through the opening. They dangled over nothingness. Don't think about the distance, she ordered herself.

She heard the kitchen door close sharply. That left this bedroom, Alec's parents' room and a closet left to search. Galvanized, she pushed herself off the ledge before she could change her mind. The actual falling took a lot less time than she thought it would. She hit the hard ground and rolled into some bushes, more out of accident than intention. Alec grabbed her arm before the shock of landing had even penetrated her consciousness. He hauled her to her feet.

"Run," he urged unnecessarily.

Her ankle hurt. Not enough to prevent weight bearing, but enough to slow her to a hobble. She glanced behind and upwards, just in time to see Peter, his legs flailing and an expression of pure horror in his eyes, fall with Darius's arms still wrapped around him in a vice.

She didn't see them land but heard the impact. Focusing every ounce of her attention on keeping upright and ignoring the pain, she tried to keep up with Alec. They ran down the weed-choked lawn, skirted a couple of bikes lying abandoned on the sidewalk, and between two parked cars to cross the street. With every step, she expected

9

to hear "that's them" and feel the cruel hold of Tyon power wrap around her, dropping her to the ground like a sack of bricks.

Riley followed Alec up a slight incline and into the shadow of another rundown apartment building. Between that and a midrise tenement block, a small grove of spindly trees created a temporary hide-a-way. Alec ducked under the nearest branches, finding the worn dirt path easily in the early evening gloom, and disappeared. Riley plunged in behind him. After only ten steps they exited to a cleared gravel space that had once been a children's play area. No one would let kids play there now; the obscene graffiti alone would put most mothers off.

"Keep your hands off your orb," she warned breathlessly as Alec's free hand came to rest on the pocket that bulged with his small crystal ball. He sat in the only unbroken swing and wrapped his free hand around the chain.

"Yeah, I know." Alec sighed deeply as the toes of his shoes scuffed the dirt. "Logan will find me if I touch it."

Riley leaned up against the broken frame of the teeter-totter and waited for her lungs to catch up. She eased off her tender right ankle. "You okay?"

For a moment he didn't answer. There was a small cut on his left cheek and a swelling over his right eye. And those were just the injuries she could see; the hidden ones were probably a lot more painful and would take much longer to heal, if he had experienced the same mind-gutting terror in the rip that she had. Add to that the strain of teleporting them back in time and it was a wonder he was still standing. Sometimes it was hard to remember that he was only fifteen. "I feel like crap, actually."

"You look like crap, actually," she replied.

He gave a short laugh. "Thanks a bunch, Cohen."

"Any time, Anderson," she answered as she nervously scanned the trees for movement. Where was Darius? They'd been right behind them. Had Logan looked out the window? Was he forcing Darius to tell him where they were, right this minute? She shook the thought from her brain and forced herself to be rational. Logan didn't know about them. He hadn't had them in his clutches, hadn't chased them across the country, and hadn't ordered Alec's death, because all that was in the future now. And by coming back, they'd changed everything. All Logan knew was that *somebody* had shifted time. And besides, she hadn't panicked through the last few weeks. She didn't panic when she was hunted, when she was captured, or even when she'd been sucked into the dimensional rip. She was not going to start now.

"This is a totally bad idea, bringing Peter with us," Alec muttered as he stared at his shoes. "He's the most stubborn person you've ever met. He'll slow us down, refuse to believe Darius, and call attention to us. Just you watch."

"We don't have any choice," Riley sighed. "You heard Darius, same as me. Peter has the same genetic aberration we do. The Tyons will come after him, same as they're after us. Your parents' only chance for safety is if Peter is removed."

"I heard him," Alec replied. "Doesn't mean I have to like it."

There was a rustle of branches and suddenly Darius burst into the clearing, dragging Peter along with his arm forced up behind his back. Peter looked as if he'd gotten off with the worst of the fall; both knees were filthy and his forehead was scraped. If the situation hadn't been so serious, Peter's outraged expression would have been funny.

"You two okay?" Darius panted.

Alec jumped off his swing. Two steps had him towering next to Riley. "Was that him?"

Riley noted the break in his voice but kept her eyes on Darius.

Darius gave Peter a yank to stop him struggling. "Scout party. Didn't hear Logan's voice and I doubt he's with them, but I can't be certain without using my orb."

Peter tried to jerk his arm from Darius's grip but couldn't budge him an inch.

"Keep quiet," Darius warned. "Kick me again and I'll break your arm."

"He means it," Alec said.

Peter continued to struggle. His eyes locked on his brother's face and shot daggers. Clearly Darius's mental hold on Peter's vocal cords was better than his hold on Peter's legs.

"Where do we go?" Riley asked with a worried look back at the pathway through the trees. "They can track us anywhere we hide."

Darius nodded. "And the scouts aren't the only problem. I've had two requests for information from Anna I haven't responded to. I'm guessing you're both feeling the call too, right? When she catches up with us, there'll be some tough explaining to do. Why I'm not answering. Why I've got the three of you with me. Why two of you have orbs. Remember, we're now a month before Anna met you and the fact you know about us and have learned some basic orb skills is a huge complication. Add in Logan zeroing in on the time-shift coordinates and you can see the disaster brewing. I need to put as much distance as possible between us and the transport site. And fast."

"We should steal a car," Riley suggested.

Darius shook his head. "We can't touch our orbs to unlock anything and only a fool would leave a car unlocked in this neighbourhood. We'll have to hike on foot."

"I've got a friend near here," Alec offered. "We could hide in the basement of their convenience store. Logan would never think to look for us there."

"Good thought, Alec, but no," Darius replied. "I'm not endangering any more civilians than I have to. Logan will track me by my orb signature once he realizes I've been here. I think we should leave town."

"There's a bus every fifteen minutes," Alec pointed out. "It goes right downtown. We could be in the middle of massive crowds in less than an hour."

"That'll work. Lead the way." Darius yanked Peter's arm back until he blanched with pain. "You will go with us. *You will not fight me*. Are we clear?"

Riley shivered as Peter's eyes widened and his limbs slackened as Darius's control surged over him. It was amazing what he could do even without an orb. Alec turned and ran lightly away from the pathway, ducking into the dimness of the ring of trees on the far side of the playground without giving his brother another look. Riley followed. They burst out of the shade a moment later and circled another apartment building. There weren't too many people, considering the time of day and the number of occupants in this part of Scarborough, and the few that passed barely gave the four of them a second glance. Alec pointed to the bus stop, half a block down and across the street. With a quick nod of his head, Darius headed directly towards the glass enclosure where several other passengers waited.

"Hope someone has some money," Riley muttered.

"We can just—" Alec began before he cut himself off. "Guess we can't."

"No orb, no power, no free bus rides," Riley ruefully agreed.

They jogged across the street at the first break in traffic. Riley noticed Alec's long look at his former home in the distance and the sudden agonized expression that crossed his face. "We fixed your dad's arm and made a serious dent in his depression. Your mom will wake up in an hour or so. Darius made certain they won't remember us at all. I'm sure they'll be fine."

Alec averted his eyes and said nothing. With a burst of speed, he tore ahead to the bus stop. Riley followed more slowly. She didn't need an orb to feel his sentiments—now that the genetic traits bred into her DNA by the Tyons had been fully activated she could feel strong emotions just being close to him. Swallowing the sudden lump in her throat, she crossed the short distance to the bus stop.

There were three other passengers waiting. A woman in a hijab stood to one side and eyed their approach warily. A young couple engaged in a vigorous game of tonsil hockey leaned up against the graffitied walls of the bus shelter. Riley avoided Alec's eye as she entered the glass enclosure and hoped she wasn't blushing.

"I'm not going anywhere," Peter said loudly. He tried pulling his arm free of Darius's grip again. Darius's hold over Peter was fading too quickly.

"And *I* told *you*, there was no point arguing. I am in charge. You will obey me. Like it or not." Riley's skin prickled with Darius's words.

"No, I won't, you crazy lunatic," Peter replied, but his voice wasn't nearly as emphatic as it had been. The kissing couple seemed oblivious but the third passenger eased away from them with a dark sideways glance.

"Do you want Mom and Dad to get killed?" Alec turned to face his brother, his voice low and insistent. "Do you? Because every minute we're around them, we put them in danger."

"Alec," Riley warned quietly, giving the necking couple a pointed look.

"I think they're occupied." Alec faced Peter again. "Well, do you?"

"Piss off," Peter said and gave Alec the finger with his free hand.

Alec took a step closer and his eyes narrowed dangerously.

"Boys," Darius interrupted, "*please* stop it now."

"Don't tell me what to do," Alec said out of the side of his mouth. He took a step backwards and Riley watched his shoulders drop as Darius's control affected him.

"Yeah, don't tell us what to do," Peter mimicked.

"When you two are finished comparing sizes, we have a bus to catch." Riley pointed. All of them turned towards the street. A lumbering city bus trundled towards them, its directional signal flashing. At the same instant, the orb inside her pocket buzzed again. The vibration was a lot stronger than before. She jumped. "Jeez, can't we turn these off?"

"Don't answer that," Darius warned.

"I wasn't going to," Riley said, pulling her hand away from her pocket.

"No one touch their orb," Darius ordered.

Alec exchanged a tight glance with Riley.

"What is it?" Peter looked at all three of them in turn. "Why aren't you answering your phone?"

"It gives our location away," Darius said quietly, "and as I told you a few minutes ago, there are people out there that we definitely don't want knowing where we are."

The bus slowed as it approached. The woman in the hijab quickly moved out of the shelter towards the curb. The kissing couple didn't stir.

"Everyone sit near a door," Darius ordered, "just in case we have to jump off quickly. Peter, you have your wallet so you'll pay."

"I won't," Peter protested.

"*You will.*"

The orbs buzzed again, this time more insistent and painful. Riley gasped with the discomfort but prevented herself from yelping. The compulsion to pull out her orb pulsed through her bones. She clenched her fist until her nails bit into her palms and, not for the first time, cursed the entire Tyon Collective. *Next time* someone told her she was special and needed training to save the world, she was going to stab them in the eye with a pencil and run like hell.

The bus ground to a halt with a squeal of brakes and the woman in the hijab muscled her way on before the doors had fully opened. Alec quickly followed her and Riley dashed on board immediately behind him. She turned and paused on the step as she heard the commotion. Peter had ducked around the couple and with a sudden violent tug pulled Darius off his feet. Darius's grip on Peter's arm hadn't been broken but now Peter was stomping as hard as he could on Darius's leg. Darius gave a vicious scissor kick and knocked Peter to the ground.

"Are you getting on this bus or not?" The bus driver's huge tortoise shell sunglasses slipped down her beaky nose. "Move it. I have a schedule to keep."

"Hold onto your Pampers, Grandma," Riley muttered as she moved to put her body in the way of the doors.

Darius got a hold of Peter's neck and instantly the fight was over. Riley couldn't hear what he said into Peter's ear and she couldn't read his lips through the filthy bus shelter glass but she did see the fight go out of Peter's body as Darius hauled him to his feet. The kissing couple didn't even come up for air as they passed. Filthy and disheveled, Darius literally dragged Peter up the stairs and onto the bus. He gave the driver his most charming smile and indicated with a nod towards Peter, "He's got the fare."

Satisfied, Riley headed towards the middle of the bus. She sat beside Alec and gripped the metal bar on the back of the seat ahead of her. The bus started with a lurch before pulling into traffic. "You're right," she murmured to him. "He is a pain in the ass."

Alec gazed out the window and sighed. "He hasn't even started yet."

Alec leaned his forehead against the coolness of the window and shut his eyes. The bus lumbered along the main thoroughfare, hitting nearly every possible pothole as the sun sank in the west and his life spun further out of control. It didn't seem to matter that moving the three of them back in time had probably saved their lives and everyone around them. Darius was sure it was a big mistake and that both the Tyons and the Intergalactic Council would be after him.

He shifted in his seat, weariness and despondency washing over him with every breath. He was so tired it was hard to think. Somewhere in his core a trembling was building—the usual reaction to teleportation and the effects of an unbelievably difficult battle with Rhozan. He wished he could curl up and fall asleep for the next forty hours. Riley's warm thigh touched his as she shifted beside him and his breath caught in his throat. He was even too tired to think about her, but that didn't stop his heart from giving an unexpected leap the instant she accidentally nudged him.

2

"How long are we going to stay on this bus?" Riley spoke to Darius in the seat behind them in a tight voice.

"We'll go all the way downtown, as close to the train station as we can. We can't fly anywhere because none of you have passports," Darius replied.

"I'm not getting on any train." Peter sounded sulky and wasn't bothering to keep his voice down.

It sounded like his lips were swollen.

"Keep quiet," Darius muttered.

Peter kicked the back of Alec's seat.

"There aren't too many places to hide," Riley was whispering. "I mean, Canada's a wicked big country, but the train only goes from East to West. What are we going to do? Jump off into a wheat field somewhere and hope no one notices?"

"Yes, Riley, jumping off a moving train was just what I was thinking," Darius replied. "We'll let you go first."

"I have a better suggestion." Alec could almost hear her unspoken words. Obviously so did Peter. The back of their seat was forcefully kicked again.

"Now, now," Darius rebuked saucily.

"What about your training station in Toronto?" Riley asked in a more serious tone. "Is Anna there or could we hide there, say we've been there all along?"

Alec could hear Darius's sigh. "Anna's in and out of the station frequently. At this present time, we're on observation mode, not collection. I show up with three Potentials, one of whom won't keep his mouth shut, and the cat is out of the bag. We're going to have to disappear."

"But won't they be able to find you with the implant?" Riley asked.

Alec felt his stomach drop. He'd forgotten the Tyons had embedded a translation device like Darius's just behind his ear. He had no idea what other functions it might have. Could he be tracked by it?

"Good thought, Riley." Darius sounded frustrated. "You're right. They can and I suspect eventually will, once they've narrowed the field and realized we're high on the list of suspects. We've got to think of a convincing story for Anna that will explain where I've been and why you three are with me by the time she shows up."

The bus jerked to a halt. The front doors opened and a laughing group clambered on board to the soundtrack provided by a boombox thudding a heavy bass line. Alec cracked open an eye as the profanity-laden music got closer. Great, gang-bangers looking for trouble. Alec closed his eyes and pretended to be asleep. With any luck they'd head to the back of the bus and harass someone else.

The bus pulled away from the curb and entered traffic. In the distance a horn blared. The music got very loud and didn't fade.

"Hey, look at this. We got two lovers on this bus." The young man's voice was thick with an unidentifiable accent and oozed menace. It was right beside him, Alec realized with a sinking feeling.

"Go harass someone who cares," Riley snapped. Alec reached out, grasped her hand and gripped it tightly. This was not the time to antagonize anyone. Especially gang members who just lived to make someone's life miserable. He opened his eyes and twisted in his seat.

The leader was nearly as short as Riley, but his neck was probably as thick as her thigh, and his dark skin was a mass of tribal African tattoos, even over the dome of his shaved head. The three others with him didn't look any friendlier, especially the one carrying the boombox on his shoulder, whose head almost brushed the roof of the bus.

All four were staring at Darius and Peter with a mixture of glee and loathing. Darius had his arm around Peter's shoulder and his hand gripped Peter's upper arm tightly to keep him under control. Darius was eyeing the gang with mild fascination but Peter was sinking lower in his seat, showing the haunted look Alec knew so well, despite his attempt to conceal it. Here we go again, Alec sighed to himself.

The gang leader poked Darius's shoulder with a finger. "Hey, boy, he your sweetheart?"

Darius cocked one golden eyebrow upwards.

"I'm talkin' to you." The poke became a shove. The other gang members sniggered. Alec felt Riley's tremor. He squeezed her hand tighter.

"My aural acuity is not compromised," Darius said. On the surface, his tone was quite reasonable. "Merely the inanity of the request that precludes a response."

It took a minute for the gang to realize the insult. "Shut his trap for him, Leon," the boombox owner encouraged.

Leon needed no encouragement. He twisted his fingers into Darius's shirt, bunching the fabric tightly, and pulled upward. A slight tearing sound provided the background for the string of profanity. Darius didn't blink.

"We don't like your kind on our bus," said one of the quartet, who was missing two of his front teeth.

"Because you're worried about your own latent feelings or because your own equipment is so pathetic?" Riley piped up.

Alec groaned.

Leon growled as he let go of Darius's shirt and reached for Riley.

Alec didn't hesitate. He knew from experience that the best defense was a painful and unexpected offence. Leaping over Riley, he dove into the boom-box carrier and belted him as hard as he could. The man crumpled under the well-placed cross. An elbow to the jerk behind him had blood spewing from the guy's nose. Anger surged in Alec's blood. He was sick and tired of this kind of idiot. Sick of having to fight other people's battles. Sick of *everything*.

The swaying bus didn't give much room to maneuver but Alec managed a straight kick and a powerful uppercut before the third thug knocked him to the floor. He was aware that Darius had entered the fray only by Riley's shouted warning, "Darius, look out" and her furious command to Peter to "help them, you dipstick." Alec didn't have time to argue that Peter never fought his own battles. Someone was holding him down, grinding his face into the accumulated dirt in the rubber flooring and twisting his arm behind his back so painfully he cried out. He managed a kick that connected with solid flesh before a heavy blow to his back stopped everything.

For a moment Alec wasn't sure what had happened. Only that his heart nearly stopped as his body acknowledged the horror his brain was slower to admit. Something warm and sticky soaked through his shirt and trickled down the small of his back.

Riley screamed.

Alec could feel the bus slowing down, heard the shouts, felt the sizzle of orb power as Darius ended the fight. He was aware of Riley dropping to all fours beside him and yelling something as she pressed her hands into his back. The pressure hurt it more and he opened his mouth to tell her so, but strangely the words wouldn't come. A hazy sense of fear surged through him but he was oddly distanced from it. It would be pretty stupid to die now, he thought feebly as the world around him faded into nothingness. The guy who saves the world falls victim to a cheap switchblade. He could see the headlines now.

Riley's heart was in her mouth and pounding so loudly she almost didn't hear Darius's hurried instructions. The world around her—Alec's limp body, the warm blood between her fingers, the crowd on the bus craning their necks to see—disappeared with a frisson of electricity and the usual surge of Tyon Power. Darius's work, clearly.

3

Riley focused her attention on Alec the instant they arrived wherever Darius had sent them. The blood was still welling up through the attempt at a seal she'd made with the palm of her hand against his tee-shirt. She could feel his heart labouring through his ribs. She'd only seen the silver blade for a second but the sight of its bloody emergence from Alec's back was seared into her memory.

"Get your orb out. Heal that incision." Darius's words seemed to come from far away. Without hesitation, Riley reached into her pocket and pulled out her orb without question. Hands trembling so hard she could barely hold onto the slippery crystal, she applied it to Alec's back, just at the opening of the knife wound. She closed her eyes. *Concentrate*, she urged herself. She tried to visualize the injury. The torn and bleeding skin, the ripped muscles, the veins spilling his precious life blood into the cavity. She shuddered. She prayed that his kidneys weren't damaged or, worse, a main blood vessel.

The orb began to heat up as the Tyon power sizzled underneath her skin. She tuned out Darius's urgent voice and Peter's whining responses. She didn't pause to notice where Darius had brought them. She didn't pause to even think how to do what she was doing. Urgency was her teacher. *Heal.* She pushed the power through her hands into Alec. Please heal.

The floor underneath her knees lurched slightly and she nearly fell. Instantly righting herself, she focused harder. The lurch repeated twice more then settled into a steady movement forward. Someone dropped down beside her. A second pair of hands bumped up against hers.

"Don't stop. I'm helping," Darius gasped in her ear.

Riley nodded. Darius's orb clinked with hers as he shoved his closer to the wound. The heat grew stronger.

The pulsing of power steadily increased, with one orb feeding off the other, amplifying in strength. Riley became entranced in the effort. She lost track of time. She was vaguely aware of her knees becoming sore, of movement around her and sounds of traffic. She felt Darius's arm and shoulder against hers. His exhaustion and concern penetrated the healing fog but she pushed that awareness away. The only thing that mattered was saving Alec's life.

Someone was shouting. The noise was insistent and irritating. Her concentration broke. She opened her eyes and blinked with amazement.

He'd transported them to a camper. A massive, top of the line, over-decorated RV, she corrected. Alec was lying on the floor in between the faux marble table and the matching plush velvet sofa bed. Darius was squished against her and Peter was ensconced in a beige leather captain's chair and steering. The tasselled curtains over the wide window above the sofa swung rhythmically back and forth and something inside the mini-fridge to her immediate right was sloshing with each sway. Someone had paid a ridiculous fortune for a made-to-order mobile palace in gold and fawn.

"Do I turn east or west?" Peter repeated loudly.

"East," Darius said weakly. Riley turned to stare at him in shock.

Darius's skin was pasty white, his freckles stood out in frank relief and his lips were bloodless. She shoved him with her shoulder. "Are you okay?"

Darius swallowed and gave a slight nod. "Hate the sight of blood," he whispered.

Instantly relieved and not a little annoyed, Riley focused her attention back to Alec. He was breathing easier she noted and his heart didn't seem to be labouring as hard as before. She peered at her bloody hands. There was barely any blood on the floor, although the back of his shirt and the waist of his jeans were soaked. She raised her orb for a quick peek underneath. The skin, puckered and angrily red, was knitted together. A wave of relief surged through her veins and she began to shiver.

"He's gonna be okay," she said to Darius.

He bobbed his head in reply.

"I can take over now. You rest," she ordered. He'd transported all three of them; a herculean task for an Operative. It was a wonder he wasn't unconscious with the strain.

"Sure?" Darius asked. But he was already pulling his orb away from hers and leaning back against the sofa with his eyes closed.

"Sure." Riley shifted into a more comfortable position. She grimaced at the cramp in her left leg and banged her heel against the carpeted floor to restart the circulation. "What on earth was he thinking?"

"To start the fight?" Darius murmured softly. "You, probably."

"I can look after myself," Riley turned her head away. She rapidly blinked the tears away. "I don't need him dying for me."

"I'd say he'd tell you that you're worth dying for."

"And you agree with him? Would you die for someone?"

"Don't be ridiculous," Darius grinned. "I'm much too

important to sacrifice myself for anyone."

Riley couldn't help the smile. It was good to see that his ego was safely overinflated, that the strain of saving them hadn't been too much. "See if there's something to drink in the fridge, Dare."

Darius sighed deeply but leaned over her shoulder to pull open the mini-fridge door behind her. The vacuum popped as it opened and the rack of cans rattled while he rooted around. The door closed.

"Here," he held out an ice-cold can of soda.

"Can you open it for me?" she asked. "My hands are kinda full."

Darius stood up instead and stepped unsteadily over her. He turned on the water in the mini-sink and washed his hands for a moment, scrubbing at the sticky blood. He then washed off the two cans of cola he had removed from the fridge, rinsing his bloody handprints down the drain. Satisfied, he stepped back over Riley and flopped down onto the sofa. There was a sharp crack and hiss as he pulled the tab. He handed her a can. In the front of the cab, Peter was swearing at the traffic and gave both of them a dark look in the rearview mirror.

Riley took a grateful swig and swallowed, while keeping the orb in place. Darius drained his can, belched loudly and sighed in satisfaction. After a couple of moments, he opened his eyes. "That feels better."

"What? The drink or the typically gross display of masculine lack of manners?" Riley said as she took another mouthful.

Darius's lips curled into a slight grin. "Both."

"I see you've got Happy Boy under control," she nodded towards Peter.

Darius rubbed his face with his hands and sighed with evident fatigue. "Maybe a bit too much," he said quietly. "I had to move pretty fast. I couldn't afford to be subtle."

"How long will it last?" Riley asked.

Darius shrugged weakly. "Who knows? Maybe it's permanent."

A horrible vision of Peter, endlessly trailing behind Darius, waiting to do his bidding, flashed across her mind. Forcibly shoving that thought away, she focused on the more pressing issues. "We've both used our orbs, Darius. They'll be onto us any minute."

"I know," Darius frowned. "I can only trust we're far enough from the time travel site that they don't put two and two together. Hopefully, my signature is distinct enough from our combined one that no one notices."

"And Anna?"

"Probably locking down my co-ordinates right now." Darius leaned forward. Just for a moment, an irrepressible spark flickered in his eyes. "You'll have to give me your orb. She can't see you using one. She'll know something's up."

"And what'll you tell her about this?" Riley placed the empty can on the counter and waved her hand over Alec's unconscious form.

"I came across three Potentials. All at once. And saved you from attack."

"And she's gonna believe that?" Darius must be brain damaged from exhaustion. Anna, his direct supervisor and ultra-strict Tyon, was anything but stupid.

"I don't see why Anna wouldn't."

"You don't see why I wouldn't what?" asked a familiar icy voice behind them.

Riley was so startled her orb slipped from her fingers and rolled off Alec's back and under the beige sofa. She barely suppressed an outright scream.

A tall, slim woman wearing a grey one-piece overall and a tight, unhappy expression stood in the middle of the camper. An orb glowed in her hand. Her white-blond hair was pulled back into a severe ponytail. Her grey eyes rolled over Darius's prostrate form, the unconscious body at Riley's knees, the teenage driver who had yet to notice her arrival, and onto Riley. The eyes narrowed as the orb flared briefly.

"I assume you have a good explanation for this," she said to Darius.

The camper momentarily swerved before Peter regained control over his surprise and pulled the wheel straight. In the rearview mirror, his eyes were huge. For a second his gaze connected with Riley's. Then he focused back on driving.

Darius blinked several times but his facial expression didn't give his shock away. "Hi Anna. Good to see you."

"You have not responded to my summons," Anna replied. Riley wrinkled her nose. She'd almost forgotten how much she disliked Anna's highhanded attitude and precise manner of speaking. "Maintaining contact with a superior officer is a high priority, Darius. As you well know."

"Don't quote regulation at me," Darius sighed.

"I've had a hard day."

"Doing what?"

"Oh, just saving lives left, right and center." Darius tried for a lofty tone but missed. He struggled to sit upright.

"Explain."

Darius poked his toe into Alec's shoulder. "This one and his brother," he nodded towards Peter, "are exceptionally strong Potentials. I've been following them for the last couple of days, studying their signal, while monitoring for signs of the Others. Riley here is Alec's girlfriend," he added with a slight smile. Riley tried not to bristle as he continued. "They're never apart. That's why she's with us."

"Non Potentials are not to be included nor should they witness Tyon power," Anna said disapprovingly. Her expression seemed to ice over even further as she gave Riley a longer and more probing glance.

"She's a Potential too," Darius added hastily. "Funny that."

"Indeed."

Anna looked like she didn't believe a word Darius was saying. Riley ducked her head and tucked her blood-covered hands between her knees to keep them out of sight. She'd have to remember to warn Alec that they were supposed to be a couple. Heaven only knew what he'd say. She could quite happily throttle Darius at the moment. She knew why he'd said it—the swine—and she was going to personally pay him back the minute she was able. But now, she had to cope with this new, imperious form of disaster.

"Have you teleported recently?" Anna continued the interrogation.

"Yeah," Darius said. "We were all on a bus. I was tailing the boys, learning about them. They were attacked by a gang of hoodlums."

Hoodlums? Riley rolled her eyes.

"Alec here was stabbed. There wasn't time to do anything else. I had to get them out of harm's way. Alec is too strong a Potential to lose. So I saw this vehicle at the side of the road and made an instant decision."

"I see." Anna bent over and placed her orb against Alec's neck. She seemed to be thinking for a moment.

"I didn't have time to summon the medical personnel of this society. Only instant orb application was going to help."

"Witnesses?"

Darius winced. "A few."

"How many?"

"Ah, twenty? But two of them were unconscious when I moved us and at least one was asleep."

Anna's frown deepened until several lines creased her forehead like fault lines. "An unacceptable number. Give me the coordinates and I will begin the modification process."

Darius handed her his orb without further comment. She touched her orb to his and there was an almost imperceptible flash of blue light. She handed it back.

"I will return the instant I have completed this task. Begin regen, Darius. I will want a complete and detailed report when I return." With one last annoyed look at Alec, Anna disappeared.

Darius flopped back onto the couch and groaned. He flung his arm up over his eye. "She'll drown me in paperwork."

"You guys don't use paper," Riley reminded him as she slumped against the sofa.

"It's a figure of speech," Darius sighed.

"Yeah, well, Tyon bureaucracy is the least of our problems," Riley snapped as she reached over Alec and stuck her hand under the sofa. She wriggled her fingers but, other than a couple of tiny dust bunnies, found nothing. "You know Miss Super-Efficient-know-it-all. She'll be back in ten minutes. Everyone in Scarborough will have had their memory wiped clean. And when she's finished with them, she'll start in on us." Riley reached further, bracing herself over Alec with her free hand, and ran her searching fingers

29

over the plush carpet. Where was that stupid orb? "I can't resist her. You know I can't. She'll take one look into my brain and see the truth."

"I'll explain."

"Darius, the woman is second in command on this mission. She's single minded. She hasn't met us before. She's not going to buy any explanation you have cooked up."

"She'll understand."

"She won't." Riley's fingers touched the cool surface of the orb but it slipped away the instant she tried to close them around it. Groaning, she strained after it. "She'll see your signature, add ours and put two and two together. The time travel thing. Remember?"

"Yeah, yeah," Darius sighed.

"You'd better think of a good method of keeping her nose out of our business and fast. Or I will." Riley said. A vision of pillows and a silently struggling Anna crossed her mind with dark pleasure.

"Tsk, tsk," Darius lay back down on the sofa and closed his eyes. "And you look so sweet. Who'd believe it?"

Riley snorted but didn't answer. He really didn't look well. Riley bit her lip and applied the orb back onto Alec's injury, focusing her attention. Time, as usual, was running out. Alec needed to heal a.s.a.p. and they needed to hit the road the second Anna learned the truth.

Alec was drifting. He had no idea where he was or what was happening to him. He couldn't feel his body or see it, but strangely, it didn't bother him. In fact, nothing did.

He was aware of his surroundings in a way that didn't seem to be connected to his vision or touch or even sense of smell. An awareness borne of *knowing* without actual experience. There was something rather familiar as well, but he couldn't quite remember what that might be. He was somewhere dark and vast and *other*; multi-coloured lights bloomed around him, flaring into something quite wonderful, then fading to nothingness, like a silent fireworks show surrounding him. The sounds were like nothing he had ever heard before; all the languages of all the worlds in creation, mixed together, muted and barely audible.

He drifted further, coming closer to the lights. They in turn receded, although whether in response to his approach or of their own accord, he wasn't sure. Not that it mattered.

Time passed but had no meaning.

For a long while Alec had no cogent thoughts; he just was. But eventually, for no real reason, his memory began to return. Thoughts drifted from one thing to another. Most made no sense. A series of images drifted into awareness; a young man, irrepressible mischief in his eyes, reaching out a hand; a girl with navy eyes, lips curled into a smirk, laughing at him; a massive cloud of pulsing, sickening lights, coming closer.

Alec felt his emotional response as if it was someone else's. The man was someone both admired and envied. The girl, longed for. The lights caused fear.

After a while those images faded. The glittering array of colour around him began to subside, slowly at first as to be almost imperceptible. Then quickly, the lights were gone. Alec became aware of pain. The pain grew. And grew. It absorbed him.

He became aware of his body again. His right arm was trapped underneath his stomach, the fingers burning with pins and needles. His face was pressed into something fibrous and scratchy. Dust tickled his nose. The back of his throat was dry and his tongue stuck to the roof of his mouth. His chest hurt with every intake of breath, but the worst pain was in his back, just below his ribs. Something hard and implacable was pressed against his skin; the pressure of it worsening the dull throbbing pain that was coming from deep inside him.

He coughed and the pain quadrupled.

He cried out and the darkness around him rapidly receded.

Something touched his mind: an alien, distant, malevolent something. Then it was gone.

Alec was swamped with exhaustion unlike anything he had ever felt before. He couldn't fight it. He didn't want to. He slept.

t took Anna much longer to modify all the memories than Riley thought it would. Evening had settled in. The windows in the houses they passed glowed warmly, and inside the RV, Riley had lit the lamps so she could see.

Peter was still driving east and hadn't spoken a word since Anna had pulled her disappearing act. Toronto had long since been left behind and with it most of the traffic. They had passed the exits for Kingston only a few minutes before and already the landscape on either side of the road was essentially empty of dwellings. Darius had fallen fast asleep from exhaustion on the couch ages ago. One hand was still flung over his eyes.

Riley rolled her shoulders to ease the kinks out of the muscles. She was still sitting on the floor with her hand on Alec's back, holding the orb in place. The second he was okay, she wanted him up and on his feet, ready to run. Anna was not to be trusted, no matter what Darius said, and likely their only hope would be to high-tail it out of there. Any extra healing she could do before 'Annageddon', she would.

6

However, she was getting hungry and the fridge—while well stocked with cola, mixes, and white wine—held nothing in the way of food. The cupboards contained only boxes of fancy crackers and tins of smoked oysters. Whoever owned this camper didn't seem to plan on actually camping in it, or else had bizarre ideas about nutrition. If Darius had been awake she would have insisted that he have Peter take them to the nearest grocery store to stock up or, at minimum, pick up a pizza. For a second she remembered the pizza she and Alec had made together. It seemed like so long ago. She smiled.

Alec stirred underneath her hand and groaned. Riley jerked her hand away as if scorched. She leaned over Alec's shoulder. His eyes were open but somewhat glazed.

"Everything is okay, Alec," she said in the most soothing tone she could manage against the lump in her throat, "You're fine."

"What...?" Alec couldn't seem to find the energy to continue.

"You got hurt but Darius and I fixed it. Don't worry."

"Oh." Alec closed his eyes and his body relaxed. Riley saw the pain dissolve from his face as he slid back into unconsciousness. Hopefully a restful sleep now, instead of involuntary coma. She sat up straighter and chewed the inside of her lip. Should she chance instructing Peter to stop at the next gas station so she could buy something for them to eat and risk that the hold Darius had over Peter was enough to keep him from taking off the second the camper stopped? Or wait until Anna decided to return and ordered them to turn around? Her stomach growled and her eyes strayed to the cupboard. Oysters would have to do.

The orb buzzed painfully. Instinctively she dropped it onto Alec's back. It buzzed again.

Darius groaned softly and, without opening his eyes, raised his own fist-clasped orb to his face and rested it against his forehead. There was a moment of silence before he muttered, "Yeah, no problem. We'll wait." He dropped his hand back to his side. "Anna wants us to stop moving and stay put for a while. It's taking her longer to track down the witnesses."

"We passed a sign for a campsite a couple of minutes ago. It should be just up ahead," Riley suggested.

Darius didn't open his eyes but he nodded. "Peter?" His

voice was weak and there was no response. He cleared his throat and tried again, a bit louder. "Peter, pull into the next campsite. Park out of the way."

There was a grunt from the driver's seat.

"Riley," Darius said quietly. "Use your orb to ensure no one remembers us."

"Will do." Riley got slowly to her feet. Muscles and joints protesting from too long in one position, she gingerly stepped over Alec and made her way to the front of the camper. She slid into the passenger seat beside Peter.

Peter's face was unnaturally pale in the reflected headlights of the oncoming traffic. His lips were pulled back from his teeth in a snarl and his hands clasped the steering wheel so tightly his knuckles were bloodless. She noticed his quick sideways glance but stayed silent. She didn't need her orb to pick up on his hatred and anger.

There was hardly any traffic and not much to look at. Just fields heading off into the distance, jagged rock cuts where the highway had been blasted out of hills, and a never-ending parade of signs: speed, deer, attractions, and distance markers. Boring as all get out.

"There," Riley pointed ahead. The teepee-shaped sign was filled with block letters indicating that Riverview Camp Ground was a destination of unparalleled beauty and that there were vacancies.

Peter only grunted in response, but applied the brakes a bit too sharply and veered onto the shoulder just in time to make a hard right turn onto the dirt road.

"Are you trying to tip us over, you idiot?" Riley gasped, her hands braced against the dashboard. Behind them there was a thump and muffled "ow" as Darius rolled off the sofa. 35

Peter swore under his breath. He swung the wheel again as the lane dipped and bent around a clump of huge trees. Riley grimaced and focused on the road, which was lurching in and out of the camper's headlights with every pothole. Clearly someone had thought the meandering pathway lent a holiday air, fooling travellers into thinking they were miles from nowhere, rather than thirty kilometers from a major city. Riley's stomach made another unpleasant lurch towards her throat as the camper skidded around a crater in the road and made the final bend with inches between the hull and a massive boulder that had, "Your almost there" spray-painted in luminous misspelled script. Peter noticed the dark metal gate at the last second.

"You keep the motor running. I'll get out and open it." Riley's hand was already unlocking her door as the RV skidded to a sharp stop. "Leave me behind and I'll pull your nuts out through your ears. Got me?" she warned.

Peter didn't speak but the tightening around his mouth acknowledged her threat.

Riley dropped down to the uneven ground and headed towards the gate. The darkness had deepened now and only the beams from the headlights behind her gave any illumination. There were lots of sounds though, above the purring of the camper's German engineered motor and none of them soothing. Night creatures of the forest chirped, squawked, and rustled, somewhere just out of sight. Riley focused on the oily latch instead of the goosebumps that were taking up residence at the back of her neck. *Who on earth would spend the night in a tent listening to this racket*, she wondered as she lifted the lever and swung the heavy gate backwards, *when you could have air conditioning, soundproof double-glazing, and Egyptian cotton sheets?* She waved at Peter, indicating he was to pull the camper forward. She stepped lightly to the side as the big machine moved slowly through the gate. Waving the exhaust fumes from her nose, she latched the gate again and climbed up into the passenger seat. Peter put the RV into gear and headed at a more sedate pace down the final stretch of the laneway.

It wasn't much of a campground, Riley decided as they pulled into the reception parking lot. The only signs of civilization were one larger rundown building with "Office" hung over a screen door and a slightly smaller building with a long porch and faux old-west styling to the right. "Ye Old General Store" was written on a sign that swung over the porch. There were bluish lights flickering in the office but no one seemed to be around.

"Cut the engine and give me the keys," Riley ordered.

Peter ground his teeth but complied.

"Leave the camper and I'll hunt you down," she added as she opened her door. A swarm of moths headed straight for her. With a grunt of disgust, she jumped down and slammed the door behind her. The moths battered against the window for a moment before heading back to the feeble naked bulb over the office door.

Riley opened the screen door and walked in. The office was larger on the inside than it had looked from the camper and the level of décor was significantly better than the outside of the building suggested. A colourful map was pinned to the wall between the two windows detailing a much larger campground than she'd expected. A long counter separated the guests from the staff, and behind it, several desks complete with computers and telephones sat vacant. The brightest light came from the private office at the back of the room. Inside it, a dark haired woman in her thirties was rising from a chair. She waved to Riley before leaning down and shutting off the television she was watching.

"Need a lot or a cabin?" she asked as she entered the main office and proceeded to sashay towards the counter in ridiculously high heels.

Riley bit down on the scathing footwear comment and smiled politely. "We have a camper. It's pretty large."

"No problem. We have lots of space," the woman said, reaching for a smaller paper version of the wall map. She expertly turned it around so Riley could read the writing. "It's still not our busy season. Would you like near the river, the pool, or the playground?"

Riley ignored the woman's searching gaze, which was

taking in her piercings and summing her up quickly. "It's a family campground," the woman said with a touch of warning in her voice. "No parties, no drinking."

"No problem," Riley answered with a direct gaze of her own. "I'm with my brother and my cousin. We'll be gone in the morning." She dropped her hand into her pocket and gripped her orb tightly. "We want to stay out of sight. *Please* forget we are even here." She pushed the Tyon *willingness* towards the woman so forcefully she almost grunted aloud with the effort. She was still very clumsy at getting people to do her bidding, unlike Darius, but she'd done it before and reasoned that she could do it again.

"I beg your pardon." The woman's eyes narrowed with suspicion. "Forget you've *what?*"

Riley forced a smile and tried again. "Forget we're here."

"And just why would I want to do that?" The woman took a step back from the counter, the forms still in her hand. She gave Riley a very unpleasant look. "Just what are you trying to do?"

"Nothing," Riley increased the wattage on her smile. "How much is it for the night?"

There was a long pause before the forms and a pen were handed over. Riley filled in the registration, remembering at the last second not to include any true information, and handed it back to the clerk.

"That'll be twenty-five dollars," the clerk said. "We take cash or credit. It's an extra fifteen if you want to empty the tanks."

Riley didn't know what tanks the woman was talking about but did know she didn't have a penny on her. Neither did Darius or Alec. "I'll get my brother to pay," she said, turning to the door. "I'll be right back."

The darkness was even more pronounced with the camper's headlights off. Riley stumbled on the rutted ground as she walked to the door. "Why couldn't that idiot keep the lights on," she grumbled to herself as she wrenched it open and clambered up.

"Dare, I need your voodoo hex on the memories here," she called out.

Peter looked up and a spasm of fear crossed his face before he realized she wasn't talking about him. Then he ducked his head and continued to stare wordlessly out the windscreen.

Darius sat up slowly and ran a free hand through his hair. He yawned as he got to his feet. "Peter, if you even try and get out of your seat, your muscles will cramp so hard you won't be able to breathe. Got it?" Without waiting for an answer he walked to the main door and left the camper. Riley watched him trudge across the parking lot and pull open the screen door to the office. He disappeared inside.

Several minutes passed before he exited. When he did, the clerk was on his heels, following as closely as a shadow and talking animatedly. Darius waved an arm at the camper as he crossed the short distance to the store. Riley hopped out and followed them, a moue of distaste crossing her face. It was clear that he'd more than gotten the woman to waive the fee.

The general store was also larger than expected, and like the office, new, well stocked and surprisingly up scale. There were several aisles of foodstuffs, one filled with souvenirs, a corner devoted to casual clothes you might have forgotten to bring, and a huge display of sporting equipment. The clerk was turning on the last of the overhead lights as Riley closed the door behind her. Her fawning expression was for Darius alone.

"We have a freezer in the back and everything you might need for a barbecue," she was saying to him. She brushed a non-existent speck of grime from her forehead and glanced ever so briefly in the shining surface of a decorative mirror next to the light switches. "It's such a lovely night for a campfire. Warm enough to sit outside for hours and talk. I could get you a couple of bottles of wine, if you'd like."

"No thanks," Darius smiled. "Just the food for now."

"You're on vacation," the woman batted her eyelashes. "A little drink won't hurt."

"As much as I'd like one," Darius replied politely, "the rest of my party is underage. If they can't, I shouldn't." He headed down the aisle to the freezer. Catching Riley's eye, he motioned towards the next aisle over, which was stocked with canned goods. The woman sidled up beside him.

"I could come over and keep you company," she breathed, leaning over his shoulder. "The kids can go to bed. You and I could have a little party."

"Sounds lovely," Darius murmured, "but no. Afraid not."

The woman was not to be dissuaded. She pulled out a card from her denim skirt pocket and slipped it into the pocket of Darius's shirt. "My number." Her grin was almost feral. "Call me once the kiddies are asleep."

Riley resisted the desire to lob a family-sized can of ravioli at the clerk's head. Grumbling to herself about Darius's need to flirt with anyone with a pulse, she grabbed several cans of spaghetti sauce instead and stalked over to the small produce section. She couldn't hear any more of the conversation while she selected ingredients for their supper, which was likely a good thing. After collecting eggs and bread for breakfast she headed to the checkout counter. Riley dumped the food next to that which Darius had collected and pointedly ignored the clerk, who was barely glancing at the keys on the cash register. After assuring herself they needed nothing else, she wandered away. There was no way she was going to let herself get nauseated listening to some idiot.

There was a pretty cotton dress in the middle of the clothing display and something about it caught her eye. She stepped closer. It was made of eyelet cotton in plainest white, with dainty capped sleeves and a scalloped neckline. A long time ago her mom used to buy her stuff like that. Riley couldn't help glancing down at her black jeans and tee-shirt.

She raised her hand and touched the fabric of the skirt. It was as soft as it looked.

Her hand was knocked away by the clerk. "'Scuse me." The woman yanked the dress off the hanger and whipped it out from underneath Riley's view.

Riley turned. Darius was leaning against the counter, an indecipherable look on his face. He caught her eye and smiled. Behind him, the clerk was stuffing the dress into a paper bag.

"That's ninety-seven, even," the clerk said.

"Put it on my tab," Darius grinned at her and his eyes almost glowed.

The clerk melted.

"Riley, take this," Darius said as he tossed her the bag containing the dress. She caught it deftly. "Thanks for everything, Laurie," Darius winked at the clerk.

"She'll pine for months, just waiting for the sound of your voice," Riley muttered under her breath as she walked out of the store behind Darius and into the inky darkness. She clasped the dress to her tightly and tried to ignore the tingle of pleasure burbling through her stomach.

"Nah," Darius smiled suggestively. He shifted the heavier bag carefully in his arms. "I only have eyes for you."

Riley couldn't help grinning back even though she knew he really didn't mean it.

They entered the RV and Riley proceeded to put the food away in the cupboards while Darius took a seat next to Peter. Alec was still sleeping on the floor. The engine purred into life and lurched slightly as Peter put the gears into drive. Riley had to hold onto the counter with one hand as the camper meandered through the campground. Clearly Darius had chosen the most out of the way site for them. She only hoped they reached it before she fell over and seriously hurt herself.

It took several minutes to back the camper in, and in the end Riley had to take over the wheel while Darius waved to her from outside. Peter sat sulkily on the sofa staring at his brother as if he'd never seen him before. While Darius covered the license plates with mud and grass, just in case the camper had been reported stolen, Riley began cooking.

It wasn't long before the appetizing aroma of garlic, sausage, and tomato sauce permeated the air. Contentedly humming under her breath, Riley stirred the bubbling sauce while the pasta cooked. Darius arrived at her shoulder after he and Peter deposited Alec in the back bedroom.

"He's still out for the count," Darius reported as he leaned over and dipped a spoon into the sauce.

"Hey," Riley admonished. "It'll be out in five minutes."

"I'm hungry now." Darius smacked his lips and nodded towards the pot. "That's really good."

"How's he look?" she asked.

"The healing's gone well but I don't want him exerting himself for several days. The tissue won't hold together if he overdoes it. I think he'll be awake by breakfast."

"If we're still here," Riley added.

"True. However, when Anna returns she'll need to rest and there's no reason why we all can't stay in this. It's big enough."

"What about Peter?"

Both turned and looked at Alec's brother. He was back on the sofa again, staring at Alec's bloodstains on the carpet.

"Hmm, good question." Darius pulled out his orb. Peter's eyes widened as Darius approached him and he flinched when Darius sat down next to him.

"This won't hurt, Peter, but it is necessary." Peter tried to lift his arm to block the touch of Darius's orb to his temple but his arm was more under Darius's control than his own. Darius's voice was cold and vibrated with power. "You follow my orders. You listen to me. You know nothing of Alec's ability to move in time. You only know that you and Alec are special and that I've told you to accompany us. Nothing more. Do you understand?"

Peter's eyes glazed over and he nodded, slack jawed. Riley turned away, sickened. Darius's power had rarely been on such blatant display. It wouldn't do to forget that she'd known Darius for only a month and that he'd spent most of his life with the Tyons and under their influence. The phrase, *he's not a tame lion*, floated across her mind.

Darius put his orb back in his pocket and got slowly to his feet again. The strain of using that amount of power showed for a second in stark reality across his face. "Is supper ready now?" he asked with a forced grin.

Darius doused the lights immediately after the dishes were cleaned and indicated that he would share the back room with the boys. Alec hadn't stirred but Darius wanted to be close by when he woke and, of course, Peter couldn't be trusted to stay in the camper, despite Darius's hold over him.

Riley snuggled down on the sofa bed and stared at the ceiling. Despite a profound fatigue, she couldn't sleep. The window over the sofa was open, just enough to let in a breeze, and it carried in the late night sounds of the forest. Somewhere, someone was playing a guitar. Outside, the darkness was thick and impenetrable but inside the trailer the lights on the microwave and some gold under-counter lighting, that none of them could find the off switch for, bathed Riley in comforting illumination.

Anna would be back sooner than later. When she returned, she'd want answers and Riley didn't believe for a minute that Darius's tale would stand up to close scrutiny. And when it didn't, and the proverbial crap hit the fan, she had to be ready to run, preferably with Alec alongside her. She fingered the soft material of the cotton dress she'd laid out on the back of the sofa. The dress was lovely and a tiny part of her was dying to wear it, but it didn't have pockets. And pockets that held an orb were essential nowadays.

S omeone hadn't closed the curtains completely and a sliver of sunlight sliced right across Alec's eyelids. He blinked several times and ran his tongue across his parched lips. His mouth tasted bitter, as if he'd been ill or something. It wasn't until he tried to lift his head off the pillow that it hit him. Pain. Severe and lancinating. Under his ribs and shooting straight down his back to his hip. *What the...?*

He turned his head to the side, suddenly aware that he wasn't alone. Darius Finn was lying next to him, fast asleep. On Darius's far side, a more familiar figure was curled up with his back facing them. Alec's brow wrinkled. How had Peter ended up with them, and for that matter, where were they, what had happened, and why was he in so much pain? Stifling the groan, he forced himself to sit up partway and lean back on his elbows. He took a look around.

The king-sized bed the three of them were laying on took up almost the entire packed space of the bedroom. There were built-in cupboards on either side of the door and a window on either side of the bed. The gold satin bedspread they were lying on matched the curtains, the ruffles on the valances, and the deep plush carpet. There were three large photographs hung on the wall, all depicting an older, bronzed and very vigorous couple, who liked sword fishing, hunting, and paragliding.

So how had he and Darius come to be sleeping

in some adventure-mad retiree's camper? And where was Riley? Alec lay back down and the pain receded to a dull thudding. He wracked his memory. What was the last thing he remembered doing?

Ah, yes. The bus. The gang. The fight. His hand unknowingly slid behind him to the wound. The skin felt raw and pain leapt with the slightest touch. He blew out a lung-full of air. The camper was probably Darius's idea. He couldn't imagine Riley picking out such an ostentatious form of transport in a month of Sundays. Of course, the camper was stationary at the moment, but he didn't have any reservation that they'd travelled somewhere. There were birds chirping outside, the steady swishing of many trees and not a car horn anywhere. He doubted they were still in Toronto.

Despite the pain, he was hungry. Ravenous actually. The air was laden with pine scent, but garlic and onions still lingered and he had no doubt that Riley, if given half a chance, had been cooking. And heaven knows, the girl could cook.

He was only wearing paisley boxer shorts and they were definitely not his, but he was decent enough and there were no signs of his clothes. He tried to sit up again.

His movements disturbed Darius somewhat, who flung a hand over his eyes and sighed deeply before resuming his even breathing. As carefully as he could, Alec eased himself off the bed and padded silently to the door. Each step gave the scar a nasty twinge but his stomach's need was stronger. He gently opened the door and blinked. The miniscule hall opened to a bathroom, this time in gold marble, and the huge living room-cum-kitchenette just beyond. He nipped into the bathroom and closed the door. He was surprised to see his damp jeans and tee-shirt hanging over the shower stall rail. The waistband of his jeans was darkened with stains that hadn't been removed fully and Alec averted his eyes. His blood was disturbing in an odd sense. Instead, he treated himself to a hot shower after a few minutes of trying to figure out the controls. Even with the bout of lightheadedness, he felt a million times better as he stepped out and dried himself with an embroidered towel.

Too hungry to go searching for other clothes to wear, he donned the boxers again, securing the waist with an elastic band he found on the counter.

He noticed Riley the minute he walked into the main room. She was tightly twisted in a blanket with her bare feet sticking out and her dark hair tousled over her face. Without the makeup and the perpetual sneer, she looked younger and terribly vulnerable. If she knew he was staring she'd make a cutting remark that would have his skin peeled in strips. Shaking his head, he tiptoed to the fridge and peered inside. His stomach growled at the plate of leftover spaghetti. He carefully retrieved it and found a fork in the drying board. The microwave would be sure to wake her up so he'd have to settle for it cold.

He balanced the plate on one hand and silently unlocked the outside door. The morning air was surprisingly chilly. He stepped down the three metal steps and onto the springy turf. He looked around as he tucked into his breakfast with relish.

The small campsite was almost dwarfed by the massive camper but had enough room for a fire-pit, empty of anything but a puddle of ashy water, a makeshift clothesline, and a picnic table that had seen better days. The surrounding trees towered overhead, limiting the view of the cloudless sky. The twinkling glint of water between the trees at the rear of the camper indicated the river. Intrigued, Alec put his empty plate on the picnic table. There wasn't a real trail, just places where the brush had been cleared a bit, allowing access through the ring of trees to the riverbank beyond. Alec pushed several low hanging branches out of his way and stepped out into the clearing. The river stretched widely, dotted with multiple rocky islands, some inhabited with cabins while others were empty of anything but a few scraggly trees. A lone hawk dipped and wheeled, close enough for Alec to notice the markings on its feathers. Near the far shore, a tiny sailboat with a rainbow-coloured mainsail tacked against the wind.

It was like an advert for Ontario Tourism. Alec hadn't done much camping before. All their family holidays had been either to visit his father's relatives in northern Scotland or his mother's family in Jamaica. But if anyone had asked him, a week in a place like this, hot dogs and marshmallows toasting over the fire and endless swimming in the river would have ranked right up there with winning the lottery. Shame he had to find this little piece of paradise while on the run.

On the run... *His orb*. Cripes, he had no idea where it was. Suddenly feeling naked and vulnerable, he whirled around and headed back to the camper. He pulled up short as he realized he wasn't alone.

A uniformed police officer was standing next to the large picture window and craning to see inside. The cop whirled around at the sound of Alec's approach, hand automatically hovering over the holstered pistol.

"This your camper, son?" the officer looked Alec up and down, taking in his bare feet, the oversized boxer shorts, and shocked expression.

"Yeah, why?" Alec answered. He forced the sullen tone out of his voice and a polite expression onto his face.

"We've got a report of a stolen vehicle, just like this one." The officer gave a jerk of her head towards the front of the camper. "The plates of this camper match. Care to explain?"

Alec shrugged. "Beats me, officer. Better ask my, ah, cousin."

"Your cousin," the officer echoed, one eyebrow inching towards her bangs. "This is your cousin's trailer?"

Alec headed towards the door and opened it. "I'll tell him

you want to talk to him. He's asleep. Just a sec." Before she could object, Alec leapt up the stairs and into the dark interior. He glimpsed Riley starting to sit up on the sofa, but mindful that the window was open, only pointed wordlessly towards the door and shook his head. Riley reached for her orb and flung the covers off her legs while Alec headed to the bedroom. He had to shake Darius awake.

"What the..?" Darius started to gasp as Alec's hand slapped over his lips.

"Cops," Alec whispered. "Did you steal this thing?"

Darius cursed quietly as he pulled Alec's hand away. He immediately jumped from the bed, pulling his shoes on and taking his orb out of his pocket at the same time. "Stay here," he said quietly as he left.

Alec sat down on the edge of the bed. His back was aching something awful now that there wasn't anything to distract him and shivers of weakness were coursing through his blood. He'd obviously been hurt pretty badly. Through the open bedroom door he could see Riley, pulling on her shoes and listening attentively to the conversation outside. Unwilling to stay in the dark any longer, Alec got up and sidled over to the open window.

"Isn't that strange, officer?" Darius was saying with false incredulity. There was the rustling of feet on twigs and dry grass. "The license plates *are* similar but you notice the last two numbers are *entirely different*."

"That's odd," the officer mused. Alec could hear the confusion growing. "I was sure they matched." Her voice tailed off as she walked away from the window.

"It's just a routine check," Darius continued. "You should carry on with your search. Head back towards Toronto. *The camper is still in the metropolitan area.*"

Well, that was that. Alec sighed with relief and returned to the bathroom. His orb hadn't been in sight in the bedroom and he knew it had been in the pocket of his jeans before he got hurt. Why anyone would wash his jeans and not take the orb out, he had no idea, but it was worth checking, just in case. The tee-shirt was almost dry and he slipped it over his head, but the jeans were still unpleasantly clammy and, he noted, orb free. Where was it? He pulled the jeans on and forced himself to ignore the dampness; he could hardly walk around in underwear. Almost without thinking, he reached for the medicine cabinet over the sink and hooked the mirror-backed door open with a finger. The metal shelves were overloaded with various creams, pill bottles, and lotions. And, sitting incongruously in the middle, one slightly bluish-white crystal orb.

Alec grinned. He scooped the crystal ball into his hand and rubbed the smooth surface with a profound sense of relief. No matter how much he might not like what had happened to him, one thing was undeniable; he felt complete with the crystal in his hand. Even the pain was better.

With a sudden splintering crack, the mirrored door shattered into a thousand pieces. Tiny shards flew out in all directions like heat-seeking missiles. Alec wasn't able to get his hands up in time and a burst of stinging bites blossomed into existence over his face and neck as the missiles found their mark.

"Ow," he gasped as he recoiled into the wall behind him.

Another outrageously loud *bang* exploded next to him as the second bullet slammed into the wall next to the open bathroom door. A third almost immediate explosion rocked the walls of the RV but sounded in another direction.

For a second Alec stood paralyzed in horrified disbelief. Someone was shooting at him. From somewhere outside, Riley screamed. His heart restarted and he dropped to the ground. His stab wound exploded in pain but he ignored it. He inched forward on his belly to peer around the corner of the doorway. The living room was empty. The soles of Peter's shoes were barely visible under the mattress of the bed.

Alec slithered into the tiny hallway and moved slowly forward towards the living room. He couldn't hear much—his ears were still ringing from the blast of the gun—but somewhere in the distance someone was shouting. He could only hope it was Darius and that he hadn't been shot.

Alec poked his head past the cupboards. The screen door wasn't latched. Alec could only see the corner of the picnic table, with his empty plate still sitting where he'd left it. Most importantly, Riley wasn't lying in a blood-soaked heap at the foot of the RV's steps. He pulled himself to his knees and stretched upwards to look outside the front windows. Over the dashboard there was only a vista of trees across the tiny roadway and a sign nailed to a maple tree indicating their location, lot 39. There was no sign of the police car, the cop, Darius, or Riley.

Where were they? He assumed it was the cop firing, but why on earth would she? Darius had told her they didn't have the stolen RV and she'd sounded pretty convinced. Had she managed to overthrow the Tyon influence and come to her senses? And even if she had, Canadian police officers hardly ever pulled out their guns and fired. It wasn't like television.

It didn't make sense. Grimacing as another white-hot spasm of pain shot through his back, Alec climbed to his feet. For a second his head spun. The instant it cleared, he opened the screen door and warily stepped outside. It was totally silent, except for the wind moaning softly through the upper boughs of the thick pine trees around them. No bird calls, no people, no sirens. A prickle of unease danced across his shoulders. Where had they gone?

50   Half afraid that any second he'd turn and discover Riley's bleeding body or, worse, a gun to his own head, Alec slowly stepped forward, heading towards the front of the camper. Figuring that if anyone was going to run anywhere, they wouldn't chose the river, he inched his way towards the deeply rutted lane that crossed in front of their campsite and

disappeared into the trees. He stayed close to the warm metal of the camper, trying to quiet his harsh breathing so he could hear if anyone snuck up on him. The nose of their RV jutted slightly out into the laneway. Alec stopped and craned his neck around the bug-pitted grill. The dirt road curved to the left and was out of sight in the space of three campsites. None of the campsites were occupied. He pulled back. In the opposite direction, the road was a bit straighter. There was an SUV two campsites down on the riverside and another mammoth camper directly across. While it was early in the day, Alec reasoned by the chilliness still tingeing the air, surely the gunshots had to have awakened someone.

Alec made a snap decision and headed along the straighter portion of the road. He kept as close to the trees as possible. Scanning the surrounding foliage while keeping a wary eye out for a deranged cop with a twitchy trigger finger wasn't easy. And to add misery, the road wasn't dirt as he'd first thought, but mostly dark gravel, sharp and unyielding to his bare feet. Why the heck hadn't he put on his shoes? He brushed another heavy pine branch away and stopped before stepping into the occupied campsite.

Two massive nylon tents were pitched side by side. A cluster of mountain bikes leaned against a spindly sapling next to the picnic table, which was laden with helmets, backpacks, and water bottles. Beer bottles littered the grass around the table and the fire pit. Someone had been partying.

Alec eyed the tents with distrust and gripped his orb more tightly. An army could be hiding behind those. He listened intently for the sound of breathing but heard nothing. He took a deep breath and dashed across the open area, ducking into the trees again, just as his energy failed. He leaned against a pine trunk for support and fought to catch his breath. He peered back at the campsite but nothing was moving and no one seemed to have noticed him. Before he could sigh with relief, goosebumps rose across his neck and down his arms. It was creepy how silent it was. Creepy and...

He didn't get to finish that thought. The warm metal of a pistol jammed up against the base of his skull. He froze with the words whispered in his ear.

"We meet again, Potential."

Riley lay on her stomach under a small pop-up camper and scratched as silently as she could at a mosquito bite on her nose. The view was lousy. The grass underneath was too long to see past and while it was decent cover, it tickled her nose something awful. Great time to develop an allergy, she thought darkly to herself. She'd lost sight of the cop and Darius. Losing the cop was a good thing. The woman had nearly taken her arm off with that last shot as Riley barrelled through the RV door. If her reflexes hadn't been as fast…

Where Darius was, Riley had no idea either. Even with her orb clutched tightly in her left hand there was no inkling of his location. She'd had a microsecond's glimpse of his back as he tore after the cop around the front of the RV, then nothing. By the time she'd pulled herself off the ground, they were both gone.

8

She hadn't waited for Alec and now that she thought about it, that hadn't been a great idea leaving him on his own. Knowing him, he'd be wandering around looking for her and Darius and thinking he could take on the gun-wielding maniac with his overconfident karate whatchamacallit. He'd get himself killed.

But getting back to their camper wasn't going to be that easy. She'd seen the police cruiser at the last second and had managed to duck under the closest camper only in the nick of time. Now the dratted cruiser was stopped only a stone's throw away, and so far, she hadn't heard the door open or anyone get out. That meant the driver was sitting there, watching, and that was odd. Hadn't the gunshots alerted anyone that there was trouble?

She rubbed her nose forcefully to avoid the building sneeze. Carefully she inched closer to the edge of the camper on her stomach, staying within the shadows. If she craned her head she could just make out the rear passenger tire of the cop car. A hand-span away from her nose, a small spider lowered itself on a microscopic thread into the grass. Riley bit her tongue, stopping herself from squealing in disgust, and forced herself to not scramble away.

The static of a two-way radio broke the morning silence. She was too far away to hear the conversation but a premonition slithered along her skin. A minute later, the driver's side door opened and booted feet crunched on the gravel. The sounds of the footsteps got louder. Uniformed trouser legs and polished black boots came into view as the cop walked around the back of his cruiser. He walked slowly towards Riley's hiding place and came to stop right at the camper. Riley watched his feet as the cop leaned forward, probably to look inside. She heard louder static from the radio as she strained to hear the words.

"…The second male has died as of O-six-forty. Repeat. Suspects are considered dangerous. Approach with extreme caution."

The cop grunted. Riley heard the rustle of fabric against leather. She swallowed convulsively. If the gang members Darius had fought actually died, that meant Darius had committed murder, and *that* meant the cops wouldn't stop until they'd hunted them down and had them in custody. Darius had no identification. In fact, he was probably on the list of missing children in his former homeland, and *that* was probably on an international database. How would he explain where he'd been all those years? And if the cops couldn't figure out his name, they'd resort to dental records, fingerprints and stuff. One medical scan of either him or Alec would have the entire government breathing down their necks and who knows what kind of secret service involved to discover who Darius really was. What if they took their orbs? Worse still, she shuddered, if her father got a call saying his daughter was in custody and wanted for murder and theft, the last battle with Rhozan would look like a summer picnic.

She held her breath and gripped her orb tightly, willing the officer to return to his car and *just drive away*. A trickle of sweat ran down her forehead.

The polished boots took a step back from the camper and stopped. Knees bent into view. Riley silently groaned as the cop's face dipped below the camper's edge.

"On your feet, miss," he ordered.

Biting the profane comment that would only get her into deeper trouble, Riley shimmied to the edge of the shadowed grass and, minding her head, clambered out from her hiding place. She kept her eye on the officer, noting that his gun was still in his holster and his expression neutral. She pasted a nonchalant look on her face and waited.

"Are you staying at this campsite, miss?"

Riley nodded. Her mind leaped ahead. He'd want to know where, and if she showed him the camper he was sure to notice the license plate and *that* would be major trouble. "With my parents. In a cabin."

"And what are you doing under this tent trailer?"

She raised an eyebrow. "Haven't you ever played hide and go seek?" She hurried on before he could answer, her voice rising with the feigned indignity. "Obviously *you* don't have two little brothers, who could drive a saint crazy with their never-ending whining. Or a mom who thinks your allowance includes watching the rug-rats for like hours and hours and hours, every weekend, even when you have way too much homework to do and Mr. Donahue is like way too stupid to stop giving assignments during exams. And it's so unfair I could just spit."

55

The cop actually took a step back and eyed her uneasily.

Riley carried on, really getting into her role now. "What are you looking for? Thieves, rapists, murders or what? Like they're gonna hide out in this totally sucking campground for losers."

"Sorry to bother you," the officer's Adam's apple bobbed.

"You've blown my cover," Riley accused. "I've gotta find somewhere else to hide. It's the only peace and quiet I'll have for this whole, entire, *stupid* weekend. If you see two ankle-biters tell them you saw me at the playground." With that, she turned on her heel and stalked off, heading back towards their RV in the distinct hope the cop would leave in the opposite direction just to get away from her. She forced herself not to turn around to look but strained to hear. There were no following footsteps. That had been too close. She had to warn Darius and Alec that the police were searching for the stolen RV. While Darius was as good an actor as she was, Alec's guilty expression would give them away in a second.

The instant she turned the slight corner of the roadway and was sure she was out of sight, she launched herself into a grove of trees. She scampered into the cool dimness of the pines and, keeping her hand in front of her face to protect her eyes from the numerous pine needles, headed back the way she'd come. It was slower going inside the woods than on the roadway, but infinitely harder to be spotted.

It took several minutes before their RV came into view. Riley paused to catch her breath before leaving the cover of the trees. The little campsite was empty and only Alec's plate on the picnic table indicated that anyone was up and about. She strained to hear above the cawing of distant crows and the moaning of the breeze in the upper regions of the trees. If Alec, Darius, or even Peter was around, there was no sign.

Riley gave the surrounding area one last quick look before dashing out of her hiding spot and across the little campground. She grabbed the door handle and flung herself inside. She pulled the door closed behind her as quietly as possible and pulled down the blind. She looked around. Other than the mess she'd made of the covers of her makeshift bed, there was little disturbed in the living room and she didn't get the uneasy sense that someone had been in to rifle around. She climbed onto the sofa bed and pulled down the blind over the large window. She headed back to the master bedroom. The door was closed. Riley bit her lip. She didn't remember Darius closing it after he left but, of course, he'd done so in a hurry and she was too interested in the cop's arrival to think about the door. Hopefully, both Alec and Peter were still waiting inside for Darius's return and had the sense enough to stay put. Although, in Alec's case, she doubted it.

She turned the handle and pulled the door towards her.

If her nerves hadn't been on edge her reaction time might have been slower. As Peter jumped out towards her, a tennis racket swinging in his hand directly at her head, she managed to duck in time. The racket smashed against the wall with enough force to dent the panelling. Peter nearly fell into her with the momentum.

"What the hell are you—?" Riley gasped as she scrambled away from him, barely managing to get her feet underneath her as he dove forward.

Another swing and another resounding *smash* that could probably be heard back at the campsite office.

"I am not staying here with you a second longer," Peter grunted loudly. He swung again, this time scarcely missing her forehead.

"Keep it down," Riley yelped as she tumbled against the pulled-out sofa and landed on her back on the bed. She rolled away from his next chopping swing. The feather pillow next to her head exploded into a cloud of angel dandruff as the racket burst the seams. "There are cops outside."

"Exactly." Peter was gloating. He was fast too. The racket swung again and this time Riley's luck ran out. The edge of it glanced across her forehead with just enough force to stun her but not enough to knock her unconscious. She cried out and clasped her hand to the blossoming pain. Her own orb banged against her skin.

"Enough," she yelled, putting every ounce of Tyon willingness into it along with the fury that was building like a volcano under her skin. "You idiot."

Peter was in mid-swing. Riley's gift wasn't focused strongly enough to stop him but it did slow him down enough so that she was able to roll away. The racket hit the foam seat cushion and bounced harmlessly off.

"Who's the idiot?" Peter growled. "Me, for knowing you're full of crazy ideas or you for actually believing them?" With that he threw the racket with enough force it cracked the window over the little kitchen table. He leaned over Riley and grabbed her shoulders before she could dodge him. His fingers bit deeply into her skin. He gave her a rough shake then threw her down onto the mattress with disgust. "You're stupid enough for Alec."

He turned and with two long strides was at the door.

"Don't leave," Riley gasped. She struggled into a sitting position. "The cops think we've killed someone. They'll shoot first and—"

It was too late. The door swung closed behind him. With a frustrated moan Riley crawled to the window and peered under the edge of the blind. She caught a glimpse of Peter as he ran down the roadway.

Riley dropped the blind with disgust and closed her eyes. She let her head fall forward to rest on the back of the sofa. Darius was going to kill her.

Alec's heart literally stopped beating. It contracted and held position, while his brain did a double backflip in recognition. A hundred thoughts, all terrible, all gut-clenching, slammed through his mind in the instant before his heart painfully restarted.

Emissaries. Rhozan. Rips. It was starting all over again. His knees nearly buckled and he barely managed to keep standing. His fingers clenched spasmodically around his orb.

"If you try to teleport, I'll find the girl and Finn and make them pay," the cold, empty voice behind him whispered. "You know how I can make them suffer."

"I'm not going anywhere." Alec could barely get the words out past his numbed lips. It took a fair bit of strength to move through space and time, and the flood of weakness and pain he felt growing as the adrenaline ebbed away had him suspecting that any jump would be a disaster. And besides, even if he got away, what would happen to the others? Rhozan knew a lot about torture. He also knew Darius and Riley's unique essence and would be able to track them in a heartbeat. Alec had been inside Rhozan. He knew what the alien was capable of.

9

"What do you want?" he croaked.

"What do I always want, Alec?" Alec could hear the smile in the voice behind him and a wave of despair washed through him. He'd beaten this guy only yesterday and it had cost him dearly. The struggle inside the rip had been horrific and even *trying* to remember what he'd done to overcome the invader made his mind scream in terror. He couldn't do this again. He didn't have it in him.

"I don't know," he answered wearily. Rhozan wanted so many things. How to pick just one?

The gun rapped against his skull for emphasis. "Think."

Alec shuddered as another wave of pain ran through his flank. He pushed it aside and concentrated. Was it the same as last time? World domination and the total destruction of everything Alec held dear? All his memories; all that he was; his very *soul*? Inside he was screaming but he forced himself to voice a response.

"You want me."

"Ah, clever. You do remember. Excellent."

A hand shoved his shoulder, spinning him around. He stumbled back and fell against the tree trunk as he got a look at the Emissary. His first suspicion was right. It was the cop he'd met outside the RV. But the intelligence and humanity he'd seen in her eyes a few minutes ago was missing. In its place was the blank, creepy nothingness of one of Rhozan's lethal puppets. The gun barrel was only an arm's length away. Alec could barely wrench his eyes from the darkness inside the gun.

"You will come with me," the Emissary said in a harsh parody of the cop's natural voice.

"Where?"

"Where the Guardian can see you." The Emissary waved her gun indicating Alec should head towards the road. "Move."

Sweat dripped into Alec's eyes. He felt shivery and a bit unsteady on his feet, but his mind was now rapidly moving into overdrive. He had to keep his head. He had Riley and Darius to think of, not to mention the entire world. He swallowed the bile at the back of his throat and forced himself to push the overwhelming fear away.

If Rhozan wanted Darius to see them, it could only be a trap. There was no way he was going to let that happen.

"Now." The Emissary struck Alec across the forehead for emphasis. The blow wasn't hard enough to do serious damage but hurt anyway. Alec jerked backwards and nearly lost his balance. He ducked his head to miss a second strike and pushed himself away from the tree and the Emissary. He dragged his feet as he tried to give himself time to think of a plan. Running wasn't an option. Police were trained to hit a moving target and even with Rhozan in charge of the cop's body and what that might mean to a reduction of accuracy, Alec wasn't going to take the chance. He'd hardly be able to run fast enough in this condition to put enough distance between him and the cop to improve his chances of escape anyway.

Overcoming her physically wasn't an option either. Normally his reflexes were great and his kickboxing skills were good enough for winning a few tournaments and, he remembered, fighting off Emissaries. But now, the world was spinning around him and he might pass out any minute. Besides, kicking a gun out of someone's hand and not getting shot only happened in the movies. There had to be another option. *Think.*

The gun poked him in the middle of his back and he stumbled forward. He had hardly traversed any distance when a familiar shout broke his concentration.

"Hey, Alec, are you okay?"

Oh no. Alec shook his head mutely and tried to will Peter to run in the other direction. His hand clenched tightly around his orb and he stopped walking as Peter ran towards them.

Peter skidded to a halt the instant he noticed the gun aimed at Alec's head. His eyes raked Alec, then the police officer, and settled back on Alec. A look of uncertainty warred with wariness. Peter slowly raised his own hands into the air. "Is he under arrest?" he called.

The Emissary stepped to Alec's side and cocked her head. Out of the corner of Alec's eye he could see her, assessing the physical similarities between them. He sensed Rhozan's perception of them both and internally groaned.

"Ah, the other one," the Emissary said quietly, as if speaking to herself. "Two for one."

"She only looks like a cop, Peter," Alec said. "She's just Rhozan's puppet."

Peter frowned but before he could respond the cop spoke. "You will die too. The signature is weak but present. Finn was wise to collect you both."

Peter took a step back. "What do you mean die? You can't kill me. I'm unarmed. And who's Rhozan?"

"I am Rhozan," the Emissary said. "I will take your life and Alec's suffering will feed me. Won't it, Alec?"

"He's nothing to me, Rhozan," Alec said. "I won't suffer at all. I hate his guts."

Alec watched the flash of what might have been pain cross Peter's face before the veil of antipathy fell into place. He might have bought Peter some time but he'd just widened the canyon-like gap between them.

"You little—" Peter started.

He never got to finish. Moving almost too fast to see, Darius rocketed out of the trees behind them. His flying leap and kick at the cop's head was as close to poetry as Alec had ever seen. There was a sickening crunch as her neck snapped and a deafening bang as her finger tightened spasmodically on the trigger of the gun. The bullet went wide, missing Alec and slamming into a tree trunk across the roadway. Peter dove to the ground and Alec followed.

62   Darius landed, rolled like a cat and was on his feet and wrenching the cop's gun from her hand in one smooth motion. He straightened, raised his orb in Peter's direction and said loudly, "Obey." A flash of white light left the orb and almost instantly circled Peter.

Alec watched the expression drain from Peter's face and an uneasy blankness replace it. Uncomfortably, he glanced over at the police officer. Already her open eyes were glazing into death.

"Jeez, Darius, I think you've killed her," Alec's voice broke.

"Alec, get a move on. There's another one." Darius ordered as he flung the gun into the trees.

Alec tried to reply but the pain in his back roared into life again as Darius spoke and a shivering chill drenched him. He started to get to his feet but the world around him slid into a sickening grey.

Oh crap, he thought as he fell into nothingness.

Riley followed Darius's lead and leapt out of the rowboat into knee-deep water. The instant her feet landed on the slippery riverbed she lost her balance and fell onto the oarlock with a nasty *thud*. She stifled the cry and ignored the pain in her arm. All they needed was to alert the local inhabitants that someone had illegally landed on their property.

She grabbed hold of the boat and began to pull it up onto the miniature beach while taking a wary look around. For as far as she could see there was nothing but trees and scrubby bushes jutting over the water and rocks. The tiny pebble-covered beach had been the only place to land for the last hour and Darius had finally agreed to pull ashore only when Riley threatened to jump overboard. She rubbed her nose. It was stinging and probably horribly burnt by now. She was going to look like Bozo the clown if she didn't either get some sunscreen or get into the shade.

10

"Peter, get out and pull the boat up onto the grass," Darius ordered as he sloshed to the bow.

Peter threw his oar to the bottom of the boat, barely missing Alec. Giving Darius a malicious look he carefully lowered himself into the water and grimaced as the cold penetrated his jeans.

"We'll be safe on this side of the river," Darius grunted as he heaved the boat onto the narrow shore. "We're in the United States now. Peter, push a bit harder."

"Don't be naïve," Riley shot back as she pulled her sleeve up to examine the rapidly forming bruise. "I told you, the cops think we're murderers and every single one of them will have our description by now and be on the lookout for us. It doesn't take a genius to figure out, hey, we've probably stolen a boat and, wow, we could be out of the country by now. Even the dimmest bulb on the OPP knows the States is on the other side of the St. Lawrence."

"Anna will take care of it."

"Anna is going to wipe the memories of the entire Ontario police force?" Riley raised an eyebrow as she stood up straight. Her hands went automatically to her hips. "Yeah, right."

Darius shrugged one shoulder. "She's relentless. Now, pull."

"You mean ridiculous. There are thousands of cops in Ontario. *Thousands.* And just how is she going to accomplish this little venture? Skip alongside each and every one of them and tap them on the head with her orb?"

"The Tyon Collective is extremely effective in erasing any knowledge of contact with us or our technology. We'd infiltrated Earth long before you people even had television," Darius replied hotly. Then he amended. "Not that I was there, then."

"Sure you weren't, Grandpa."

Darius pulled a face as he tugged the rowboat higher on the shingle. "That's not the point. The point is, you, I mean the collective you, had no idea that aliens walked the streets, studied your culture, and infiltrated your gene pool. Go on, argue that. You didn't know."

Riley turned her back on him and tugged. "Don't get me started on the genetic manipulation," she growled.

"What genetic manipulation?" Peter let go of the rowboat and frowned.

Riley jumped in before Darius could reply. "Ever

wonder how you and I got picked by the Tyons, huh? What makes us special?"

Peter's face was easy to read. She could see the possibilities flit by inside his brain as easily as if they had been hers. His sudden understanding that he was somehow unusual, somehow different, somehow modified.

"You mean someone fiddled with my genes?" Peter sounded as aghast as he looked.

"'Fraid so. But years ago. Back before television," Riley replied.

"The Tyons infiltrated several locations and introduced the Tyon resistance gene into the population. We had hoped that by the time the Others came here to invade, it would have sufficiently spread through the population to confer adequate resistance." Darius had grabbed the painter from the rowboat and was now looking around for something to tie it to.

"But the Others arrived too soon," Riley added. "Or our grandparents didn't have enough kids. Either way." She slashed her hand across her neck. "We're toast." She smiled to herself at Peter's appalled expression.

"Which one of my grandparents, er, consorted with you weirdos?" Peter took a step back, slipping slightly in the uneven riverbed, his gaze fixed on Darius with a new, enhanced loathing.

"Your paternal grandmother, Peter, and man, she was hot," Darius said with a straight face.

"He's kidding you," Riley leaned over and smacked Peter's upper arm. For a moment, he looked like he was going to cry. "Darius, that's enough." She never thought she would be taking Peter's side in anything, but Darius's teasing had a cruel edge especially with the mind control he had over Peter. "We need to get into town and borrow a vehicle as quickly as possible, and without attracting attention by arguing among ourselves. Or had you forgotten we're fugitives from the law?"

"How could I with you reminding us every thirty seconds?" Darius replied.

Once the painter was securely tied to an overhanging branch and Alec was hoisted over Darius's shoulder, they set out. Darius reasoned that waterfront was prime real estate and there was bound to be lots of homes within an easy distance, all with the plethora of vehicles rich people liked to own. But as the minutes passed and all they found were trees, trees and more trees, Riley decided they'd stumbled upon the only stretch of uninhabited prime real estate in the country.

She swatted at yet another wretched mosquito with the back of her hand and thought dark thoughts. If Darius had any clue as to her opinions, he said nothing. He was cheerily bounding through the miserable little forest as if they were having the time of their lives instead of racing against time. Peter, on the other hand, was sharing her bad mood. He was slouching beside her, the invisible chain between him and Darius still clearly in operation, and muttering under his breath as he constantly waved his hand at the swarms of flies and bugs intent on a human feast. She noted he kept his eyes studiously off Alec and Darius, as if even acknowledging their presence would crack his ability to stay in control. She didn't need any orb-enhanced ability to tune into his emotions. The fear and anger radiated off him in waves.

Riley shoved another intruding bough away from her face and contemplated Alec. He was still very pale and she couldn't help but be worried. And, if she was honest, not a little annoyed with him. Honestly, what had he been trying to prove, running off and getting into a fight with the cop? Didn't he realize how badly hurt he'd been? The Intergalactic Council had him on their most wanted list; why kill himself and do their job for them? That reminded her.

"Just where do you plan for us to go, to evade the Council, Dare?"

Darius gave her a quick look over his shoulder. "We'll start with Home Base. If I can arrange it, I'll get us off planet. The sooner Alec's Tyon signal is dissociated with Terra, the better."

A shiver that had nothing to do with the cool, shaded air rippled across Riley's skin. She wasn't totally surprised. Other than Alec not using his Tyon talents ever again, where else could he go? The Council would be searching Earth. Not to mention the police.

"And the Tyons are going to send us on somewhere else?" Riley caught herself before she tripped over a root. "Won't they want us to stay and fight the Others, if they show up again? I mean, that was the reason you were looking out for us in the first place."

She saw Darius's shoulder rise and fall but didn't hear the accompanying sigh. "If there are any signs of the Others, the operation will move into high gear. You remember what that means."

"I don't." Peter spoke up beside her but so quietly she barely heard him.

"You don't want to," Riley answered.

"Your training will begin, Peter," Darius spoke over her. "You'll learn to use an orb, like Riley and Alec. You'll learn how to protect your planet from invasion."

"I don't want to learn anything from you people," Peter replied. "I don't have to do anything I don't want to."

"You sound like a two-year-old," Darius gave a short laugh. "In case you haven't noticed, Peter, I can make you do anything I want. You've *already* been doing what I want. How much more evidence do you need?"

"You think you've got me right where you want me, but you don't," Peter shot back. "I know all about you guys now. Just wait until the police catch up with you. I have a photographic memory. I can tell them everything."

"And they'll believe you?" Darius threw an amused look over his shoulder. "I have two witnesses, including your own brother who will contradict everything you say. Forced to come with me? Lots of witnesses to the contrary. Mind control using a crystal? Fantasy novel mumbo jumbo. Alien invaders ready to take over the world? They'll ask you what medications you take as they drive you to the hospital. Get real, Peter. You aren't wearing handcuffs and are walking beside us under your own steam. No one will believe you."

"You'll still go to jail," Peter replied hotly. "You killed two gang members."

"*That* was a public service," Darius said as he shifted Alec a bit. "And self-defense."

"What about the cop? They'll nail you for that."

"There's no evidence I did it. And neither you nor Alec would tell."

"I would," Peter spat. "And when I do, you'll go to jail."

"Nope."

"He won't," Riley butted in. "He'll transport us out the minute the cops close in. You've forgotten how we moved from the bus to the RV."

Peter turned his head away. "I blacked out."

"You didn't," Riley smiled. "Darius teleported us with his orb. I helped. We can move in space using our orbs."

Peter blanched. He'd clearly forced that unbelievable event out of his brain but now had no option but to face it. "That's impossible," he said weakly.

"I think you need to check the dictionary, Peter," Darius said as he clambered over a rotting tree trunk. "You misunderstand the meaning of that word."

There was silence for a while as Peter retreated into a simmering rage and Riley focused on her own uncomfortable thoughts. Around them, the sunlight streamed in green banners through the thick summer foliage and birds called in constant chatter. The ground underfoot was thick with rocks and springy moss and rather treacherous if one didn't pay attention. Riley was about to ask Darius to slow down when he came to a sudden halt. He raised a hand to indicate they were all to be quiet. He pointed straight forward.

There was a clearing just up ahead, just visible through the trees. And as if the fates had conspired to fulfill their wishes, the entire field was full of RVs and campers.

Darius turned and gave Riley an evil grin. "Which one do you want?" he whispered.

"I'm partial to blue," Riley answered as she squinted through the trees at the selection of motor homes. Oddly enough, there didn't seem to be any people.

"Wait here," Darius instructed. "I'll go and see which one has keys in it and, if worse comes to worse, you can hotwire it, Riley. Wait for my signal. Peter, stay here and stay quiet. Do anything to jeopardize this little mission and I'll have you eating that earring of yours. Got it?"

Darius gently laid Alec on the ground and slipped off silently through the trees. Riley dropped to her knees and wiggled her orb under Alec's back to the approximate area of his injury. She didn't bother to watch Peter. Darius's control seemed tighter than ever. She closed her eyes and concentrated.

Almost no time passed at all before the gentle purring of an engine cut through the birdcalls. She glanced upwards. A square camper was turning an awkward and jerky circle inside the ring of RVs. It stopped as close to the trees as it could and the window rolled down. An arm waved at them.

"Come on, lift him up and carry him," Riley ordered as she got to her feet.

"I don't have to do anything you say," Peter grumbled.

70   "Sure. Don't bother. I'll just call Darius over and see how he likes you holding us up." Riley crossed her arms. She overcame the urge to stick out her tongue.

Peter cursed but obeyed. He struggled to pull Alec up into his arms and Riley had to help hold Alec's ankles. Swinging him gently between them, Peter walked backwards towards the clearing. Darius opened the side door of the camper and transferred Alec to his own arms. He carried him inside. Peter slowly followed and Riley closed the door behind herself.

This camper was a much cheaper version of their previous mode of transportation. Plain, more compact and clearly much older, there was a bed tucked over the driver's seat, a roundish bench with a table jammed in the middle that probably folded into a bed, a miniature kitchen, and a miniscule toilet cubicle between the bedroom and main space. They would have to take turns walking around.

Riley didn't waste time dissing the worn and discount-store décor. She plopped herself in the driver's seat and clicked the seatbelt closed.

The RVs were parked in a ring around the perimeter of a huge field and interspersed with several cars and a couple of motorcycles. On the far side of the field a wide gap beckoned and she headed for it in low gear. Behind her, she heard Darius's instructions to lay Alec on the bed. She carefully steered the little camper between two very large motor homes and onto a gravel road. It suddenly became apparent where all the people were.

The next field over was filled with hot air balloons. A fairly large crowd of spectators were scattered across the grass, standing around each of the seven balloons, most of which seemed to be nearly fully expanded. Riley couldn't help but grin. The balloons were bright and cheerful, the piping gas fires that filled them surprisingly noisy, and the smiles and cheery expressions of the people ringing the balloons as they waited their turn for a ride, infectious.

An alarming thought crossed her mind. Riley slammed on the brakes and peered at Darius. He had that rapt expression and gleam to his eye that only spelled trouble.

"No," she said shaking her head firmly and putting the little camper van back into gear, "Absolutely not."

"It's faster," Darius protested.

"It's incredibly obvious. Honestly, Dare, you think no one will notice we've stolen a balloon. Do you believe for a second the police won't think to look *up*. We'd be totally easy to track. They'd just have to wait for us to come down."

"It'd be fun," Darius said quietly as he craned his neck for the last view of the balloons above the treetops.

Riley sped up. The camper rattled as it bumped along the rutted dirt road. No one seemed interested as she drove past.

She turned her attention back to the task at hand and carefully maneuvered the small vehicle down the road. It was a generally straight path through a series of fields, most tilled and planted with a variety of crops, but a few, like the one filled with balloons, fallow and allowed to grow grass unimpeded. There were no buildings. It only took a couple of minutes before the road ended at a busy four-lane thoroughfare. To her left a huge sign indicated, "Turn here for Sky-high."

"Which way?" she called out.

Darius held up his orb and peered into it. "East," he said.

Riley just looked at him.

"Left," he amended.

"Thanks," she muttered and switched on her directional signal. It took a few minutes before there was a sufficient break in traffic for them to safely make the turn. Once on the highway, Riley quickly accelerated and pulled into the right lane. "Look for a map," she instructed. She glanced down at the dashboard. "And figure out how we're going to pay for gas."

72 Darius rummaged in the glove compartment but, other than a handful of wadded candy bar wrappers and a flashlight, it was empty. He searched in the door pocket and above the visor but there was no map.

"We'll keep heading east," he finally said. "Eventually we'll hit the ocean. I'll go in the back and work on Alec's healing. You just drive."

"Can't we just," Riley gave Peter a wary glance in the rearview mirror, "teleport?"

"Too much baggage," Darius replied. "I can't manage all three of you except in an emergency and then only a very short distance. The rules of physics apply to orb power too, you know. We either wait for Anna to show up and help or get as close as we can and summon a transport ship."

"But you don't like either option," Riley said quietly. "Do you?"

Darius pursed his lips and frowned. "No."

"Why not?"

"Anna is going to have some questions I just can't answer. Lying to her will be nearly impossible for me. Asking the Collective to bring three Potentials into the Base when they haven't ordered it is going to be even trickier. We're not on collection or training mode. Just observation."

Riley thought it over. There had to be another way.

"Peter's going to be a huge problem too," Darius continued as he rubbed his forehead. A couple of pine needles fell out of his hair and onto his collar. "I can't silence him without keeping him unconscious. He's wearing off my control faster each time. I won't be able to keep it up indefinitely unless I seriously damage him and make the control permanent." He caught a glimpse of her expression. "And no, I'm not willing to do that to him." He sighed deeply and shook his head. "One good scan or a telepath and the jig is up."

"We could just toss him into the Atlantic," Riley suggested. "Tie his ankles with lead weights and heave ho. I won't argue if you suggest it. I doubt Alec would either."

Darius grinned. "Don't tempt me."

Riley bit her lower lip as she worked on phrasing the enquiry. "Why do you believe Anna won't turn us all in?"

For a long moment Darius was silent as he stared

straight ahead. "Anna was the first I came in contact with." He gave a ghost of a smile. "I come from a large family, Riley. Having anyone's undivided attention is heady stuff. Especially when that attention isn't a smack to the head."

Riley glanced sideways at him, struck by the aching tone of his voice. "How long ago was that?"

Darius gave a slight shrug. "I was about fourteen and in foster care and really angry at the world. The Tyons offered stability and made me feel special for the first time in my life. Anna was the one who convinced them to train me. I owe her a great deal of loyalty, not to mention my life. If they hadn't found me I'd be in jail or dead by now." He got up out of the passenger seat. "I'm going to work on Alec now."

Riley nodded but Darius was already gone. Well that was certainly food for thought, she mused worriedly. Darius had several reasons now for his blindness about Anna. There was little she'd be able to do to counteract years of obligation and love. And if she couldn't get Darius to open his eyes about Anna, then she'd have no choice. She and Alec would have to disappear without him.

Alec poured the last of the cereal into his bowl and reached for the small container of milk. It was his third bowl and he was still starving. Apparently massively accelerated healing used a great deal of energy and his body was desperate to catch up. Darius was rooting in the cupboards for something else for him to eat and Peter was driving. Riley had done several hours and was having a nap now, her head likely pillowed exactly where his had been only half an hour before.

He shovelled a heaping spoonful into his mouth and chewed contentedly. Nothing much had seemed to happen while he was sleeping. Anna still hadn't returned. There had been no police chases or interest in them by anyone, despite the fact that they were now driving through New Hampshire in another stolen camper with three first-degree murder charges hanging over their heads.

11

"Have you warned Peter about the rips, yet?" Alec asked. A few crumbs fell to the tabletop and he wiped them away with the sleeve of a borrowed shirt before Darius noticed.

"No." Darius closed the cupboard door and opened another.

Alec swallowed and took another mouthful. "Have you seen any?"

"No, and don't talk with your mouth full. It's rude and a choking hazard."

Alec raised his hand and gave Darius the finger as he grinned.

"And that's rude too," Darius pointed out with a returned smile. His face suddenly became serious. "I haven't told Riley about the Emissary either."

Alec nearly choked even though his mouth was empty. "What? Darius, she has to know. There'll be millions out there. She has to be on her guard."

"Hear me out." Darius abandoned his search and sat down next to Alec. He lowered his voice. "Rhozan tracks us by the use of our orbs, right? And we've had to use them a lot over the last few hours. But if we keep our hands off them and keep moving, he won't be able to find us that easily. Once we're in Home Base, we're safe."

"He found me easily enough, long before I ever got an orb," Alec reminded him.

"He found you through me. I was using my orb and he picked up your signal in the vicinity."

"Okay, fine. That's how he tracks us." Alec was willing to concede the point. "But still, Riley has to know."

"Riley has had enough on her mind lately. You aren't in touch with her feelings the way I am but I'll tell you that your injury nearly broke her heart. Worse still, she's done a lot of the healing and while she might not feel the effects, I can see them. Any more emotional trauma at this point and she'll collapse."

Alec sat back in the seat and dropped his spoon to the table. She had been worried about him. A lot. Good.

"Healing takes emotional energy, focused through Tyon power. When you heal someone you deplete your own resources. It takes time to replace and, in the untrained, is highly dangerous. It was only because it was such a dire situation that I allowed her to help out. First with your father, and then with you."

Talk about guilt. Alec turned his head to look out the window. She'd put herself at risk and didn't even know it.

Darius continued. "I want you to keep an eye on things, Alec. Make sure she stays clear of any rips. At least until I know she's strong enough to mentally cope. All right?"

Alec didn't look at him. He nodded his head mutely. Darius got back up and continued his search but Alec's appetite was gone. The rips in the fabric of time and space were seriously dangerous things; he should know, he'd jumped into one and just barely made it out alive. Last time they'd lived through this month, Rhozan had caused the rips to multiply until they were nearly everywhere. Hundreds, maybe even thousands of people had disappeared into them. If Alec hadn't defeated Rhozan, all those people would still be stuck there. Or will be stuck there if time repeats itself. Alec frowned. This time travel stuff was mind-boggling. Without thinking, his hand reached for his orb. He stopped himself just in time from slipping his hand into his pocket. He clasped his hands together firmly instead.

"Darius," he began slowly, "what will happen if—"

He didn't get to finish. Suddenly, right in front of him, Anna appeared. Alec was so startled he nearly knocked over his half empty bowl. Milk sloshed onto the Formica tabletop.

"Ah, Anna, welcome back," Darius said smoothly, as if Anna had merely been out for a walk. He closed the cupboard and leaned against the countertop. "All returned to normal, I take it?"

"No," Anna fixed him with a sharp look. "We need to talk."

"Didn't you find everyone?"

She didn't bother to answer his question. "We've received a transmission from the Council, Darius. It's troubling and important. I wish to discuss it with you."

"Okay." Darius slid himself into a seat beside Alec. He patted the bench seat with his hand. "Come and sit down."

"This is a private matter, of utmost importance. Potentials should not be included." Anna hadn't changed one bit, Alec thought, watching her ramrod posture and implacable features. If anything, she was colder.

"All right," Darius replied easily. "I can't move Riley coz she's fast asleep." He gave Alec a pointed look. "Go and stay with Riley until I call for you. Practice your skills the way I've shown you."

Alec tried to keep the puzzlement out of his expression as he got up and inched past Anna to go to the bedroom. Hadn't Darius just gotten through telling him not to use his orb? The little swaying bedroom was in darkness. Alec could barely make out Riley's form on the double bed. He gingerly sat on the edge of the foam mattress and inadvertently sat on her foot.

"Hey," she muttered, kicking sleepily at him.

He leaned over and whispered. "Anna's back."

She sat bolt upright. "When?"

"Shh," Alec hissed. "You're supposed to be asleep."

Riley pushed the covers away and reached up to jerk open the curtains, enough to flood the little room with light. She crawled over to his side and hunched on her knees beside him. "What's she know?"

"I'm not sure. She just got here. But the Council's twitchy and has more questions than is good for us."

He barely heard her mutter the profanity. She was obviously as scared as he was. "Get your orb out," she ordered. Before he could tell her not to, she had her own in her hand. "Hurry up," she whispered as she grabbed at his hand and folded his fingers around her own.

It was as if Alec had turned on a radio, but only inside his head, and with several channels playing at once. He had no idea Riley was so gifted in this area. For a second it was almost overwhelming and he was tempted to jerk his hand out of hers. Then the images and sounds cleared and he heard Darius speaking.

"…Show me what you've got." Images of weird symbols suddenly scrolled across Alec's mind. They looked familiar but moved too quickly for him to decipher. This must be what Darius was looking at. Alec was stunned. Could Riley see inside him the same way?

Impressions of someone else's emotions slipped inside him too: *worry, fear, uncertainty*. Were these Darius's feelings or were Anna's in there as well? Was either of them aware that he and Riley were eavesdropping?

"See, here and here." Anna's voice. *Suspicion, concern.* Her emotions likely. Alec tried to keep up but everything moved through him so quickly.

"What does this mean?" Darius, sounding more nonchalant than he felt.

"Temporal distortion. Someone, somewhere has moved in time. It's not specific enough to pinpoint, but you see here, and this? Clear indications. There is no other explanation. They've sent a directive to Logan to determine where this came from and who is doing it."

"Could it be a natural phenomenon?" Darius again.

Riley and Alec looked at each other. Instantly their hopes were dashed.

"No. Logan's reviewed the power signature. It's human."

Carefully controlled sensations emanated through the orb. *Consideration, interest, willingness to cooperate.*

"If Logan is sure, then it must be correct. Does he have any idea who might have done this? Is it someone we've been following or one of us?"

"Don't be ridiculous, Darius. None of the Collective has this aberration. It must be native. And we must find it as soon as possible. Time shift is dangerous and unlawful. You know the consequences."

Riley tried to pull away but Alec tightened his grip, maintaining the contact. It was about him after all.

"Let me inside your mind."

The demand was politely made but firm. Alec and Riley exchanged horrified glances. If Anna got inside Darius's head there would be no secrets he couldn't hide. Anna might care for Darius and he might be in love with her, but she worked for the Collective and personal feelings didn't get in the way. They were screwed.

Alec's free hand hovered over his pocket. She'd have to catch him first.

"Not now." Darius's reply was tinged with humour. "Later. When we've got a bit of privacy." A definite overtone of amorous intentions suffused the words. Alec mentally backed away. This he did not want to see.

Disappointment and a certain flavour of suspicion seeped into Alec's mind with Anna's next words. "We'll wait then. In the meantime, we must take these three Potentials to Home Base and have them begin their training. There is merit to your suggestion that assistance provided by natives may be of benefit. I will discuss this concept with Logan upon our arrival. He will decide. Keep them ignorant of the potential power of the orbs. Keep the driver under control through any means. I do not wish to manage an uncontrolled teenage male."

Riley jerked her hand out of Alec's just as the door from the camper bedroom opened. She held her orb in her palm and frowned as if unable to figure out what to do with it as Anna stared at them both. Alec leaned over and stared at Riley as if enthralled with her efforts. The second the door closed behind the departing Anna, he urged Riley to put the orb away. "She might pick up any of your thoughts."

Riley nodded. "Good idea." She paused then added, "Darius was boosting our reception. I usually can't hear anyone that clearly. In case you're wondering." She turned away and stowed her own orb in her pocket, keeping her back to him. It was too late. He'd already seen the blush tingeing her cheeks.

"Yeah, well," Alec cleared his throat. "You're still really good at it. Amazing actually."

Riley picked up a tiny porcelain figurine from a shelf across from the bed and examined it carefully. "Uh, thanks," she said.

Alec sat immobile and watched her, but despite his assumption she'd leave, she didn't. After a moment she sat back down beside him. He bit the inside of his lip and wished for something really clever or witty to say to break the increasing tension, but nothing came to mind and he felt like an idiot. Still, it was far better than thinking about going back to Home Base. And Logan.

Riley thought innocuous thoughts about her orb, her hair, and her clothes as much as she possibly could, just in case Anna was listening in. It was a strain to keep it up but she felt she'd been pretty successful. Anna hadn't given her any strange looks or indication that she thought Riley was anything but a vacuous teenager while they ate their meal. But in a couple of minutes, Anna would return from the take-out restaurant's bathroom and Riley knew that Anna would soon consider teleporting to Home Base. It would be next to impossible to keep any secrets there. There were so many Tyon Operatives wandering around and lots of them were telepaths. The instant anyone realized Alec could move people through time he was a goner.

And even if she could convince Darius not to take them back to the Tyon Base, Peter was the other problem. Riley couldn't be sure that Darius's hold over Peter would continue or even extend to Peter's thoughts. She couldn't be sure what Peter felt about Alec's situation or if he even remembered it—she hadn't had a chance to touch Peter with her orb to explore his thoughts, and for some reason, she wasn't as in tune with his emotions as she was Alec's.

Either way, it was a lousy situation.

They were parked at the farthest edge of the drive-through parking lot. Darius watched through the front windscreen as Anna crossed the parking lot to the restaurant. The instant she was inside he grabbed Peter's arm, dragged him into the bedroom

12

and shut the door. Riley waited, chewing her nails until she couldn't stand it any longer. She might not have a chance like this again.

Peter was sitting on the bed, his back against the head-rest. A trickle of sunlight through the crack in the drapes glinted off his miniscule diamond stud. He looked scared to death. Darius was sitting on the edge of the bed on the far side. Both his hands were curled into fists and the glint of an orb peaked from one of them. Both looked up as she entered.

Riley didn't bother to soften the blow. "We've got to get away from her. If Logan gets within ten meters of Alec he's gonna know."

"Tell me about it," Darius said. He glanced at Peter then back at her.

"I think you should kill her," Riley continued.

Darius jerked back as if he'd been scalded. "Are you nuts?"

"Dare, I know that you've got a thing with this woman. Beats me why, but who knows how men think? But the hard fact is that Anna'll turn you in as quick as she can blink. You know it. You can't trust her. And she's dead in the last future too. So it isn't very different."

"I've just got to set it up. Get her on board. That's going to take a bit of work."

"Forget it. She'll turn your ass in."

"You're wrong, Riley. And *you* have to trust *me*." Darius stood up. His face had hardened, as he brushed past her and closed the door.

"He told me everything," Peter said, injecting the gloom with an even more somber tone.

"What?" Riley lifted her head. Had Darius completely lost his mind?

"About Alec. What he can do. What'll happen to him if anyone finds out." Peter's expression momentarily morphed into one of extreme dislike, although Riley had no idea if it was that the idea of his brother being murdered was un-palatable or that Alec was so powerful. Or both. "So?"

"So," Peter shrugged. "I can't let Alec get whacked."

"Thought you hated him."

"I do." Peter pulled his knees up and balanced his crossed arms upon them. He was struggling with something and waves of an emotion she couldn't quite place rolled off him. For a moment he didn't speak. "I'm his older brother. I have a responsibility."

"Like I said, so?"

"My parents would kill me if I let anything happen to Alec. And it would break my mom's heart. She's had enough trouble lately."

"True." Riley didn't add that having only one son come to her rescue when she was about to be decked by her husband was also a heart breaker. Annoying Peter at this point was not a good idea, no matter how big a jerk he was. "So, you're going to play along, keep Alec safe and keep your mouth and your mind off the topic of Alec's little abnormality. Right?"

"I'm not saying anything to this Anna person," Peter affirmed.

"And Darius reminded you that Anna is highly adept at plucking the most private thoughts out of your brain and inspecting them without your knowledge or consent, right? You know how to keep your thoughts off Alec entirely, right?"

Even in the gloom she saw him blanch. "No," he replied warily. "What do you mean?"

"She's a skilled telepath," Riley informed him quickly, aware that every moment she was in the bedroom was a moment she was not out with Alec, keeping an eye on things. "And she is not, no matter how much Darius wants to believe it, on our side. Her main loyalty is to the Tyon Commander, Logan. Hope you never meet him."

Riley returned to the empty main room of the camper,

Peter on her heels. She dropped to her knees on the couch and peered out the window. Alec was standing by the side of the trailer tossing pebbles into the ditch. Sunlight glinted off the expanding rings of water. Farther along the roadway, Darius walked side by side with Anna. They were too far away to hear what was being said but Anna's posture was worth a thousand words.

"Rats," Riley hissed. She was out the door and at Alec's side a moment later. She grabbed his arm just as he was about to launch a handful of stones at the stagnant water several feet away.

"What?" He jumped with fright.

"Anna's about to hear about your special gift, buddy boy. You and I need to be ready to zap out of here the minute she comes gunning for you, that's what. Get your orb out." Riley didn't take her eyes off the pair now nearly half a kilometer down the road.

"I thought Darius wanted to get back into the Base?" Alec pulled his arm away from Riley, gave his approaching brother a wary look, and then swung the stones away. They splattered into the ditch with a dull *plunk*.

"There are dozens of mind readers there. You'll be toast in seconds."

"You don't have to keep going on about it. I'm ready." He pointed to the bulge of his orb. "And if I'm going any-where, I'm going alone."

"Are you crazy?" Riley gasped.

"I'm faster on my own. I'm less of a target on my own. It's me he's gonna come after. You're better off out of the way."

Riley peered intently at him. He was serious. "I disagree." He wouldn't last a minute without her planning for him. "We're in this together. You can't just dump me. Who'll do the thinking?"

"I'm not stupid," Alec flared. He leaned over her, eyes blazing. "I may not get the best marks in the world and I suppose, by your estimation, that makes me nothing, but I happen to be a great strategist. I never panic in tough situations and I'm a hell of lot tougher than you are. It's my mind they want. My superior abilities. Not yours. So piss off."

For a horrible moment, Riley thought she might cry. She hastily brought her emotions under control. *No one* told her to piss off.

"I think he's right. A separated target is a harder one to find." Peter scuffed at the gravel with a toe, looking at neither of them.

"What would you know about it?" Riley rounded on him angrily. "Ten seconds ago you were hoping he'd get run over by a truck and now you're trying to convince him to go it alone because he'll be more successful? Neither of us is about to take anything you say seriously."

"I'm just pointing out that he's making sense." Peter folded his arms. "And you're yelling."

"So?" Riley screeched.

"They're listening." Peter nodded towards Darius and Anna who had stopped and were now staring back at them. "Your thoughts are probably in bold caps."

Sickened, Riley slapped her hand across her lips before she could say another thing. A deep hurt was spreading throughout her chest, like someone had stabbed her.

"I need a diversion," Alec said. He was speaking to his brother, over the top of her head as if he couldn't be bothered to look her in the eye. "The second you think she's gonna come after me, take Riley, and teleport somewhere. Anywhere. Just don't go where I'm going."

"And just where are you going?"

"Can't tell you. In case she reads it off you."

"I can't teleport or whatever. I don't even have one of these crystal balls of yours," Peter reminded him.

"Orbs. And Riley has one. She needs help but if you've got any power like me you can boost her. Just think really strongly of disappearing and it should happen."

Peter shrugged but his face betrayed his uneasiness. "Don't go home. That's the first place they'll look."

"Don't worry."

"I won't."

"Yeah, well, thanks anyway."

Riley stamped her foot. They were talking about her as if she wasn't there. Idiots. If she weren't such a lady she'd have smacked their heads together. "I am not," she repeated, "*not* going to run off with Peter, and you can just get that stupid thought out of your mind, because—"

"Hey!"

She didn't get any further. A shout from the distance interrupted her rant. Anna was bolting towards them at a dead run, Darius right behind her.

Oh no. Darius had told her. She was going to kill Alec.

"Run," Riley screamed.

Alec glanced around to see Anna. Almost instantly he turned back to Riley, his face set with a determination she'd never seen before. He leaned forward, grabbed her upper arms and pulled her up and into him. He kissed her hard. Her heart zoomed up into her throat. Something inside her exploded into being. "Take care," he whispered before letting go and winking out of existence.

Too stunned to grasp what had just happened, Riley felt Peter's hand clutch her own. The power surged from the orb clasped between them, up her arm and into her torso.

"Make it go," Peter urged frantically, his eyes wild with shock.

Riley had one last glimpse of Darius passing Anna, waving his arms frantically, the sound of his shout lost in Peter's urgent cry. Then she focused her inner attention on getting them out of there.

Alec materialized on the edge of a massive crowd of people. The acutely disorienting effect of teleporting caused him to fall backwards onto a tiled wall. He flung out his hands to stop from toppling over. The instant he was steady he shoved his orb into his pocket.

He was in a huge hall. Lined with tiled walls and vending machines, it contained far too many people all hurrying in various directions. Signs hung down from the ceiling slightly off to his right above a series of escalators heading down into the bowels of the earth. The coloured ceramics surrounding the escalator openings made his eyes water. The instant the vertigo left him, he stepped out from the slight alcove he'd arrived in, and peered upwards. *Northern Line, Platforms 3 and 4.* Alec swallowed the bile at the back of his throat and took several deep breaths. The air was congested, filled with dust and the odour of underground circulation. Not entirely displeasing and certainly distinctive.

He glanced around. No one seemed to be paying him any attention. He didn't have the strange sensation that preceded seeing an Emissary. He wiped his sweaty palms against his jeans. A tingle of excitement shuddered through him. Now he just had to figure out which subway station he was in and where he wanted to go.

He turned away from the escalators and followed the trail of people. There were many tourists holding maps and peering intently at the signs, as well as

13

shoppers and the occasional businessperson. Slipping into the busy summer crowd was easy enough and Alec let himself be washed forward with the surrounding swell of humanity.

The wide hall opened up to a huge central station. Here the milling crowd separated into several streams and surged through what Alec quickly determined were ticket collecting machines before emptying out of the station to the surrounding streets. Alec eased himself off to the side. He didn't have a ticket and it appeared that you had to slip one into the machine for the gates to open. He bit the inside of his lip. He could steal someone else's ticket he supposed, but in all honesty his pick-pocketing skills were pretty abysmal. His orb might be of use to trick the machine into thinking it had a ticket but Alec wasn't going to touch his orb again unless it was an emergency. He was going to have to try and slip through unnoticed and, if worse came to worse, run like crazy.

He read the street signs—*Tottenham Court Road, Oxford Street, Charing Cross*—that hung above the steps leading up to sunshine. None were particularly familiar although Charing Cross had a ring to it he liked. Impulsively deciding, he eased back into the crowd and headed obliquely towards the wheelchair exit. Two tottering, elderly Japanese tourists each wheeling a huge suitcase preceded directly ahead of him. Perfect.

Alec waited until the man's ticket triggered a green light and the wide exit doors swung open. Dashing around them, he cleared the exit before the man could shout in anger. Alec looked back for a second. The doors had permitted one person through and the man was now stuck, half- way through the barrier, his wife yelling at him that the trip to England was a huge mistake and that he couldn't do anything right. Alec chuckled and ran.

He took the stairs three at a time and dodged several slower moving commuters with ease. He emerged onto the wide street and came to a sudden stop.

The street in front of him was packed with double-decker buses, cars, motorbikes and at least a dozen beetle-shaped black cabs, all jockeying for far too little roadway. The smells of diesel fumes, cigarettes, and several types of foods assailed his nostrils. There were people everywhere: gazing in shop windows, streaming purposely past each other, chatting, smoking, and talking on cellphones. Tourists with cameras were taking photos of the street and the grey stone buildings that lined each side of the road above the stores and businesses. Alec had no idea where exactly in London he was, but it didn't matter. This was a huge city and he was just one of millions. Darius would never find him here.

And every single one of those millions could turn into an Emissary. Alec blew out a lungful of air with the realization and vowed to keep his hands off his orb.

The next several hours were spent wandering without plan or destination. When his feet began to ache he realized that taking one of the on-off tour buses that wove through the city would be the smartest idea. He'd get a better lay of the land that way and save the rubber soles of his runners from wearing out. Surprisingly, it didn't take long to find a discarded ticket in a garbage bin near one of the bus stops.

He clambered aboard the first double decker that stopped, flashed his ticket to the collector and made his way up the narrow circular stairs to the upper deck, two at a time. The only empty seat was near the back. Alec kept his balance as the bus lurched forward and he dropped into the seat with a contented sigh. He fished the earphones out of the sealed plastic bag and, after selecting the English channel on the dial next to his elbow, shoved the ear buds in his ears. The commentary didn't quite muffle the constant comments from an obnoxious group of tourists behind him, but it helped.

The traffic was heavy and the going slow. The sun was gloriously warm and with the steady drone of the commentator in his ear, Alec found himself getting sleepy. The bus turned into Trafalgar Square and came to a stop. Alec felt his head bob and he straightened up in his seat, afraid that someone had witnessed him dozing off. He rested his arm on the rail and cupped his chin. Soon it would be time to get off and find something to eat.

His orb began to burn. Alec jerked upright and managed at the last second not to reach into his pocket to grab it. A distinctly cold, unpleasant feeling pulsated from the crystal and a creepy sensation ran down Alec's back.

Trying not to be obvious, Alec scanned his surroundings. The crowds were still pretty heavy even this late in the afternoon. On the steps of the National Gallery, a crowd of high-school students were laughing and cavorting, despite the harried instructions of their teacher. Tourists were feeding the pigeons by the monument and taking pictures of each other, covered in the filthy birds. Businessmen and women were striding impatiently through the crowds, laptop bags swinging and cellphones out and to the ears.

The feeling persisted as the bus restarted its journey. Alec slumped down in his seat. It didn't feel like Rhozan. It felt different, like...

Something caught his eye. There, by Nelson's column. There were three of them. Two very tall individuals and one smaller. Another double decker, travelling in the opposite direction, stopped right in front him and blocked his field of vision. Cursing the stupid bus Alec stood up. It was no use. He couldn't see over it.

The burning sensation worsened just as his bus jerked out of its standstill and the other bus did the same. The traffic suddenly cleared enough and the driver took full advantage, speeding up around the corner. Alec craned his neck but the odd trio was nowhere to be seen. Puzzled, he sat back down. The orb's burn slowly dissipated and disappeared completely a moment later. That was strange. Were those three actually looking for him? Were they a part of the Others he didn't know about? Could it have been the creepy Council that Darius was always ragging on about? Or was it his imagination working overtime and the orb just doing some weird orb thing he hadn't noticed before?

With more questions than answers swirling around in his head, Alec sat back and tried to relax. Regardless of who those three oddities were, no one seemed to notice him. As long as he kept his hand off his orb, he'd be fine.

He ended up near Parliament by late afternoon, hungry and moderately annoyed at the continuous hordes of tourists. Alec came to a weary stop on the bridge under Big Ben's shadow. He leaned over the stone balustrade and watched the tour boats chug below him in the murky water of the Thames.

The city was great. There were masses of things to see and he'd made up an entire list of things to do and places to go. The problem was money. Getting money the legal way, like a job, was out of the question. Panhandling wasn't a viable option either; he'd have to stay in one place for too long and he doubted he'd get the kind of cash he needed.

There was nothing else for it. He'd have to use his orb and take money, preferably from someone who wouldn't even miss it. He ignored the twinge of conscience. Was it his fault he was alone, broke, on the streets without any supports? No, it wasn't. Darius was the one bossing him around, putting him in danger, flirting with Riley. If Darius hadn't followed him and opened the way for Rhozan to find him, everything would have been fine.

Galvanized with anger, Alec set off again, a vague plan in his head. Stealing a wallet was too risky. It might not have any cash in it and if he was caught, he'd be in serious trouble. Most credit cards needed pin numbers nowadays and without them they'd be useless. He needed cash.

The now familiar red circle with a blue line cutting it in half indicated a subway or, as he now knew it, an underground station, just up ahead. There was probably an ATM near the ticket booth. Time to see if the orb he carried really did work on machines.

He crossed the busy thoroughfare with the crowds and entered Westminster station. Sure enough, within a few heartbeats he'd located the bank machine and joined the queue. There were several people ahead of him and it seemed to take ages before it was his turn. He had to keep the time he held the orb down to the very minimum and be prepared to run for his life the instant goosebumps crawled over his skin. He pulled his orb out of his pocket and, furtively looking around to see if anyone was watching, he pressed it against the machine and closed his eyes.

Money. Lots and lots of money. He focused his attention on the machine ahead of him. Pictured twenty-pound notes slipping out of the dispenser. Willed it to happen.

Nothing did.

He opened his eyes. In the line behind him, someone coughed with annoyance.

Screw them, this was important. He could almost feel the machine, as odd as that was. He was close. He tried again.

Money. Dispense the money.

Nothing.

"Hey, are you going to take all day?"

Alec squared his shoulders and ignored the sharp comment. If this didn't work, he'd have to try robbing someone and he really didn't like that idea at all. He'd been holding the orb far too long now.

Concentrate.

Five hundred pounds. Come on. Give it to me.

The sharp whir of the money dispenser almost made him shout. He opened his eyes to see the opening widen and a thick wad of paper notes protrude out. Alec didn't waste a moment. He grabbed the cash, his heart hammering wildly, and ran.

Riley fell into an exhausted heap the second she materialized. Peter was still holding her hand. This transport thing was way harder than she'd ever thought possible and she had a dark suspicion that she'd probably still be at the side of the road if Peter hadn't unknowingly helped. Not that she was about to tell him.

She cracked open an eye. It was hard to tell exactly where she was as Peter was standing directly in front of her and his legs blocked her view. She leaned over weakly, pressing her forehead on his shins. She felt awful. She closed her eyes and waited for the vertigo to pass.

14

There was a pleasantly cool breeze blowing and, somewhere nearby, the origin of the saltwater tang. There was grass under her hand and she let Peter's hand go so she could rest both on the ground. In the distance, the low, lonely horn of a ship sounded.

"Is this Vancouver?" Peter asked, his voice breathy and quivering.

"Hope so," Riley muttered. Any long conversation was likely to make her throw up. She took a shaky breath.

"Any particular reason you brought us here?" Peter wasn't using the scathing tone he normally spoke in. She could only imagine he was in shock. Teleporting did that to you. At least, the first time.

"Yup."

"Because Alec won't be here?"

Alec. Her stomach flipped. Dear God, was he

okay? Did he get away? Why had he kissed her? "Yup."

"Good idea. We've never been to British Colombia. It probably wouldn't cross his mind to come here. How did you do that transport thing anyway? I want to learn."

"Gimme a second," Riley murmured. Thoughts and emotions were screaming inside her head so loudly she could barely hear herself think. They were on the run. She didn't have Darius with her. Alec was completely by himself. Where would they go? How long could they hide out? Had she kissed Alec back or just stood there like a complete idiot?

"Sure. I don't feel so great myself." Peter's legs moved away from her and he walked several feet away. Riley looked up. They were in a storage yard for shipping containers somewhere near the waterfront. Several empty railway boxcars dotted the landscape here and there in between the islands of scrappy weeds. Between them and the distant blue water was a high barbed-wire fence. The mist-shrouded mountains beckoned across the inlet. Somewhere nearby the thudding drone of a plane sounded overhead.

Riley tried to think of the map of Vancouver she'd memorized before setting out for her sister Deborah's place last July. Amend that, this *coming* July. And she hadn't memorized it yet, in this reality, because she hadn't left for out west until that lady at the concert attacked her and her exams were over. And that would be in another week.

"What do we do now?"

Peter was talking again. Riley shook her head to clear it but the wooziness persisted. She heard his footsteps crunching in the gravel. Maybe he'd find a coffee shop and bring her back a double espresso with a dash of peppermint flavouring?

Barking started in the distance.

Maybe he wouldn't.

The barking got louder. Didn't some companies use dogs to guard their properties? Riley groaned.

She had just gotten to her knees when the Alsatian rounded the corner of the nearest boxcar. Pebbles flew out from under its scrabbling paws. The dog was snarling. Riley could see how white the canines were.

The dog charged.

Riley was aware of the fleeting thought that animals responded to commands even in times of stress, and that a guard dog might halt if ordered. But her throat closed in with terror as the beast rushed her, saliva flecking from its jaws. She tucked her head with her hands and curled into a ball.

"No, no. Go away." Peter's high-pitched cry came from somewhere far away.

The first scream-inducing pain began in her right shoulder where the jaws clamped down. She was going to die, eaten by dogs in a shipping yard.

Peter didn't run away. Riley entirely expected him to. Hands gripped her, pushing and slapping the animal away. The hands plundered her body, searching for something. The dog bit again.

"Riley, your orb," Peter shouted.

Riley let go of her head for a moment and scrabbled to find the orb. It must be in her pocket. *Think!*

Peter's hand found it first. "Go away," he shouted hoarsely.

The barking stopped. For a moment there was utter silence. Then Riley heard the plaintive whine.

Opening her eyes, she was astounded. Peter was holding her orb at arm's length as if it was radioactive. The guard dog was laying on its stomach several meters away, a contrite and pathetic look on its face. The tail thumped in the dirt twice and then was still.

"Is this you doing this, or me?" Peter's voice cracked.

"You." Riley gasped with pain. Her shoulder was bleeding and she hurt in more places than she could count. Reaction engulfed her and she began to shake all over.

"Cool," Peter breathed.

"Yeah, whatever." Her teeth were chattering. The dog's head lay on the ground between his paws and the gaze he gave would have melted her heart. If he hadn't bitten her first.

"Do you think I can make this dog do anything I want?" Peter's grip on the orb hadn't lessened. His head was cocked to one side and he seemed oblivious to her distress.

"Just keep it away from me," Riley groaned.

"I don't really like dogs." Peter was chatting rapidly, as if the ideas couldn't come out of his mouth fast enough. "All animals really. I just don't get why people like them. I mean cats are basically evil. You can't train them or anything. And they'll eat you if you die. Alec was always bugging Mum and Dad for a dog. He loves them. Especially big dogs like this. But they make too much mess and are a lot of work. Are you hurt?"

Riley got shakily to her feet. She pulled the orb slowly from Peter's hand. The dog lifted its head but did nothing else.

"Nothing that time won't heal." She gritted her teeth. Her shoulder was throbbing horribly. Hopefully Deborah had a good supply of painkillers and antibiotic cream. This was going to be a lousy day. "Tell it to stay," she advised Peter.

Peter shrugged. "Stay."

The dog whined again, as if mounting a feeble protest, then laid its head back down and closed its eyes.

Peter took a step to the left. The dog didn't move. Riley started to walk away. She held the orb tightly and Peter stayed right by her side, but the dog didn't watch them. After several steps, both picked up speed, resisting the temptation to run. They rounded the closest container and both noticed the far gate of the facility in the distance. Wordlessly they headed for it.

Riley was a bit surprised that no one rushed out of the

portable that serviced as an office, and that the gates swung open at their touch. There wasn't a car in the small parking lot or on the paved road that passed in front of the compound. It took a couple of moments to realize it was much earlier in the day here. Peter didn't question her choice of turning left towards the distant city nor did he speak as they trudged along the side of the road. Riley was too uncomfortable to talk; she could only guess why Peter was so silent.

It took nearly an hour until they'd entered the industrial area of the city and a cab passed by. Peter had to run out into the road to get it to stop. Riley was in tears as she collapsed in the back seat. She gave her sister's address in a barely audible voice, clutching her orb and *willing* the cab driver to get them there quickly and for free. She was so uncomfortable when they arrived at the small, upscale apartment building she couldn't speak. The cab driver didn't ask for money. He peeled away from the curb the second Peter's feet touched the pavement.

Peter helped her up the steps to the tidy foyer where polished parquet flooring gleamed in the morning sunlight. Riley pushed the buzzer beside the calligraphied 𝔇 Cohen and leaned against the wall. If Deb wasn't home…

"Hello?"

"Deb, it's me," Riley gasped. "Let me in."

"Riley? Is that you? What are you doing here? I thought you were—"

Riley buzzed again, holding her finger on the button. "Open up. Now."

"Jeesh, no reason to get snotty," the disembodied voice muttered before the interior bevelled glass door gave an audible click.

Peter pulled it open and allowed Riley to proceed. She mounted the marble steps slowly, pulling herself up each separate tread like an elderly woman. Thank goodness her sister only lived on the second floor. By the time Riley reached the wide, carpeted hall, the door of the closest apartment was open and a slim, dark-haired woman wearing a velour tracksuit unzipped to the pierced belly button was leaning out.

"Oh my God. Riley, what happened?" The woman dashed out and grabbed Riley. She pulled her into the apartment and shoved the door closed with her hip. Peter just made it in before the door could slam shut on his fingers.

"Dog bites," Peter said before Riley could get the words out. "They might be infected by now."

"Wow." Deborah pulled Riley down the hall of a light-filled space decorated by huge black and white pictures of attractive strangers posed provocatively. They entered the black and white tiled bathroom and Deborah shoved Riley onto the edge of a claw-footed bathtub.

"Let's see."

Riley barely heard Peter mutter something about waiting outside before Deborah yanked off her ruined tee-shirt. Deborah's long hair brushed against Riley's face as her sister peered at the wounds. Years ago they'd played hairdresser and Riley had spent hours brushing her sister's hair. It was another life then.

"I'm going to run a bath and dump some of the anti-septic stuff you gave me in that first-aid kit. I want you to have a good long soak. Then I'll stick a few bandages on these. I'm guessing you don't want to go to the hospital?"

Riley wearily shook her head. They were taking a chance even being here. Darius knew she had a sister.

"'Kay. Get your clothes off."

The bath was soothing and would have been much more pleasant without the smelly disinfectant, but Riley felt a million times better after she'd pulled the plug. She did her own dressings with the first-aid kit and donned one of Deborah's tracksuits before heading to the living room. Deb was on the elliptical in front of the television. She had headphones on and had worked up quite a sweat. Knowing that nothing but a nuclear war—and then only if it was in her own backyard—interrupted Deb's workout, Riley went into the kitchen. Peter was already there, the remains of breakfast in front of him. He was reading the paper.

"Did you leave me anything to eat?" Riley peered inside the fridge. There wasn't much. Deborah had very specific ideas about food, which generally meant as little as possible.

"There's a couple of eggs left. And some bread." Peter nodded towards the counter. "Coffee if you want it."

"Please," Riley replied knowing full well Peter hadn't offered to pour her a cup. She swallowed the smile as he sighed and got out of his chair. "Did she ask you anything?" she queried as she popped two slices of bread into the toaster and took the eggs out of the fridge.

"Just my name. I told her we were friends travelling together. She didn't ask why you were here or anything."

"Okay. I just want to keep our stories straight."

Riley was just finishing wiping down the countertops when Deborah walked in. All the time in the bathroom had not been wasted; she looked like something from a fashion runway. Peter hovered by her shoulder.

"We were mugged," Riley began, before Deborah could ask. "Everything gone. Cards, money, ID. Both of us."

"Wow, that's awful. Do you know who did it?"

Peter raised his eyebrows at the question but said nothing.

"We didn't get his name. We were too busy looking at his gun. Can you help us or not?" Riley suppressed the urge to roll her eyes.

"Sure. But why don't you just call Dad? He'll wire some money."

Riley turned away. "No."

"Are you still pissed about Alison?" Deborah brushed past and picked up her designer handbag that was slung casually over the back of a chair. "Honestly, Riley, grow up. He's single. He can marry whomever he wants. It could be worse."

"She's a complete cow, Deb. You know it. You've seen how she treats him. Ordering him around like some *slave*. She's only a couple of years older than you. She wants to have a *baby*."

"If Daddy is stupid enough to reverse his vasectomy, he's more than welcome to being up all night with a screaming kid. Rather him than me. Riley, you'll be on your own in a few weeks. Why on earth should this matter so much to you?" Deborah pulled a lipstick from the interior of the bag and applied a generous coating to her lips while peering in the small mirror next to the door. "Look, I've got an audition this morning and I'm meeting Lionel for lunch. You and…" she paused to give Peter a vague look, "What did you say your name was?"

"Peter."

"Oh, right. Sorry. You and Paul make yourself at home. Here's my card. Take some moolah out of the bank, have a nice quiet day in town and we'll talk over supper. 'Kay?" Without waiting for an answer, Deborah handed a card to Peter and slipped out the door in a cloud of perfume.

Peter raised an eyebrow.

"Say anything and I'll bite you," Riley muttered.

Alec stepped out of the fitting room and stared at his reflection with satisfaction. The new jeans were far tighter than his previous baggy ones and there was no chance these would fall down around his ankles if he had to run for it. The shirt was the softest cotton and the sky blue colour very flattering. The suede jacket fit him as if it had been specially ordered. This was much better, he told himself. He peered closer. He definitely looked older. Seventeen at least, maybe even twenty, if the light was right. He turned to check out the back of the jacket. Sophisticated. Riley would be impressed.

"I'll take all of them," Alec said to the sales clerk.

"Very good, sir," the man gave a slight bow. "Would you prefer to wear them now or shall I wrap?"

"I'll wear them. Just cut off the tags. You can throw my old stuff out."

Within minutes the clerk had run through the sale and Alec had handed over a sizable chunk of his cash. He hadn't realized just how expensive Harrods was but for the first time in years money wasn't an issue. Alec picked up the small package that contained the gold earrings he'd bought for his mom and shoved it into the jacket pocket along with the receipt for the new clothes. He'd have to find a post office and send them off to her, before he lost them. He grinned as he imagined her opening it. She'd probably cry.

15

He turned and headed towards the escalators, his thoughts filled with plans. He was going to need another withdrawal for supper and a hotel room. There was an ATM in the store. He remembered seeing a sign for it when he came in. He'd just nip downstairs, grab some cash then snare a taxi. Suddenly, as if someone had punched him in his guts, he realized. His orb. Where was it?

Frantically he patted the pockets of his new jeans and the jacket. Nothing. *Cripes.* He was sure he'd transferred it to his new jacket. Could it have fallen out onto the carpeted floor and he hadn't heard it? He was defenseless without the orb. He turned, intending to run back up the escalator stairs but there was no room. Other than tossing shopper after shopper over the side of the movable stairway he wasn't going to be able to make it.

It seemed to take ages to land at the next floor down, run around to the up escalator and propel himself ahead of the people already waiting. He ignored the outraged comments. The second he was off the step he broke into a run and headed back to the fitting rooms.

"Excuse me, sir, that room is occupied." An unfamiliar salesman appeared out of nowhere, brandishing a measuring tape and supercilious expression.

Alec tugged on the locked door of the change room. "I was just in here," he said. "My old clothes are there and I left something important in a pocket. Or on the floor."

"I'm sure you didn't," the salesman sniffed. "I personally noted this cubicle was empty."

"Where's the other guy?" Alec snapped. "The skinny one with the mustache. He helped me buy these clothes and he said he'd get rid of my old ones."

The salesman pursed his lips. "I'm sure I don't know."

"You do," Alec almost shouted. "He was just here five minutes ago."

"I believe Mr. Steiner has left on his dinner break. You

may check back in an hour or leave your telephone number and I shall be sure to pass it to him."

Alec let go of the door handle and took a step towards the clerk. He reached out and poked the man in the chest, just above his nametag. "Look, Geoffrey," he said as he read the tag, "I need my clothes. Now. Or else."

"Are you threatening me?" Geoffrey's eyes narrowed and he straightened to his full height, which was several inches taller than Alec although most of that height was neck.

"Not yet," Alec growled.

"Is there a problem?" The elderly man that emerged from the cubicle was almost wider than he was tall but he carried himself with the bearing of a Navy Rear Admiral. Alec dripped his hand to his side and unconsciously took a step back.

"I left my old clothes in this change room." Alec heard the respectful tone of his own voice in surprise. "I've lost something important."

The customer sidestepped and waved at the interior. "You are most welcome to take a look."

Alec didn't hesitate. Pushing past the clerk he leaned around the door. Other than the portly gentleman's trousers, neatly folded on the velvet wing chair and a hanger on the hook above it, the cubicle was empty.

"He's taken them then," Alec addressed his comments to Geoffrey. "Where would he take my clothes? He was going to throw them out."

Geoffrey gave a sour look and his generous Adam's apple bobbed a few times before he wordlessly turned and led the way out of the fitting room. Alec followed immediately behind, a sick feeling growing in his stomach with every step. If his clothes were already in the incinerator he'd be up a creek. He'd have no choice but to eventually call his parents and have them bring him home. The airline ticket alone would doom them.

"I can't leave the floor, at this hour," Geoffrey said, "and

I suspect your clothes, if they were for disposal, have been taken to the basement. But perhaps it's worth checking the bins, just in case."

Alec pushed past him and reached for the garbage container under the cashier's desk. There were several wads of crumpled packaging and someone's leftover sandwich, but Alec didn't care. He shoved his hand as far into the bin as possible and rummaged around.

Geoffrey had just opened his mouth to clearly tell him off when Alec's hand touched cloth and the distinct bulge of rounded crystal. "Got it," he gasped with relief. It took both hands to pull the worn jeans out and extract the orb. Paper and bits of bread rained onto the floor. Alec gripped the orb tightly and leaned against the counter as the adrenaline ebbed. Thank heavens.

It was the horror reflected in Geoffrey's eyes that had Alec ducking. The *swoosh* of the golf club slicing the air just above his head was the signal to run. That and the goosebumps that had sprung to life all over. Alec caught a glimpse of the customer from the change room wielding the club like a samurai and Geoffrey's shocked face before he dropped to the ground and rolled. *Crack.* The golf club hit the counter with enough force to split the surface and throw the box of paperclips into the air. They rained down on the floor where Alec had been a second before.

"Oh please, sir, no," Geoffrey cried. He was abruptly silenced as the golf club whirled again and hit him with a dull *splat* across his face. Alec saw the splash of blood and internally cringed. But there was no time to help the salesman. Already the club was sailing through the air in his direction.

Alec scrambled to his feet and ran. The store was too crowded to get any real speed but Alec had years of zig-zagging through opponents on the soccer field and he put every skill to use now. He dashed around shoppers and baby carriages, careened around displays of mannequins—one of which depicted a golf scenario and was missing a club—and jumped over a toddler who was taking a tantrum on the floor. He heard the shouts of outrage from the patrons he knocked over but there was no time to apologize. The crazed rear admiral was right behind him.

If he could get to the escalators he could push himself in between people and escape to another floor much faster than the Emissary. His assailant was too fat to get by anyone on the stairs. He glanced around at the signage hanging from the ceiling as he darted into an area full of racks of clothes. Nothing. He gritted his jaw. He was sure he'd come this way before, but there was no sign of the escalator and he must have gotten turned around.

He ran out of the racks on the other side and skidded to a stop. Right in front of him a huge crowd waited at the wall of elevator doors. And a light glowing above the one to the far right indicated it was heading downwards. Alec didn't hesitate. He ran around the crowd and thrust himself through, stepping into the elevator right in front of an elderly lady and almost pushing her back out. The doors slammed shut in front of him, trapping him in a tightly packed space with almost no room to breathe.

He sighed with relief and closed his eyes.

"That, young man, was incredibly rude."

Alec didn't crack an eye open at the matronly voice beside him and, with great restraint, refrained from giving her the finger. He concentrated instead on keeping his hand off his orb and catching his breath. That had been too close. Rhozan had found him when he least expected it and if he'd been half a second faster, it would have been Alec's brains all over the countertop, not paperclips. There was no way he was going to use an ATM in this store now. Better wait and find one with plenty of space for a quick exit.

The elevator jerked. For a second Alec lost his balance and bumped into the cranky woman who'd told him off.

"Sorry," he muttered.

"I should think so," she replied haughtily.

Alec didn't get a chance to reply. The floor of the elevator abruptly dropped away from Alec's feet.

16

The sun was hidden by a slow moving band of clouds that threatened only shade as Riley and Peter made their way slowly up the steep hill that preceded Deborah's neighbourhood. The day hadn't been an entire loss, she thought to herself. They'd managed a type of truce. As long as Riley said nothing about Alec or the situation they were in, Peter managed to keep a veneer of politeness over his feelings. There had actually been seconds when she hadn't minded his company. Riley pulled a brochure out from her pocket and stretched the accordioned page out.

"Look at this," she said, peering more closely at the pictorial display of a crowded beach she'd picked up at a travel agent's. "Even in winter, people in Sydney can go swimming. It's winter there now."

Peter glanced over her shoulder. His new sunglasses hid his eyes. "I have a pen pal there," he said.

"Pen pal?" Riley laughed. "Like, with letters? Who does that these days? Everyone emails and Facebooks and stuff."

"Letter writing is a lost art," Peter said in a chilly tone. "Some of us still appreciate it."

Riley shrugged. "Each to his own, I guess." She stuffed the folder back. "So, Australia next?"

"Sure," Peter nodded.

"Okay. We'll spend the night at Deb's. Rest up. Tomorrow, when she goes out for the day, we'll...," Riley waved her hand to indicate their special mode of transport, "and see how we get on."

"I've always wanted to see the Outback," Peter said as they turned the corner onto Deborah's street.

Riley glanced up. "Sure," she started to say. But the word died on her tongue as she froze in place and Peter stumbled into her. Up ahead, on the steps of Deborah's apartment building, two very familiar people were talking to an even more familiar, dark-haired woman in stiletto heels.

"Stop." Riley grabbed Peter's arm. She swung him around. "Walk quickly."

"What is it?"

"I think that's Darius and Anna. Talking to Deb. No, don't look!" Hurrying back the way they came, Riley turned the corner, Peter right beside her. She ducked into the side of the building and peeked out. "Get behind me," she ordered.

"Stop telling me what to do." Peter elbowed her out of the way and poked his own head around the brickwork. He immediately ducked back. "I think it's them."

"We'll run down this road and grab the next bus. There's one every five minutes. I don't think they saw us."

"No. Transport out." Peter was already reaching towards her pocket where she kept her orb. "Let's go."

"Don't be crazy. They'll feel the power so close. He'll be right behind me. We're better off running."

"Gimme the orb."

"No."

He was bigger and stronger and her shoulder still ached terribly. Riley didn't stand a chance. He pulled it right out of her hand. He backed away, holding the orb above his head. His face was a mask of triumph.

"Who's in charge now, huh?" he hissed. "Either you do what I say for a change or I leave you behind. Got it?"

Riley's voice was low and urgent. Even now Darius could be sensing Peter's touch on the crystal. "You don't know what you're doing with that thing and I do. Your best chance of surviving is to do what I tell you. Give me back my orb before you totally screw things up."

Peter backed away, his steps taking him further into the shadows between the buildings they were hiding behind. "You had your turn. Now it's mine."

"This isn't an issue of what's fair, you idiot," she spat.

"You guys think you're better than me, don't you?" Peter taunted. "You thought I was coming around nicely, all afternoon, didn't you? Play Peter along and he'll do everything you want. Well, I'm not going to. I'm not Alec. You mean nothing to me."

Riley was slightly shocked at the vitriol. She hadn't sensed this, not once. "I've trained for weeks to do this and you—"

Riley didn't get out another word. A firm hand came down on her sore shoulder, sending her into spasms of pain. She dropped to the ground with a scream.

"Don't even think about it, Peter," Darius warned. He dropped to his knees to cradle Riley as she rocked in agony. "What happened to—?"

Anna flew around the corner and skidded to a stop. She took in the scene in one glance.

Peter cursed. Clasping the orb with both hands, he squeezed his eyes shut tight and grimaced. For a second nothing happened and Anna calmly reached for her own orb and raised it. Then he vanished.

Alec had paid enough attention in physics class to know that falling seven stories totally sucked. There was no choice. Turn into a bloody pancake or use his orb.

He shoved his hand into his pocket and tightened his fingers around the crystal. *Move it*, he ordered. The satisfying surge of Tyon power made his skin tingle and his heart race. Around him, panic seized the other occupants of the elevator. Their screams filled the air and elbows and hands beat futilely at him and the walls. Alec didn't have time to pick a destination or to fight off the wildly terrified people around him. He just left.

He was vaguely aware of the usual pulling and pushing sensations and that he was not alone as he travelled. He was also aware of a growing sense of guilt. He had left at least ten people to die. It didn't matter that there was nothing he could have done to save them; no one had the power to move so many through space with a Tyon crystal. But those people were dying directly because of him. Rhozan wouldn't have cut the cable otherwise.

Sickened, he landed with a thud and toppled backwards into the tiled walls. Someone fell on top of him and someone else gave a loud grunt and shoved him from behind. An almost-familiar voice was screaming. Alec opened his eyes as he jammed the orb back into his pocket.

He was back in the same subway he'd started in, he realized with a start. Clearly his subconscious had been driving and had recognized the tube station as a safe place. But on the other hand, he'd brought four people with him, which explained the massive headache that was now making its unpleasantness known. Groaning, he clasped a hand to his forehead and checked out the vicinity. Five people winking into existence in the middle of a very public space was not going to be missed. Especially by the people who'd done the travelling.

The matronly woman who'd told him off in the elevator had landed several feet away and was lying on her back, her wool skirt around her waist and her knee-high nylons kicking in the air. Alec groaned. What a horrible sight. Directly on top of him was a businessman. The man was struggling to right himself and grabbing at the papers that had escaped his briefcase and were floating downwards to settle all over the filthy floor while his eyes darted all over the subway station, Alec, and the screaming matron. The businessman gibbered something unintelligible, gave one final terrified look at Alec and bolted. Alec pulled himself to his feet and turned to see whom he'd landed on. It was actually two people and one of them looked enough like Riley that Alec's heart zoomed right back up into his throat. He couldn't tear his eyes away and for a long moment stood entranced.

A closer inspection showed that the Riley look-alike was actually much older and not nearly as pretty. Especially as her eyes narrowed and she snarled, "Who the hell are you?"

Okay, that was more like Riley.

Alec was just about to take a step away when a heavy hand dropped to his shoulder and spun him around. Off balance and sickened by the teleportation and the headache, Alec fell against the uniformed chest of a burly man.

"'Ere, young man. What's going on?"

Alec blinked at the shiny buttons under his nose. The hands gripped his shoulders again, this time both sides, and pulled him upwards to stand about a foot away. Alec craned his neck upwards. The police officer was nearly a foot taller and twice as wide. He stank of nicotine and his hazel eyes didn't have a fraction of kindness anywhere.

Alec tried to moisten his mouth enough to unstick his tongue from the roof. He was about to protest his innocence, when the matron shoved herself between the officer and Alec and started screeching.

Alec watched the bobby's face harden as he focused on the woman. The second the grip on his shoulders slackened, Alec was off. Head still pounding, vertigo threatening to topple him to the ground with every step, he ran. He heard the shouts behind him. The cop's thick baritone brogue, the matron's shriek of indignation and the Riley look-alike's profanity. None of it mattered. The icy sensation of being targeted galvanized his feet. An Emissary. Somewhere nearby and moving in fast.

Alec tore through the station. He vaulted over the exit turnstiles and took the stairs upwards three at a time. There were more shouts but he ignored them. The instant he was out of the station and on the street he turned on the speed. He didn't spare a look behind.

He ran down the street for several blocks before the goosebumps faded and the uneasy feeling disappeared. He slowed to a walk and tried to catch his breath. That had been far too close and way too scary.

He forced himself to take a few slow and deep breaths. He would have to grab a cab and get something to eat and find a place to stay for the night. He had only a few pounds left in his pocket so another ATM was on the list too, and he didn't fancy that at all. Rhozan was getting faster at showing up when he touched his orb. One of these times his luck was going to run out.

He buttoned his jacket and rammed his hands in the pockets, mostly to keep them well away from his orb. The lights in the shops on either side of the street were coming on and the crowds thinning. All the cabs seemed full and now that the adrenaline rush was over he felt drained and weary. He had just spotted a bank machine on the other side of the street when the freezing sensation started in his orb again. Without pausing to consider it, he ducked in the closest shop, scurried around a rack of clothing and slipped up to the window, hiding behind a mannequin. He peered through the glass and waited.

A minute passed and Alec saw no one who might be anything of significance. No obvious Tyon Operative in dull grey overalls, or blank-eyed puppet of the Others. As for the trio he'd only briefly glimpsed while on the tour bus, not a sign. He ran his fingers through his hair and leaned a little closer to the window. Why did this odd sensation he was being watched persist? Who was out there?

"Excuse me, young man." A hand came down on his shoulder. Alec leapt a foot off the ground. He whirled around.

The saleswoman was middle aged with bright blue stripes in her hair and nearly purple lipstick. She had a half annoyed and half amused expression on her face. "May I help you find something?"

Alec cleared his throat. "I just…," he started to say as he glanced past the woman to the store beyond her. There were racks of filmy lace and shelf after shelf of satin. His face flushed a brilliant crimson as realization hit him.

"No, I er, just made a…" He stepped back and bumped into the mannequin. His eyes rolled over the scantily clad all-too-realistic dummy and his throat closed. He didn't finish his sentence. With a strangled gasp, he bolted from the store.

Deborah placed the steaming mug of tea on a coaster in front of Riley's better arm without taking her eyes off Darius.

"Sure I can't get you anything?" she simpered while eyeing him like a starving vulture.

"No, thanks, I'm fine," he replied with the kind of smile that made Riley's heart flip over. Inwardly she groaned. Despite the fact that his current lover was seated across from him on an armchair looking as if she'd like nothing better than to smack the stupid grin off Deborah's face, Darius was flirting outrageously.

Riley shivered. So far Darius and Anna had been the soul of polite company, solicitous about her welfare, but something about it was wrong.

18

She felt like a total failure. She'd been on the run for what, six hours? And she'd been found at the first place she'd hidden, had completely forgotten to warn her sister not to tell anyone she was there, and had her entire body bitten by a savage guard dog. Not to mention, she'd lost her orb. What had happened to the cool and implacable young woman who'd faced not one, but two attempts on her life and barely blinked? Alec would laugh his head off when he heard about this. *If* he heard. If Darius blabbed about this, she'd kill him.

"I was, like, really surprised when Riley and Patrick showed up here." Deborah was batting her unnaturally thick eyelashes and pouting prettily as if auditioning for a Marilyn Monroe look-alike calendar.

"It's Peter," Riley interrupted.

"Yeah, sorry. I was, like, what are you doing here? It's still exams. Riley is really into school, you know. Me, I'm finished. Just the occasional acting class. Not that I need them. I'm a natural actress."

"I'm sure you're very good," Darius crooned. Anna stiffened almost imperceptibly. Riley sunk lower in her seat.

"I've done tons of modeling. Petites and catalogue mostly. I've done six commercials and an infomercial. Lionel says that he's got a TV pilot that I'd be perfect for." Deborah leaned forward even further and licked her lower lip.

Riley was about to mutter, "Get a room," when Anna held up her orb and said firmly, "Sleep." There was a slight flash of pale bluish light and Deborah keeled over in her chair. Riley gave a brief struggle to move towards her sister but Darius pushed her gently back into the soft cushions of the sofa and his grip on her shoulder tightened.

"Finally, peace and quiet." Anna leaned forward to peer down at the draped body. The ever-present chain around her neck threatened to spill out but with an unconscious movement, she tucked the pendant below her collar. Her orb was still in her hand and she was frowning. She glanced up at Riley. "Have some of the tea and swallow the tablets. You will feel less pain if you do."

Riley looked at the two white ovals lying on the coaster next to her mug. What kind of drug were they going to give her to keep her under control?

"It's a common muscle relaxant. Your sister had them in the bathroom cabinet. I'm assuming they're safe," Darius said.

Riley squirmed a bit to dislodge his hand and slowly picked up the tablets with her good arm and inspected them. They certainly looked normal, and even with Darius working on healing the bites, the pain was pretty bad. Taking a deep breath she popped them in her mouth and took a large swallow of tea to wash them down. Darius resumed the contact with her shoulder immediately. He held his glowing orb in his right hand as he directed the healing energy.

"Care to explain yourself?" Anna crossed her arms.

"We've been worried sick," Darius interjected, a bit too quickly.

Riley turned and looked him in the eye. Darius was the most accomplished liar she'd ever met and she had no way of knowing what was really on his mind. She wished she could believe him but the odds were against it.

"Riley?" Anna prompted.

"You're after Alec, aren't you? You want him to die."

Anna's pale brows rose into her fringe but other than that there was no change of expression. "How did you come to that conclusion?"

Riley looked from Anna to Darius and back again. Did she know everything or had Darius managed to keep her in the dark? Had she made a huge mistake? "You were yelling at us," she began carefully, "and I thought that you were mad or something and I just panicked."

Anna's head cocked slightly to one side. "Why would you ascertain that I would harm you in any way, when our acquaintance has been so limited?"

Good question. *Think.*

"Well, I know that you're an alien. I watch a lot of television. Guess I put two and two together and came up with five. Sorry." Inwardly Riley cringed. No one was that stupid.

"Riley, Anna knows. You can quit with the excuses," Darius said, giving her shoulder a slight squeeze. "You think fast on your feet, but it isn't necessary." Riley winced with the pressure. "Sorry. Forgot."

"You were leading me on," Riley accused. *Was Anna on their side or not?*

"She is," Darius answered out loud. "I've told her everything. The past, the future, all of it. Anna has agreed to help us." He smiled warmly at Anna.

Riley swallowed her disappointment. The last person in the world she wanted on their team, snuggling up to her and Darius, was the Ice Queen. "You were yelling and running towards us. Why?"

"There was a truck veering towards the camper. It had swerved several times and we both thought it would hit your vehicle and subsequently injure the three of you." Anna's gaze didn't waver. Darius was nodding in agreement.

Riley thought it over. "We didn't hear it."

"I think you were, um, otherwise preoccupied." Darius was smiling broadly and clearly trying not to smirk.

Angrily, Riley changed tactic. "She'll tell Logan. She's more loyal to him than you, Dare. Aren't you?" Riley turned to face Anna. There was no need to beat around the bush any longer. If Darius had thrown them to the proverbial wolves, then she might as well lay all her cards on the table. *And* stop thinking in metaphors.

"I must maintain some loyalty to the Collective and my commander. However, if I deem a situation to be exceptional, I may, within reason, act on my own volition. I have assessed the situation regarding Alec and have agreed to keep Alec hidden and not inform the Collective and the Council."

It was quite the speech and Riley didn't believe a word of it. Darius was in love with her and Anna would use it to her advantage. And yet, in the future that was no longer, she'd died rather than kill Darius, Alec, and herself. Riley ground her teeth and remained silent. She didn't know what to believe: her intuition or her reasoning.

"So you know that Alec has a special ability and you also know that everyone who finds out about this is going to want him dead," Riley said. "There'll probably be a huge reward, maybe a commendation. And you're trying to tell me that, hey, that's okay, you'll give it all up for love. Puhleese. Try someone else."

Anna cocked her head "You did warn me about her," she said to Darius.

"See why we all adore her?" Darius replied.

"What?" Riley demanded.

"Although our interactions have been limited in this reality, Darius informs me that we have never seen eye to eye on any subject and that your emotional response to me has been more negative than positive."

"True."

"Then perhaps we should declare a truce. We both care for Darius. Your feelings are quite obvious to me and, as you know, I have affection for him, despite his Terran birth. This should be enough to establish a sense of rapport and bonding. In addition we are both concerned for the life of your companion, Alec. He is in considerable danger, as much from himself as from the Council. The power he wields is formidable and he has limited training and is prone to negative emotions. I am informed that he opened the first rip and allowed the Others to maintain a connection. We cannot permit that to happen again."

"Alec didn't know about Rhozan last time. He's on his guard now," Riley reasoned.

"True. He is forewarned. But he is still an untrained adolescent and prone to serious mood swings."

Riley hadn't thought about that. The whole business with the Intergalactic Council and Logan breathing down their necks had totally preoccupied her. She hated to admit it but Anna was right. Rhozan hadn't been defeated, merely postponed. And Alec—impulsive, headstrong Alec—was out there, alone and undefended.

Alec lay on the wide bed and stared at the massive plasma-screen TV with rapt enjoyment. The remains of his delivered meal was spread across the plush brocade bedspread beside him and on the nightstand two empty cans of beer made wet rings on the polished wood surface. He slung another satin pillow under his head.

This was the life.

He hadn't had the feeling for the rest of the night that he was being watched or followed, even when he used an ATM to get enough cash for supper and the hotel.

The meal at the swanky hotel overlooking the Thames hadn't been quite as much fun as he'd thought it would be—there were too many forks and he could tell that the snotty waiters were just waiting for him to use the wrong utensil and snigger. The boutique hotel staff was better. Used to actors and music industry types, no one batted an eye when Alec used a fake name or objected to buying him beer and a pizza when he called down later.

19

He glanced at the clock radio on the low glass table. It was late evening at home. His mom would probably be pacing the halls with worry. She might even have called the police.

Decision made, he pulled the phone off the night table beside him, knocking both cans to the floor. He leaned over woozily. A small amount of beer soaked into the plush carpet with a slight fizzing. Alec stifled the giggle and sat up again. He squinted at the phone, then at the rather complicated instructions for international calls on the bedside table. It took five tries before his fingers stabbed the correct numbers in the correct sequence and the ringing indicated the call had gone through.

"Hello?" His mom sounded frantic. A stab of guilt coursed through his chest. Better mail those earrings first thing in the morning.

"Mom? It's me, Alec. I'm fine."

"Where on earth are you?" The panic was subsiding and replaced with anger. "Is Peter with you? Are you two okay?"

"Mom, I—"

"The school's left a message that you'd missed your exam. Alec, what in the world is going on with you?"

Alec took a deep breath. "I can't tell you where I am right now. I'm just calling to let you know I'm okay."

"Are you with Chin?" she continued as if he hadn't spoken. "You know that boy is trouble."

"No, I'm not." The searing memory of Chin dying in the previous future flashed across Alec's mind and he forcibly pushed it away.

"Well, I want you and your brother home in the next hour. Do you hear me?"

"Yeah. I do. I mean, I hear you but I can't come home right now. But I will. Soon. I promise." Alec's throat ached. He dropped the receiver into the cradle before he could change his mind. For a long time he didn't move, then he crawled off the bed and headed for the marble bathroom and the fancy steam bath.

Alec woke the next morning with a nasty headache and a feeling of doom hanging over his head. For several minutes he lay back on the huge bed, nested in a pile of cushions and pillows, and stared at the high ceiling and the exposed pipes that crisscrossed above him like the tangled pathways of his life and those of his family and new companions. Only a few weeks ago the most difficult things in his life were his failing grades in French and social studies and managing to stay on the provincial soccer team, despite not having the money for the out-of-town tournaments. How had he ever thought his life sucked back then? Now he was on the run from everyone. He couldn't go home again. Power to destroy everything he knew bubbled constantly under his skin. And the one person who could guide him through all of this, Darius Finn, might now be working for Anna and out to get him. He couldn't take the chance of contacting him or Riley. He'd have to go it alone.

He stared at the room as if seeing it for the first time. The black gauze drapes with the lightproof backing were haphazardly pulled to meet only partway over the massive window. The wildly patterned carpet made him slightly nauseated with its unrelenting multicoloured zigzags. It was a sterile loneliness Alec hadn't noticed last night and suddenly couldn't stand. He'd check out and find something else, he decided. Something homier.

Head pounding dully, he showered, finagled a couple of headache tablets from the sympathetic desk clerk and went to the hotel restaurant for a late breakfast. The service was slow and the prices ridiculous. However, the food was hot and very tasty when it arrived. The morning paper was filled with reports of fights, arrests, and at least three incidents of arson. Alec shook his head and tossed the paper to an empty seat. The last thing he needed to read about were other people's problems and London's soaring crime rates. There hadn't been anything but a short paragraph about the elevator crash at Harrod's and absolutely nothing in that report about him.

Feeling somewhat better with a full stomach, he headed back towards his room. He'd grab his new jacket and the tourist map and head out on the town. Probably hit an ATM first before checking out the London Dungeon.

He pressed the third-floor button in the lift and leaned

back against the shiny black-mirrored walls. It gave a slight lurch before starting its quiet trek upwards and Alec's heart did the same thing. It was a wonder he could even get into an elevator after yesterday. He forced his mind away from the death and destruction Rhozan had wrought.

He could get quite used to having this kind of money, he mused. People calling you "sir," getting you whatever you wanted. He could just hear Riley's scathing comments. Mind you, it would have been pretty nice to have her with him, teasing aside. They could have watched pay-per-view movies for hours, ordered room service and got increasingly more, well, *relaxed*.

Lost in this progressively interesting train of thought, Alec barely noticed as the elevator came to a gentle halt and the gilded doors slid silently open. Grinning slightly foolishly, he stepped out and headed down the narrow hall towards his room. He almost walked in through the open door without thinking. At the last second, he jerked out of his daydream with the horrible realization that someone was in his room.

"Time to play the game, Alec," said a female voice.

Not again. Alec turned and bolted down the hall without a second's hesitation. With a burst of speed he zipped around the corner into a secondary hallway and flung open the fire door to the stairs. He headed upwards one floor before exiting the stairwell. He pulled the door silently closed behind him and ran as fast as he could down the hall, slowing only as he grasped each consecutive door handle and attempted to open them. No good—they were all locked. There wasn't much else to do. Grimacing, he chose a door at random and grabbed his orb, focusing his attention on the lock.

The lock clicked and the knob turned. He leapt inside then closed the door as quietly as possible. He instantly pocketed the orb and kept his hand away from it. Trembling, he stood still. There was no outraged shout and after ten seconds he was able to penetrate the gloom enough to tell that the previous occupants had likely long gone. The drapes were pulled tightly shut against the summer sunshine but there was enough to see the unmade bed, the scattered newspaper, and a heap of soggy towels by the foot of the bed.

Alec leaned against the door and listened. Sure enough, pounding feet approached from the elevator end of the hallway. Alec peered through the peephole. He had a momentary glimpse of a short, dark-skinned woman in a maid's uniform, brandishing a mop and a blank expression. For a horrible second the woman paused, right outside his door and stared at the peephole. Alec held his breath. Then without a sound, she continued down the hallway.

Alec blew the breath out of his pursed lips and leaned his forehead against the door in relief. It took a minute before the trembling in his legs stopped. That had been too close. His hand must have brushed up against his crystal when he put his hand in his pocket. How incredibly stupid to be so lost in thought he hadn't even noticed. He'd have to be constantly on his guard now.

"Who are you and how did you acquire an orb?"

The deep and familiar voice startled Alec almost out of his skin. He whirled around, heart in his mouth, his hand automatically going to the orb in his pocket. *Ohmygod.*

Logan.

Riley sat on the edge of the bunk and thought black thoughts. She was back in the bunker in Toronto. Her orb was gone. She was covered in half-healed dog bites. Her sister was still in a deep sleep in her Vancouver living room, maybe to never wake up. Peter was presumably in Australia, but she hoped he'd missed and landed in Antarctica. Alec was on the run and nobody seemed to have any idea where he was.

So far this day *really* sucked.

She picked at the peeling polish on her left thumb and watched her companions out of the corner of her eye. Across the bunker, Darius and Anna were peering intently into the transparent computer screen Anna had conjured out of thin air with her orb and they were ignoring her. Had anyone asked if she was hungry? Tired? No. For the last hour or so since they'd teleported back, the two Tyons had hunched over the screen—well, Anna didn't hunch, she had perfect posture—while page after page of unintelligible symbols scrolled past.

20

Typical. As soon as Anna was back in the picture, she, Riley, ceased to exist. Well, that was going to have to stop right now. "Is this going to take much longer?"

"Yes," Darius muttered as he squinted and leaned forward. "See that," he pointed with a finger, "it could be him."

"The signature's distorted. Distance I assume," Anna agreed.

Riley glowered at her thumbnail. Screw Alec's older and clearly weirder brother. If he were having a terrific time soaking up the sun on Bondi Beach right now, she'd make him pay the minute Darius got a hold of him. *Nobody* stole her orb and made her look like an idiot.

"I would have thought that big, strong aliens like you would be able to track a couple of teenage boys like this." Riley snapped her fingers.

Darius turned around in his chair to face her. "There are signals all over the world from Operatives using orbs. We have to correlate each signal with the whereabouts of a known Operative, and because, as you'll remember, we're trying to keep this quiet, it means doing a manual search. So, if you don't mind, Riley, you've caused enough trouble for us lately and we'd both appreciate it if you'd let us work in peace." He turned back to the computer screen and muttered, "And I'm not an alien."

Riley snorted and lay down on the bed with a flounce. *Fine. Don't ask for my help. See if I care.* The minutes crawled past.

"What the hell is that?" Darius's sharp exclamation broke her reverie. He was leaning over the console and pointing at something on the screen she couldn't see.

"The signature's distorted. Derive the coordinates," Anna ordered.

"I'm on it," Darius replied. He waved his orb in a complicated series of movements and then nodded. "Do we have anyone in the South Pacific?"

Riley's stomach gave a leap.

"Tor and Paran are reviewing a potential rip in a country called New Zealand. I believe that is in the Southern portion of this planet. The distortion is too large for an operative. Unless they were attacked during teleportation?" Anna sounded completely blasé. The fact her colleagues might have suffered a serious problem didn't seem to faze her at all. Unfeeling cow, Riley thought.

"Looks more like an incomplete to me," Darius mused quietly. He half twisted around in his chair to look at Riley. "Was Peter on his way to the South Pacific, Riley?"

Riley crossed her arms. "Like I'm gonna tell you."

"Peter didn't know what he was doing," Darius said testily. "He needed you to guide him, didn't he? So, what do you think? Maybe he's in trouble?"

Riley shrugged. Peter could be hanging by one ankle over Sydney Harbour as far as she was concerned.

"Have you considered the effects of not fully knowing how to teleport?" Anna was frowning.

"No," Riley conceded after a long and rather uncomfortable silence.

"Not every Potential has the ability to instinctively travel by orb in the same way that each person's range of abilities are unique. There isn't always an innate ability to understand the process or the power. Without that, teleportation may not proceed fully. Incomplete transfers often result in death or a situation where the individual lingers in something we call the Alter."

"Forever," Darius added. "If this signature is his, I need to know. We don't have much time to reverse the process."

"What if it's not him?" Riley asked. "It might be something else."

"Want to take the chance?" Darius retorted.

"Well," Riley muttered, "he *is* a total ass."

"True," Darius agreed to her surprise. "But he's Alec's brother. Letting him die, even if Alec is chronically annoyed by him, will hardly endear you either to Alec or his parents, should that be important to you sometime in the future."

"And just what do you mean by that?" Riley picked at another chip of polish.

"Take a whopping big guess, sweetheart."

Riley pursed her lips and refused to take the bait.

"Every minute we spend in argument and innuendo reduces the chance to reverse the teleportation process."

Anna's droll tone cut the silence. "The longer the individual is within the Alter, the less chance of success."

"He's heading for Sydney, Australia. Happy now?" Riley flung herself off the bed and stamped across the room to stand behind Darius who was waving his orb urgently at the screen. She tapped her foot in annoyance. "Well, is it him or not?"

"Gimme a minute," Darius murmured.

Riley watched the symbols flicker across the screen, sideways and up and down, almost too fast for her eyes. A flicker of worry twisted her stomach for a moment. Unconsciously she leaned forward, resting her hands lightly on Darius's shoulders as she squinted at the computer screen. She nearly jerked back when she realized that his thoughts were slipping up through her fingertips into her mind.

He was worried; seriously concerned about the possibility that Peter was hurt or worse. There was conflict, distrust, and anger flitting across his thoughts but these were too abstract for Riley to fully comprehend. She was so engrossed in the transmission of his feelings and the heady sensations of his muscles moving slightly under his shirt that she neglected to be aware that the transfer might go in both directions, until Darius pulled himself away, breaking the contact and piercing her with a sharp look and a raised eyebrow.

"It's him." Anna stood up. "The signature is almost identical to his brother albeit quite a bit weaker. There are at least three locations. We must leave now."

"I need an orb," Riley said quickly. There was no way she was being left behind without one.

Darius practically leapt to his feet before Anna could draw breath to disagree. "There are a couple of extras. Riley can protect herself. She needs to have one."

"I disagree," Anna frowned. "She is untrained."

"She learns fast," Darius said as he made several complicated waves in front of a blank section of wall with his orb. A small cupboard door appeared and opened. Darius reached in and pulled out a yellow-tinged orb. He tossed it to Riley who caught it before thinking. She immediately pocketed the crystal before Anna could disagree.

He reached out and clasped Riley's fingers with his own, grabbing onto Anna at the same time. Riley caught a pungent sense of urgency from both of them in the instant before Anna forced the jump.

There was the usual disconcerting sensation of nothingness, moving through space and yet not doing so, the unpleasant pull and tug of elements beyond her recognition before the sharp reversal of movement. She landed on the ground, her head spinning nastily. Each teleportation seemed to be worse than the last.

It took Riley a moment to clamber to her feet and orient to an upright position. She had to wait until she could blink several times and look around without feeling she might lose the contents of her stomach.

She was standing in the shadow of a large building on what appeared to be a wide pier facing the harbour. The distinct smell of seawater mixed with fried foods and diesel fumes assailed her nostrils. Straight ahead a huge bridge soared majestically across the wide span of deep blue water, which was dotted with boats of all descriptions. Behind her the iconic clamshell roofs of the Sydney Opera House reflected the sunshine off their beige and cream tiles. The large paving stones under her feet with their granite chips almost seemed to shine the further away she looked. The air was alive with the sounds of the milling crowd in front of the building and on the lower balcony, which jutted out over the water, and the motors of the ferries pulling out from the multiple wharves on her far left. A street musician's plaintiff violin created a mournful undertone to the squeals of excited blue uniform-clad schoolchildren who were resisting a harassed teacher's effort to keep them in line.

The scene was straight from the travel brochure. The air was humid and much warmer than the bunker had been. Riley looked carefully around but no one was pointing and shouting in their direction. It didn't seem like anyone had noticed their arrival.

Darius was already walking around in a circle like a water diviner, his orb glinting in the palm of his hand. His eyes were almost closed. Anna, on the other hand, had moved out of the Opera House's shadow and was leaning over the edge of the pier, staring down into the lapping water. She too had her orb out but didn't seem to be using it.

Riley pulled a face in her general direction. She leaned against an Information sign and focused on Darius, who was walking in increasingly wider circles. If he didn't watch where he was going, Riley grinned, he was going to topple right over the wall and into the mucky harbour. She crossed the stone walkway to intersect his next circuit.

"There." Anna raised an arm and pointed towards an impressive sailboat with gold trim and two women lounging on the back deck. It was bobbing at least a hundred meters directly between the Opera house and the swanky neighbourhood across the bay. "Beside or under."

"I don't see him," Riley said.

"Incomplete teleportation means the physical configuration has not reformed from the transfer through the Alter. This is one location where Peter's signature is present. He is not physically located here."

Darius noted Riley's facial expression at Anna's incomprehensible explanation and added, "Peter was thinking of this location when he tried to transfer but either he wasn't clear enough or he had other thoughts intruding. Either way he's physically not through yet and somewhat split."

"And you have to find the places where he nearly came through?" Riley offered.

"And push it the rest of the way, yes," Darius smiled.

"Hope you can swim." Riley gave Anna an insincere smile before shading her eyes and squinting at the sailboat. Both the sunbathers had eyeshades and earphones on. Neither wore much more than suntan oil.

"I'll go," Darius said a shade too quickly.

"Big surprise," Riley smirked. "Interrogate both of them while you're at it."

Anna didn't seem worried. "I'll take the next location. Riley will come with me."

Darius was already scanning the nearby boats for something he could use for transport. He muttered "uh huh" and walked away with a distinctly preoccupied air.

"You know he'll be seriously distracted," Riley said. She hoped the jealously wasn't audible.

"With what?" Anna took hold of Riley's arm and led her back to the shaded side of the Opera house. Darius was already several meters down the pier and within a moment disappeared into the crowd.

"The bimbos on the Lido deck," Riley replied as she allowed herself to be led. She nodded in the direction of the sailboat. "Women fall all over themselves around him. I'd of thought you would worry about it."

"Why should I worry?" Anna seemed genuinely puzzled.

"Coz he's your lover, that's why." Riley shook her head. "You aliens have weird relationship issues I can't get my head around."

"Then don't try." Anna ended the conversation. She pointed upwards towards the highest peak of the bridge. "Take a deep breath."

131

This transport was quicker and less distressing but the sudden materialization one hundred and thirty meters above the water on the narrow strip of metal planking was anything but. The wind tore at Riley's hair and buffeted her against the thin metal railings. She grabbed on and gasped. Dear God in Heaven. She was on top of the freaking bridge!

Anna appeared as unconcerned as ever, turning her face into the wind so wisps of hair pulled from her ponytail would not obstruct her vision. Already her orb was out and working.

Riley couldn't help herself. Her entire body broke into a drenching sweat and her knees threatened to give way altogether. She grabbed onto the metal rail with both hands and muttered a prayer her grandmother had taught her in childhood.

"Take your orb out and focus your attention on the flag-pole on the right," Anna instructed. She seemed oblivious to Riley's distress.

"Ergh," Riley muttered through clenched teeth. Her stomach was heaving and there was no way she was letting go of the rail to reach her orb. She didn't even raise her eyes to the wildly flapping Australian flag.

"You will not fall," Anna instructed. "Look around you. Several people are walking unconcernedly along these catwalks. You are in no danger."

"Easy for you to say," Riley whispered.

"You must concentrate on the area next to the flagpole and await my signal," Anna continued. "I will find the last location and report back immediately."

"Whatever."

"Take out your orb," Anna instructed before she winked out of sight.

A bone-jarring shudder wracked Riley's entire body. The wind was too strong. If she let go for a second she'd be whisked right over the side and fall to her death. If she let go of the railing she'd slide right down the metal catwalk and fall right off the end. Why hadn't she volunteered to get the part of Peter that was in the water? Drowning couldn't be worse.

Cursing Alec's brother fluently in English, French, and

a smattering of her grandmother's Yiddish, plus a few made-up words that sounded suitably horrible, Riley wrapped her arm around the railing, moving it only a centimeter at a time, until the fingers of one hand were free enough to pluck the orb from her pocket. The fear of dropping it overcame her before she could pull it free.

What on earth was she supposed to do? Her palms were soaked and she couldn't let go of the rail long enough to wipe them on her clothes. She blinked the sweat out of her eyes.

"Hey, you!"

The shout was so unexpected that for a moment Riley didn't realize she was being hailed. It was only with the third, "Hey girl, what are you doing?" that she bothered to look up.

A tall, suntanned young man wearing a gray and blue coverall, not dissimilar to the Tyon Home Base uniform, was rapidly striding towards her, a frown marring what was otherwise a handsome face. A belt or chain was around his slim waist and seemed to be attached in some way to the railings; Riley could hear the sliding *clink* as it moved from one section to the next.

"You aren't supposed to be up here alone," the young man called. He was only meters away. "Where's your group?"

"Oh no," Riley groaned. Any minute now Anna would begin the process of pulling Peter through from wherever the bits of him were located and they did *not* need an audience.

"Are you hurt, mate?" The man squatted down beside her. Riley tore her eyes away from the horrors below to look at him.

He was younger than she'd first thought. Maybe a few years older than her. Sun-bleached curls clustered tightly around his head. His nose was peeling and his greenish-brown eyes twinkled with humour despite his obvious concern. "Your group isn't supposed to leave you behind."

He had a distinct Australian accent and fabulously white teeth. "It's against the rules. Who's your guide?"

Riley just shook her head. She looked around quickly. Sure enough, a group of a dozen or so similarly clad people were trouping in single file downwards on the opposite side of the bridge. The catwalks were organized like a kind of high-rise sidewalk. She shuddered again. What kind of lunatics would do this for fun?

"And where's your jumpsuit, mate?" He reached out and tugged the edge of her sleeve. "You are with a tour, right?"

Riley opened her mouth to reply but before she could get any explanation out, the orb in her pocket shuddered and emitted a low buzzing sound. Riley startled.

"Here, your phone's ringing." The boy reached towards her pocket. "Don't worry, I'll get it."

"No!" Riley yelled as a vision of her orb slipping from his hands swam sickeningly in front of her eyes.

It was too late. The boy unbuttoned the pocket with a quick flip of his fingers and pulled the orb out. Sunlight flashed into the crystal and for a moment blinded both of them. The boy gave a sharp cry and stumbled backward.

"My orb," Riley screeched.

The memories of Logan's repeated attacks on his mind surged through Alec on a wave of adrenalin. Not again. *No way.* Alec took a step back. He forced the words out of his dry mouth and tried to unobtrusively drop his hand close to the pocket with the orb. "Who the hell are you?"

Logan's pale eyes watched the movement with unmistakable discernment. "Answer my question. Where did you get that orb?"

Before Alec could even begin to think of a response, the orb in his pocket shivered slightly and a cold burning sensation flashed from within the crystal's center to sear the skin against his pocket. Alec couldn't help the yelp of surprise and pain.

Logan's orb had simultaneously glowed wildly between his fingers. The big man raised his fist in front of his eyes and peered intently at the orb for a moment, before the glow settled. Inside his jeans' pocket, Alec's own orb stopped moving and the burning sensation ceased. Logan's stern face wrinkled into a severe frown and he crossed the couple of steps to Alec's side in less than a heartbeat. Alec backed up quickly, desperate to put as much distance between him and the Tyon Commander as possible, but his foot tangled in the bundle of bedcovers on the floor. He just regained his balance as Logan's iron grip encircled his upper arm.

"Don't move," Logan commanded.

Alec did as he was told. Logan had his right arm in a vice grip and his orb was in his right front

21

pocket. There was no way to reach it, and even if he did, teleporting with Logan holding on to him would only bring the two of them to whatever destination he chose. If that happened, there would be no way to talk his way out of things. And besides, Logan was nearly a foot taller and probably could bench press Alec with one hand.

Alec ground his teeth together and tried to keep his mind as clear as possible. His only hope was to play stupid; to lie and say he'd found the orb and discovered by accident that it disabled ATMs. Just how he was going to make that credible he had no idea. Fortunately, Logan appeared to momentarily have forgotten him. The commander was peering deeply into the depths of his orb.

"Report," he ordered.

Alec startled as the reply sounded in his own ear. The clipped accent-less voice was familiar. He was touching Logan and therefore receiving the message too.

"Rip in quadrant alpha one zero," the male voice reported. "Exceptionally large. No Potentials in the vicinity. However, witnesses confirmed. Evidence of contact. Priority index, one."

Logan swore under his breath. "Who is the closest Operative, Tyrell?"

"You are, sir."

"Anna's location?"

"Momentarily off the grid."

Logan scowled. "I will investigate." He gave a piercing glance at Alec and his eyes narrowed. "I don't know who you are, boy, or how you acquired an orb, but I will find out." He leaned in a bit closer. Alec could see the tiny

flecks of silver inside the pale blue irises and the coldness that glittered within. "You will come with me. Take a deep breath."

The hotel room faded quickly from view, the push and pull of moving through space drenched him with a sense of claustrophobia and breathlessness. Then as quickly as it started, it was over. They materialized outside. Alec landed on his knees, his upper arm still in Logan's tight grip. The view in front of his eyes swam for a moment as the vertigo rose to an unpleasant level before starting to subside much faster than usual. Alec gave his head a slight shake. He squinted at the brightness around him.

They had arrived in a large rolling meadow that was an incredibly vibrant green. The undulating terrain was checker-boarded by crumbling stone fences. Overhead, fluffy white clouds scudded past while, in the distance, fluffy white sheep grazed contentedly. Alec had no idea where he was.

He scrambled to his feet. His heart sank when he spied the shimmer of sparkles hovering, chest high, only meters away from where the two of them stood. The rip was the size of a suitcase, pulsing with faint multicolour lights inside.

Alec couldn't help himself. Terror had him twisting his arm as hard as he could. The sudden pain was sharp and biting, but he paid no attention as he managed to pull free. He instinctively scrambled away.

"You know what this is," Logan rumbled. A small muscle jerked spasmodically in his jaw. "Tell me how."

Alec instantly recognized the Tyon persuasion and clamped his own jaws tightly together, resisting the compulsion to spill his guts. There was *no way* he was giving in and telling Logan how he knew about Rhozan and orb power. He reached for the orb in his pocket. The second his fingertip touched the warm glass, Logan's effort to control his mind eased off.

A sneer curled Logan's upper lip. He lunged, faster than Alec could prepare for, and once again grabbed Alec's arm, this time more painfully. He jerked Alec closer, pulling him almost off his feet to look directly into his eyes. "Who are you? How do you know how to use an orb? Why do you fear the rip? *Answer* me."

"Go to hell." Alec found the words leaving his mouth before he could stop himself.

For a second it looked like Logan might hit him, but then his grip on Alec's arm slightly lessened. Alec was lowered to stand on his feet again. Logan smiled tightly. He raised his fist and the orb within his fingers glowed brightly for a second. A sensation of ants crawling all over Alec's skin preceded the more internal feeling of something moving swiftly through him. It took only a minute. He had the distinct impression that if he hadn't been holding tightly to his own orb, the invasion would have been far more unpleasant, as it had in the past. As it was, he managed to keep his mind closed and his gaze steady.

Logan's smile could have frozen lava. "I thought I detected his stink off you."

Alec didn't move a muscle. *Whose stink?*

"Teaching you to use an orb. Recruiting you, was he?" Was Logan thinking about Darius or was there someone else Logan had in his gun sites? "Did he think I would not suspect? Fool." Logan's free hand pulled Alec's wrist clear of his pocket. Alec tried to grip his crystal tighter but Logan easily began to pry his fingers off it, one by one. "He has tried it before. But I found them all."

Who'd tried *what?* And what had Logan done with the ones he found? Alec couldn't waste the effort to think about it. If he lost his orb, he was done for. Another finger was painfully pulled away.

"Tell me his name, boy, and I'll let you live."

Logan was toying with him. Two fingers were all that remained between some semblance of self-preservation and being solely within Logan's power. The man could easily have wrenched the orb from him, had him on his knees in pain—he had done it before and Alec hadn't been able to even slow him down—but the creep was lengthening the moment before his complete defeat, almost glorying in it. Alec twisted to the right, pulling his orb hand underneath him, using his weight as leverage. Useless.

"What has he recruited you for?"

The second-last finger was peeled away.

"I don't know what you're talking about," Alec gasped. Agony built as his last finger was slowly and brutally pulled back. He bit down on the whimper. Logan took the orb easily and held it aloft. He let go of Alec's arm at the same time.

Alec crumpled to his knees, cradling his throbbing hand and wrist. He was dead meat now. He caught the movement out of the corner of his eye. Sparkles, glittering evilly in the bright sunlight, right behind Logan's left shoulder and zeroing in.

"Look out," Alec shouted instinctively.

Logan ducked and twisted fluidly. The rip advanced like a puff of smoke through the space Logan had occupied only a second before, drifting over Alec's head and moving on past him, the outline of the cloud of otherworldly lights pulsing, changing without design.

The rip stopped. It reversed direction, moving towards them both again.

Logan stepped to the side and his eyes narrowed dangerously. The cloud of sparkles did not float past but stopped and hovered as if it noted its quarry had moved. Alec quickly glanced around, keeping one eye on the floating rip. There was no one in sight and nowhere to hide. He didn't have the second-fastest time trials in winter training for nothing, but could you outrun a rip?

"Do not attempt to run," Logan ordered. At the sound of his words the rip began to move towards them and quickly. Logan had just enough time to dash in the opposite direction. The cloud of sparkles practically brushed Alec's shoulder. Heart in his mouth and skin crawling with remembered revulsion, Alec bolted. His legs flew into action and he tore across the grass at breakneck speed, barely registering the uneven ground and the danger of rabbit holes. He'd managed a dozen meters before Logan's power hit him, straight between the shoulder blades.

Both his legs locked together. He pitched forward. Only years of training to absorb the impact of a fall prevented him from serious injury. He rolled several times before coming to a bruised and filthy stop on his back. Within a second Logan's form had blocked out the sun overhead.

Logan held up his orb. With the sun directly behind his head, Alec couldn't make out the man's triumphant grin, but he heard the pleasure in his voice. "You are not going anywhere until I have some answers."

Alec cursed under his breath.

The sparkles floated into view, directly behind Logan's head.

Logan reached down, his orb glinting in the sunlight between his fingers. He touched Alec's wrist and the contact between the orb and Alec's skin burned.

The next words had Alec frozen in horror and completely ignoring Logan's probe. It had only been days since he'd heard the voice, felt it inside him, vibrating his bones with the sickly, terrifying sound that was not human, not anything, but it felt like a lifetime ago. The voice he'd come to know as Rhozan.

"The game begins again, Alec."

Riley was so terrified of losing her orb she let go of the railing and lunged at the young man. He took a step backwards but the impact of Riley's leap was more than he could tolerate and he lost his footing. Falling backwards with a rattling *clang* on the narrow sidewalk, he landed on his back. Riley couldn't stop her forward motion either. Both hands grasping his hand that held her orb, she tumbled into him and landed directly on top.

For a moment, neither moved. Riley's eyes opened wide with horror and something much more pleasant. Underneath her the young man was taking a few deep breaths.

"It's not a phone," he said. The beginning of a grin tugged at the corners of his lips.

22

Suddenly mortified, Riley tried to scramble to her feet, but there seemed to be nowhere to put her knees or hands other than warm, solid flesh. She could feel the blush burning into her cheeks. Her orb buzzed again.

"Give it to me," she pleaded as she struggled awkwardly in the narrow confines of the catwalk.

"You're gonna have to ask me nicely," he laughed.

"Seriously, give it to me." Riley tried to pull herself away but caught sight of the water so incredibly far below that her body seized with a sickening paralysis.

"Hey, don't worry." The boy sat up and his arms went right around her. She smelled coconut sunscreen and a faint whiff of soap. *Fabulous.* "I won't let you fall. You're totally safe up here. Trust me."

"I haven't been totally safe in ages," she whispered.

"You are now." The voice was soothing and his breath tickled her ear. "Try and stand up. I've got you."

"Don't drop my orb," she hissed.

"Got it," the boy assured her. His arms protectively around her, he helped her slowly to her feet. The wind caught at her again the moment she was standing, but the Australian's grip held her firmly. "No worries."

"That's a joke, right?" Riley said to his wide expanse of chest.

She felt his laugh rather than heard it. The orb buzzed again.

"Please, give it to me," Riley instructed. "Just be very careful. I can't drop it."

"No problem. Here." He carefully transferred the orb to her hand, cupping his own around her fingers to ensure its safety. Anna's voice was suddenly loud and sharp inside her head.

"I've found the third. Focus your will on my lead, Riley. Darius, are you in position?"

"Hey," the boy gave a short yelp, but Riley stamped on his foot.

"Shhh," she admonished. "This is important."

Darius's voice came through, inside her head, as loud and clear as if he was standing beside her. "I'm in position. Readings are distorted."

Anna cut him off. "Focus on my signal. I'll send him to Riley's location."

"No, no," Riley nearly shouted. "I'm on top of a bridge." She cracked open one eye and got a very close view of a couple of gold chest hairs curling over the V of the boy's collar. She was standing on a metal bridge higher than a skyscraper with a *witness*.

"I'm not having him drown the moment we pull him

through, Riley," Anna's curt tones swiftly squashed any refusal. "Prepare."

"Oh no," Riley moaned. But it was too late.

The temperature of the orb rose to an uncomfortable warmth. An unpleasant tingling buzzed through her fingers and likely through those of her rescuer if his shocked grunt was any indication. Riley hurriedly focused her attention, following Anna's lead that was clearly transmitted through the orb. She'd deal with Crocodile Dundee once Peter was back in one piece.

The effort was draining. Riley felt her mind almost pulled out of her skull with the force of Anna's direction. There was the sense of Darius and Anna almost inside her head and the panic and desperation of Peter's consciousness flitting in and out. Suddenly the connection was closed. Exhausted, Riley dropped to her knees.

It must have only been a moment later when Riley's eyelids fluttered open. For a second she was completely disoriented. Where was she? What had happened? Events came rushing back and she sat up quickly. She had passed out. Someone, likely the Australian, had laid her down on the catwalk. He had also tucked her orb into the side pocket of her cargo pants and buttoned up the closure. Reassured, she patted the orb before pulling herself slowly to her feet. Once again the wind caught her, knocking her into the rail, but this time she was less concerned. Her attention was riveted at the scene in front of her.

Peter was sprawled on metal girders immediately below the flagpole. The Australian was leaning over him and speaking to him loudly. Riley watched the boy take Peter's pulse and lift an eyelid. There was no sign of Darius or Anna.

143

Riley pulled her orb back out of her pocket. She gripped it tightly and whispered at it, feeling partly desperate and at the same time silly. "Darius, Anna, where are you?" No reply. She tried again, speaking a little louder and sneaking a glance towards Peter at the same time.

Anna's voice came through very faintly in her ear. "Is the process complete?"

"Looks like it. But he's out for the count. Aren't you coming over to get him?" Riley whispered.

"Darius is unable to transport at the moment and I must regen significantly before any teleportation is possible. Wait for us. It will take only an hour or so."

"I don't have an hour. I've already been caught by the tour company. I've got to get out of here."

"You do not have the energy to teleport," came Anna's curt reply. "You will either have to climb down with Peter or wait for us."

Riley was feeling woozy and she recognized the shaking that had started in her knees. Anna was right. She wouldn't have the energy to teleport after doing whatever it was they'd done for Peter. And besides, she'd needed Peter's help to teleport last time anyway, and he looked like he was in no shape to have a conversation, never mind move them in space. Riley ground her teeth together. She was not waiting on the top of this bridge for Anna to get her act together. She wanted off and she wanted it *now*.

"Hey," she shouted towards Peter.

"Just a sec," the Australian shouted back. "I've found another one."

"Yeah, I know," Riley muttered under her breath. The guy looked strong but she doubted he could carry both of them. Gingerly, heart still in her mouth and holding the railings on either side of her with an almost numbing grip, she put one foot in front of the other and took a tentative step towards them. Then another. Eight more had her at the boy's side.

"His name is Peter and he's an idiot," she said as means of introduction.

"That right?" The boy glanced up at her. "How'd he get up here?"

"Same way I did," Riley said. "Problem is, we have to get him down."

"Fair right," the boy said. "He's out for it though. I'll have to get my mates and the stretcher. Are you all right by yourself with him?"

"Look, er, sorry, I don't know your name," Riley said.

"Ah, yeah. It's Kerry. Darling. Like the harbour." He pronounced it dah-ling. He smiled. "And you are?"

"Riley Cohen." She reached out and clasped the offered hand. They shook and she gave a slight snort of the ridiculous. Next they'd be trading phone numbers and friend-ing each other on Facebook.

"Yeah, so, Riley, what are the two of you doing up here? It's illegal unless you're part of the tour." Kerry sat back on his haunches and peered up at her with the kind of guileless open expression she hadn't seen in ages.

"It's a long story. Is he okay?"

Kerry shrugged. "I dunno."

Whatever was wrong with Peter was probably due to being in some kind of suspended animation while bits of his body hung in some weird dimension in several pieces. Hardly the kind of thing the local emergency room was going to be familiar with. And, even if they did know what was wrong with him, there was no way they had time to drop him off at a hospital, without a passport, a health card, or with the chance that he'd open his big mouth and spill the beans. Which she didn't put it past Peter to do in a heartbeat. The best thing was to get him somewhere quiet and private where she and the others could regroup and plan what their next move would be. Where and how she was going to get Peter there was another question.

"I think he just needs to sleep it off," Riley said slowly as she carefully slipped her fingers into her pocket to make contact with her orb. She closely watched Kerry's face for the first sign of disagreement. "You know how it is. I just have to get him off this bridge and give him a couple of

145

hours. His dad'll kill him if he catches him like this."

"Yeah, got it." Kerry was nodding. "What about your friends?" At Riley's frown he added, "On the phone. Just a minute ago."

"Oh, them," Riley twigged. "I'll call them when we're down. We'll have to find a hotel or something for him, just for a couple of hours. Any suggestions?"

"Ah, yeah. Let me think." Kerry frowned for a moment then his expression cleared. "My place is only two blocks away. Both my roommates are working today. I don't mind if you crash there."

Riley forced her most brilliant smile and watched the returning grin with a sense of relief. "That's great. Let's go now."

"Stick with me. I know a way off the bridge without going through the tour offices." Kerry leaned over and with surprising ease, hoisted Peter over his shoulders in a fireman lift. "Ready?"

"Guess so," Riley said with false cheer. What Anna would say when she discovered Kerry's involvement didn't bear thinking about, but one thing was clear. If she spent another minute teetering on this flimsy metal sidewalk about to fall to her death, she'd scream.

There wasn't much choice but to walk directly behind Kerry. If she kept her eyes on Peter's arm, which was dangling down Kerry's back, the vertigo wasn't too bad and she could actually move her feet. The main problem was the wind, which buffeted her constantly, and the rapidly increasing downward slope. If only she had the same kind of harness chain attached to the rail system that Kerry did. She held on as tightly as possible to the parallel handrails and talked to herself constantly.

They hadn't travelled far when the first major problem arose in the shape of another man, this time several years older, wearing the identical jumpsuit to Kerry.

"Here, what's going on?" the man called out as they approached.

"No worries, Bob," Kerry called back. "Fainted."

Riley caught a glimpse of Bob's frown and saw his hand reach up to the radio on his shoulder. Riley's stomach clenched. There was nothing else for it. Pulling her orb from her pocket she aimed it right at Bob and turned her entire attention to him. "Forget we're here," she ordered, straining as hard as she could.

The orb glowed for a moment, almost imperceptible in the bright sunshine. Bob's face lost all expression and his eyes glazed over. He didn't move.

"Bob?" Kerry took the last few steps and stopped in front of Bob. The older man didn't seem to notice him at all, his face slack and eyes half shut. "Er, Bob mate, you okay?"

There was no reaction, not even a blink.

"Crikey," Kerry breathed. Unable to let go of Peter's arm or leg, Kerry used his foot to tap Bob none too gently on the shin. Bob didn't react.

Riley gulped and tightened her grip on the rail as her knees began shaking. The effort it took was considerable and after fixing Peter she had little in reserve. "He's obviously stoned or something," Riley muttered guiltily, pushing past Kerry and his load to ease past Bob. She headed down the catwalk, ignoring the screaming in the back of her head as the sidewalk began to slope even steeper. She had to get some distance between them and Bob. Kerry was hardly going to let her run off on her own.

"Hey, wait for me."

Riley ignored Kerry's shout and kept marching, one foot in front of the other. She gazed ahead at the city skyline and the myriad buildings of the "Rocks" area ahead that she'd been interested in at the travel agent's. This was hardly the way she'd planned to see the city, but then, as horrible as it was, there was no denying the spectacular view.

They met up with another tour operator at the first ladder down to a lower level. Riley focused her orb and her power and he too was rendered incapable of thought or action. She swallowed the remorse. It would wear off. Eventually. It should.

She heard Kerry exclaim, "Jim, Jim," before passing him and very slowly and carefully climbing down to join her. He gave her a distinctly odd look before she turned her back and carried on. There were two more ladders to traverse. Each time Kerry shifted Peter so he could loop an arm around Peter's knee and hold onto his wrist, freeing up a hand to hold onto the ladder. It looked remarkably dangerous, but Kerry didn't seem fazed.

It took several minutes to get down to ground level. Kerry immediately marched up the road, Peter still slung over his shoulders, towards the cluster of old narrow sandstone buildings ahead. Riley headed after them at a run.

There were several minutes of twisting back and forth through the narrow cobbled lanes before he abruptly turned into an alley and stopped in front of an unassuming door in the side of a retail establishment. A faded "live long and prosper" sticker was peeling at the edges in the tiny window.

"Key's under the mat." Kerry turned and gave Riley a slightly lopsided grin.

"And *that's* totally safe," she chided as she lifted the edge of a worn welcome mat to find a smallish key. She picked it up gingerly and inserted it. The lock turned easily.

"Normie never remembers his key. It's better than
148 having him bang on the door at three in the morning. Go on."

Riley shoved the door open and was pleasantly surprised at the clean foyer and steep stairs that ran up to the second story. There was a rubber mat for dirty footwear against the wall and several pegs had been screwed into the plaster to hold coats. Readjusting her expectations she mounted the first tread and headed up. Kerry gave a grunt, shifted Peter's inert form and followed her.

The stairway opened up to a huge loft with a wall of windows facing a large wooden deck on one side and several doors on the other. There were exposed brick walls, shiny dark wood floors, granite countertops, and a plethora of gleaming steel appliances. Real art adorned the walls, Riley noted with interest, and a vase of fresh-cut flowers sat on the coffee table.

Kerry laid Peter out on the red leather sofa, removing his shoes without any appearance of self-consciousness, and tucked a yellow throw cushion under his head. Then he straightened up and gave Riley a polite smile. "How about a lemonade?" he asked pleasantly.

Riley raised a shoulder and pretended an interest in the abstract oil hung over the sofa. "Sure." Suddenly she was overcome with an odd sense of shyness mixed with a tinge of worry. Kerry might have Darius's self-confidence and relaxed manner, but, unlike Darius, he hadn't taken any oath to keep his hands off her.

Kerry rooted in the fridge for a moment. There was the clinking of glass and the clunk of ice being dispensed into tumblers. He crossed over to where Riley hadn't moved and handed her a glass.

"Cheers," he said, raising his glass for a moment before taking a long swallow.

Riley raised her glass to her lips and took a grateful mouthful. She nearly choked as the liquid burned down her throat. "There's booze in this," she gasped.

"Sure," Kerry seemed nonplussed.

"Isn't it a bit early in the day?" She tried to recover and appear nonchalant. She was seventeen and heading to university. Or had been.

"Nah, it's afternoon somewhere." Kerry drained his glass and set it down on a table. Then he dropped down into a leather director's-style chair and leaned back. "Have a seat, Riley. I'm not going to eat you."

Riley chose a similar seat farthest from him and lowered herself carefully to the taut leather. It was pretty low and she almost spilled her drink as she maneuvered herself into it. Self-consciously she took a tiny sip.

"What do you call that glass ball of yours?" Kerry asked. "It works like a radio but obviously isn't. You used it on Bob and Jim to knock them for a loop. Who are you and what are you doing here?"

"Riley Cohen, and you invited me." Riley gave a ghost of a smile.

"Very funny," Kerry crossed his arms. "Answer the question."

"Where do you think I'm from?" she asked.

"The future," Kerry replied without an ounce of self-consciousness.

Riley raised an eyebrow. "Oh-kaay," she drawled, thinking as fast as she could. "If you like that explanation I can live with it."

"You use futuristic equipment and have some kind of weird power over people when you hold it. You seem entirely human, not alien. So, as Spock says, 'Once you have eliminated the impossible, whatever remains, however improbable, must be the truth.' Since the power you're using is not available now, it can only mean you're from the future."

In a weird way, he made sense. And she knew the Star Trek reference. Hadn't she watched that episode a dozen times herself?

150 "How about 'not the future,' but somewhere else?" she hinted. She took another sip of her drink. It was really hot inside the apartment and climbing down the bridge, coupled with her fear, had made her terribly thirsty. She took another sip, then a mouthful.

"Like another planet?" Kerry shrugged and leaned

forward, resting his elbows on his knees. "Doubtful. There isn't any evidence to suggest that human life would evolve so similarly on different planets. Humans are a product of their environment. Earth, as far as we know, is unique." He paused for a moment then got out of his seat and grabbed another bottle of lemonade from the fridge. After a couple of swallows he put the glass down and grinned at her. Riley took another mouthful. She squirmed a bit and got more comfortable in the chair. She blinked several times then yawned. For some reason she was kind of sleepy.

"You might be surprised, you know," Riley replied sagely. "If you have to put that theory to the test, you might get the surprise of your life."

"Are you saying you *are* an alien?" One blond eyebrow disappeared into his curls.

Riley took another couple of gulps. She wished the loft had air conditioning. "Course not. I'm Canadian."

"Yeah?" Kerry raised his glass in a salute. "Cheers, then. I've got cousins that are Canadian."

"Well, I don't know them," she said before he could continue. "It's a big country."

"*And* you're from the future," Kerry added.

Riley took another swallow. He wasn't *really* wrong. She was from the future in a weird kind of way. She'd travelled back to this time, which if you wanted to be totally honest, was her past. So technically, he was right. Sort of.

"You know," she said, "it's a bit surprising how fast you caught on. You know, to my orb."

"I watch a lot of sci-fi," Kerry said. He nodded towards the bookshelves on the distant wall. "I'm studying anthropology and astronomy at uni. I know what to look for."

"Cool." Riley leaned her head back on the seat. She didn't want to fall asleep but it wouldn't hurt to close her eyes for a moment. "Aren't you going to get in trouble at work?"

"Nah. I figure meeting someone from the future is way

more interesting than the tour company. I mean, I like the bridge climb and everything but it's only a part-time job. I can get another anytime. Meeting you and your mate, Peter, not so often."

"Hmm," Riley nodded. She stopped instantly. Moving her head made her feel a bit odd, like riding a tilt-a-whirl at the fair. She drained her glass and pulled a small ice cube into her mouth. It felt incredibly cool and pleasant. She tried not to yawn. It wasn't very polite.

"So, what can that glass ball do?"

"My orb?"

"Is that what you call it? What powers does it have?"

It wouldn't hurt to tell him. Darius would just erase his memory anyway. "By itself, none. It's me. The orb channels my power into a usable form. I just think something and…," she tried to snap her fingers but they wouldn't make a sound, "presto."

"Could I try?"

Riley started to shake her head but quickly stopped. "Nope. Only works for me." A giggle started somewhere inside her. "And Peter. And Anna, the ice queen." The giggle grew. "And of course, Darius Finn."

"You spoke to them, right?" Kerry was on his feet. His voice was moving around the apartment but Riley didn't open her eyes to watch him. She was incredibly comfortable and almost asleep. The thought that it was taking Darius and Anna a long time to get to her briefly crossed her mind and then drifted away in a cloud of fuzzy contentment. Her glass was plucked from her grip.

"I heard them. Inside my head when you contacted them using the orb." Kerry sounded closer. Riley cracked open an eyelid and saw his face swim into view. He was hunched down beside her chair and grinning. "See, I knew there was something going on the moment I saw you up on the bridge. No tour uniform, no group, terrified out of your mind. I'd just passed that area ten seconds before you arrived so I knew you'd had to beam down. I was watching when Peter beamed into place. That's how I knew you were from the future. We don't have transporters yet."

Riley giggled again. Someone was having trouble keeping television and real life straight, and it wasn't her.

"No transporter," she murmured. "This." Riley tried to undo the button on the pant pocket but the buttonhole seemed to have shrunk. Kerry undid it for her and pulled out her orb. Anna would not be amused to find Kerry with them and holding her orb, Riley realized with a sudden moment of clarity. It was probably a good idea if she and Peter were to hightail it out of there before she showed up. Or just her, since Peter was unconscious.

"Better give it back to me," she said.

"Yeah, just a sec." Kerry was holding her orb up to the sunlight in front of the wall of windows for a better look. "This is really cool, Riley. I mean, you can't see any mechanism at all. How does it work? What's it made of?"

"Orbs are Telurian Crystal and are grown, not made." The cold voice cut through Riley's foggy brain and her stomach lurched. Uh oh. The Ice Queen. "And you had better have a good explanation why this civilian is holding it, Riley."

Alec tried hard not to scream but a gurgled cry tore from his lips. Despite his painful wrist he scuttled backwards like a crab through the grass but the cloud of sparkles moved past Logan to hover between them. Alec stopped, his heart pounding painfully in his throat.

Logan's orb was held directly at the rip. He fairly growled his next words. "Explain, boy."

Alec held very still and his eyes never left the rip. Thoughts scrambled over themselves inside his head. How would he explain this without telling the truth?

"Alec, are you ready to play again?" Rhozan's voice rose and fell in a sibilant wave that forced goosebumps into life all over Alec's skin.

23

Stay calm, he ordered himself. "I don't want to play, Rhozan. Find someone else."

"Alec, are you ready to play again?" Rhozan repeated.

"How do the Others know you?" Logan stepped closer, bringing himself perilously close to the rip. "I *demand* you tell me."

Alec clamped his mouth shut and concentrated with all his might as Tyon persuasion flowed over him, forcing its way into his mind with an almost overwhelming compulsion to spill his guts. A sweat broke out on his brow. He shivered with the strain. I'm not telling you, he repeated over and over in his mind. *I won't.*

Logan took another step. He was practically

touching the rip. His eyes blazed and his fists curled into balls at the defiance. Alec shivered. When Logan got him he was going to be torn into little pieces. *If* Logan got him. One more step and Logan would be touching the rip and pulled right inside. He didn't know the way out of the Other's dimensional access port, whereas if he could get a hold of an orb, Alec did. He just had to make Logan so angry that he'd make a mistake, forget for a crucial second about the rip. If Logan took his orb with him into Rhozan's domain, well so be it.

Alec swore, loudly and vehemently. He forced a saucy grin in Logan's direction. *Take that, jerk.*

It might have worked if the rip hadn't moved closer to Alec at the same time Logan took another step forward.

"You will pay for your disrespect," Logan hissed viciously.

Suddenly two Operatives, both in identical grey coveralls, winked into existence on either side of him. They acted immediately. The man to Alec's left reached forward and, without a word, grabbed Alec's shoulder and pulled him away from the advancing rip with a painful tug. The second man pulled out his orb and focused it on the rip, sending a jet of blinding white light towards it.

The rip reacted immediately. It enlarged with a sickening pulse and a sound Alec had never heard before, like the hissing of a thousand insects blasting in his ears.

Alec tried to get to his feet but before he could find a purchase in the slippery grass, the teleportation process had begun. In and out, over and under, through and not through. Alec shook his head to clear the distorting sensation of travel the second his feet touched something solid. He looked around quickly hoping to bolt for safety but the grip on his arm never lessened.

High above him, a rock ceiling of carved grey stone soared as far as a football field in all directions. The familiar smell of cold rock, metal, and alien superiority pervaded his nostrils. He didn't even need to see the huge movie screens that dotted the rock chamber walls, all playing televised real-time events the world over. He knew exactly where he was. Crap, crap, and double crap. His heart sank down to his ankles.

Quickly remembering that he wasn't supposed to know anything about the secretive underground headquarters, Alec kept his head down and feigned a terror that wasn't wholly manufactured. He stole several surreptitious looks around him as his captor marched him towards the main console at the center of the station.

Not much had changed, although the last time he was here the world was deteriorating significantly, with rips opening all over the place and the malevolent influence Rhozan exerted at an all-time high. There'd been riots and general mayhem and the National Guard had been deployed in many countries. The Tyon Operatives had responded with an unemotional intentness. Now, Alec could feel relative calmness in the air. It didn't make him feel much better, though.

He didn't see anyone he knew. While Anna had kept him sequestered during his previous stay, he had seen several of the same faces over and over when she talked to her compatriots while he was supposed to be sleeping. There had been someone named Ty who'd been a frequent visitor, as well as a few others whose names he didn't know.

The Operative led him through a multitude of small corridors at a steady clip. The brown metal walls were only shoulder high, like the dividers that made modern office spaces into a series of cubicles. Alec could see across the entire cavern but, other than heads bobbing up and down as people moved in and out of the cubicles, there was nothing of interest.

Alec squirmed around for a moment to get a look at his captor's face but the firm-jawed visage was unfamiliar. He looked behind him. No sign of Logan. If the Commander hadn't travelled with them, it only meant a temporary reprieve.

The towering center console rose up ahead of him and, sure enough, his captor led him straight to it. There was a small crowd gathered in front. Four blond, uniformed women with serious expressions surrounded a wide screen and stared intently at it. All held orbs in their hands, Alec noted, and all turned as one to stare at him.

"Report," barked an older man Alec hadn't noticed. He stepped out from behind the others and gave Alec a long curious look. He was quite broad shouldered and stocky, which was an unusual deviation from the typical tall and thin Tyon. Moreover, he had a closely shaven goatee, which would have marked him as different even if his body type hadn't. He glanced at Alec's captor with sharp, assessing eyes. "What is this Potential doing inside the Base, Kellin?"

"This Potential's readings are exceptionally strong and he was in the direct proximity of a rip," Kellin said. "Logan wishes to begin his analysis as soon as possible."

Alec scuffed his toe and tried to look scared and helpless. Which was depressingly easy.

The older Operative murmured, "I did not give any such order."

Alec felt Kellin's shrug. "No, sir. Logan sent the message to myself and Irik, directly."

"Where is Irik?"

"At the location of the rip, Commander Kholar, sir. There is a serious anomaly with this particular rip and Logan wants a full scan and report. They are conducting it presently."

Kholar rubbed his chin thoughtfully. He turned his attention to Alec. "What is your name, Terran?"

His tone maintained Logan's air of authority but there wasn't the cold, condescension Alec was used to hearing from a commander of the Tyon Collective. Thinking quickly, he said his middle name. "William."

"Where are you from?"

"Toronto." Alec looked about him and let a distinct tremor enter his voice along with the most subservient tone he could muster. "I don't know where I am or how I got here. I want to go home. Please."

"How did you get to Ireland with my second in command? Did you see the rip?"

Taking a deep breath, Alec launched into a tale as close to truth as possible. "I found this big marble in a tube station in London. I got short of cash and tried to use an ATM. You know, a cash machine. But it wouldn't take my card. I got really angry and suddenly the machine just spat out all this money. It took me a while to figure out that when I held the marble, machines would give me money. It was the coolest thing. Then this big guy shows up, demands the marble back and, before I could give it to him, grabs me. I must have blacked out or something coz the next thing I knew we were in some field and this big guy is yelling at me and there's a cloud of dust coming at us."

Alec didn't need to fake the shiver. "I was totally freaked. Then this guy shows up," he nodded in Kellin's direction, "and the next thing I know I'm here. I wanna go home." He looked from one Tyon to another, pasting the pleading look on his face that had worked so often with his mother.

"I am Commander Kohlar. The man you met in London is Logan. He is my second in command and in charge of this particular mission. You will obey him, as you will me, in the future."

Alec whimpered. "Please, I don't know who you are and I don't belong here."

"You are a Potential," Kohlar continued. "One of the very few humans on this planet with the special ability to protect themselves from the influence of the Others, an enemy that invades worlds such as yours. You must learn to protect yourself from the Others' attack. If you are strong enough, you may protect your planet from destruction. It is a noble cause. You must accept this and train for it." Kohlar seemed to finish his speech. He turned to Kellin and gave a curt nod. "Since the boy is already here, we will begin the training process. Who is the Guardian of Potentials here?"

"Dean, sir. I'll have him prepared to begin his training." Kellin didn't wait for any further instructions. Grabbing Alec's arm in an unbreakable grip, he tugged him out of central command before Alec could think of an argument to stay. Kellin led him through the maze of divider walls until they arrived at a long line of metal bunk beds placed up against the rock-hewn wall of the cavern. There were small metal cupboards between each bunk and a large metal room protruding out from the wall that Alec remembered was a bathroom. A familiar young man was sitting at a table reading something. He looked up as Alec and Kellin approached.

Dean was around Darius's age but slightly taller and wider across the shoulders. His eyes were a pale, almost colourless blue, but had none of Logan's coldness. The last time Alec had seen him, he was trying to kill Riley, Darius, and himself. There was none of the hatred in his expression as Dean half rose from his seat and waved his computer screen into nothingness.

"Your first Potential. Logan found him and ordered him here. Kohlar wants him trained," Kellin said as a way of introduction. "He calls himself William."

Dean reached forward to shake hands. He had an almost crushing grip and his hand had multiple calluses. Alec tried not to shake the blood back into his fingers once Dean let go, grateful it hadn't been his aching wrist Dean shook.   159

"I thought the retrieval phase hadn't started yet?" Dean said.

"Are you questioning Logan's decision?"

Dean gave a slight grin that didn't reach his eyes. "Of course not. What the Commander wants is fine with me."

Kellin seemed to accept this statement at face value and let go of Alec's shoulder. Without another word he turned and left. There was a long pause. Alec kept his mouth shut and waited for Dean's next move.

"Well, let's get you kitted out," Dean said with a definite shade of warmth in his voice and a hint of a smile on his face. "As you can see, you're the first of the Terran trainees so you get the choice of bunks." Dean got up and crossed to a small locker behind Alec, opened the lid and pulled out a grey one-piece coverall. Alec couldn't help the grimace. "There'll be lots of things here you find different from home. The faster you give up the memories of your previous life the faster you'll assimilate to our ways. In the long run, it'll be easier."

"How do you know?" Alec asked. He took the offered coverall and held it at arm's length. "I didn't ask for this. I just want to go home."

"I'm afraid that it isn't an option. Potentials never return to their previous lives after their training. They always continue with the Collective after completion, even if their world is rendered resistant."

"Resistant to what?" Alec tried to ask the questions he was sure he'd ask if this was the first time he'd been here.

"The Others. Pan-dimensional beings with a thirst for domination." Dean began rummaging in another locker, this time for shoes. He pulled out several pairs, eyed them critically before dropping them back. "Those of us in the Tyon Collective, which by the way now includes you, have an important mission. We disseminate the resistance gene to humanoid populations throughout this galaxy, which reduces the chance of the Others decimating a world. It's important work." Dean looked up and froze.

Alec didn't need to turn around.

"Place this boy in confinement immediately," Logan barked from only a step behind. "I must interrogate him."

Riley closed her eyes and wished herself a million miles away. Why did Anna have to constantly follow her around and pick holes in everything she did?

"Riley, I'm speaking to you."

Riley wrinkled her nose. Time for the high and mighty Ice Queen to melt the attitude. Riley raised her hand and extended her middle finger. Then she burst into giggles.

"Ah, who are you and how did you get into my apartment?" Kerry sounded far away and excited. Riley cracked open an eye just in time to see Anna's face stiffen into severe annoyance. She was holding onto something, but the sofa was blocking Riley's view. Riley rested her head back on the chair and closed both eyes. That felt better. Too much sunlight was giving her a bit of a headache and she felt so tired and comfortable where she was.

"Riley!"

"Gimme a break," Riley muttered, not bothering to open her eyes again. Honestly, did that woman ever give up? She felt rather than heard Anna's approach after something heavy slid to the floor. A painful grip latched on to both her upper arms and she was roughly pulled upward, right off the chair. She could feel Anna's breath on her forehead.

"Whoa," Riley muttered, "I'm, like, so not into you."

"What have you done to Riley?" Anna's words were directed over her shoulder.

24

"I just gave her a lemonade." Kerry's tone was more amused than worried.

"She's drugged," Anna's sharp tone cut the air. Riley was dropped back into the chair unceremoniously. She cracked open her eyes as she heard Anna's steps across the wide expanse of wooden floor. Anna stopped directly in front of Kerry and held out her hand. "You drugged her and took her orb. Return it to me."

"Hey, that's mine," Riley protested weakly.

"She's just a bit sleepy." Kerry handed back the orb and Anna pocketed it without comment. "And who's on the carpet?"

Riley squinted in the direction Kerry was pointing. There was indeed someone lying on the throw rug at the top of the stairs. A pool of water had formed around the crumpled figure.

"What's wrong with Darius?" Riley tried to get out of the chair but the slippery leather defeated her.

"Why is everyone from the future unconscious?" Kerry added.

Anna didn't respond. She walked over to Darius's side and leaned over. "Have you somewhere more comfortable for him to rest?" she asked.

"Ah, yeah." Kerry launched himself away from the windows and stepped neatly over the soggy form on the floor. He opened the middle door along the wall opposite the windows and gestured inside with a sweep of his arm. "He can use my room."

Anna didn't request any help picking Darius up off the floor and carrying him in her arms several steps to the bedroom where she momentarily disappeared with him. Kerry stood at the doorway watching intently. He turned to give Riley a *would you look at that* type of glance before facing Anna who exited the bedroom and strode purposefully towards Peter. She wordlessly pulled Peter into her arms. His head lolled back and forth as she carried him into the bedroom.

"Riley," she called.

Riley strongly considered not even answering, never mind getting up out of the comfortable seat and trekking all the way across the open living room to the bedroom, just to do Anna's bidding. But she wasn't holding her orb and the Tyon power pulled her relentlessly out of the slippery chair and onto her feet. Muttering under her breath, she shuffled across the smooth floor to stop at the doorway.

The bedroom ceiling sloped downward into two dormered windows, the lower sill of each rested directly on the floor next to several multicoloured potted flowers. There was a huge king-size bed with a black-on-black patterned spread and a pile of yellow and red cushions piled against the iron bedstead. There wasn't an errant sock or piece of dirty underwear anywhere in sight. A young man who didn't live like a pig, Riley thought fuzzily; wonders never cease.

Darius and Peter were laying side by side and both were very pale and clearly unconscious. Riley instinctively went to Darius's side. She leaned over to peer closely at him.

"What happened to him?" she asked.

"Drowned," Anna replied.

"Why aren't you doing something, you idiot?" Riley gasped. Her fuzzy thinking seemed to clear rapidly. She climbed onto the bed beside Darius and urgently palpated for a pulse in his neck. He hadn't shaved recently, her mind noted abstractly as her fingers fumbled in desperation to find the right spot under his ear. He couldn't die unshaven.

It took nearly forever before her shaky fingers discovered the steady heaving of his carotid artery. Once the relief set in, Riley examined Darius more closely. His skin was warm, almost hot, and there was a definite rasp to his breathing if she listened. Pneumonia. If the salt water hadn't done the job immediately it would have another go in the long term.

"He needs a hospital," Riley pronounced.

"We are unable to utilize the medical facilities of this planet," Anna said from the doorway.

"Why not?" Kerry spoke up. He had crossed over to the other side of the bed and was standing, hands deep in the pockets of his tour company overalls, staring at Anna in rapt fascination. "I mean, do you have cybernetics or a completely different physiology that would give you away?"

"I am unfamiliar with the term cybernetics," Anna said. Her gaze never left Darius. "But we do have implants that would show up on your investigative medical technology and must remain secret."

"Ah yeah," Kerry breathed with wide-eyed excitement. "The government would be right on ya the second anything showed up on a CT scan. Area fifty-four and all that."

"I don't care what the government would do," Riley lashed out. This was so stupid. Darius could *die*. "He needs to see a doctor and get on some antibiotics right away. I mean it."

"We cannot take the chance of being discovered," Anna said.

"Bring us to Home Base," Riley said. It was the only thing she could think of. There was a top-notch medical facility inside the dreaded Tyon stronghold, and even though it was the last place on earth Riley wanted to visit again, it was Darius's only hope if Anna refused to take him to an emergency room. "Please."

"I am unable to transport at the present time," Anna replied. She didn't look happy to make that admission. "I must regen. There must be at least another Operative to take two of you with us, and Darius cannot help. Transporting three is impossible. Particularly after reorganizing Peter and bringing Darius here. I cannot leave you and Peter here alone."

"Why not?" Riley stroked a lock of damp hair off Darius's forehead. "I'm perfectly safe here with Kerry, aren't

I?" She gave the Australian a pleading look. "Darius could transport two of us at the same time. You can take Peter and him back to Home Base. Get them fixed up. Pick me up when you're done." Of course, she'd be long gone by then, Riley thought. As long as she could get her orb back, she was a free agent.

"Can I help transport you?" Kerry had his helpful face on. His eyes were bright with eagerness. "Just tell me where you want to go. I have a car. Or actually, my sister has one, but she'd let me borrow it." He turned to Riley. "Where's home base?"

Riley opened her mouth to answer but Anna interrupted with a sharp glance in her direction. "Using a gas-powered vehicle from this location would be impossible."

Kerry looked crestfallen only for a second. "Riley can stay with me. You can come back and get her, after your mates are looked after. Don't worry. I'd take good care of her."

"As you have already?" Anna asked. "You hoped she would be pliable and willing to give you information about us, were she inebriated." Riley glanced from her to Kerry and back again. The faint blush told her all she needed to know.

"Creep," Riley spat.

"Ah, come on, it was just one drink." Kerry shrugged at her before he turned to Anna. "I do want to know as much about you as possible. That's true. I'm not denying it. I've been waiting my whole life to meet people like you."

"People like us," Anna echoed as she turned her attention back to Riley. "Darius needs medical attention. We are unable to take him to a facility here and Home Base is not an option until I have regenned enough to manage the trip. I will call for assistance then. In the meantime, you must begin the healing process. Darius indicated that you have the gift. I advise you to begin the process as quickly as possible."

Riley snatched up the crystal Anna tossed onto the bed as she turned and left the doorway.

"She's a right piece of work." The corner of the bed depressed with Kerry's weight as he sat down on the edge beside Peter and stared in fascination at her orb.

"Yeah, and you're not," Riley muttered.

"I wasn't going to do anything." He sounded a bit sulky. "You don't have to be so pissed."

"I thought you were a decent guy, Kerry."

"How was I to know you're underage?" Kerry nodded in Darius's direction and changed the topic. "He'll definitely catch pneumonia if he doesn't get out of his wet clothes."

Kerry did the honours. Within minutes Darius was wearing a pair of Kerry's track pants. Riley clambered up onto the bed and placed the orb on Darius's chest.

"You can heal him with your orb?" Kerry asked.

"Yup."

"Cool," Kerry said as he climbed up on the bed beside Peter and watched her intently. He eased a few cushions under his back and appeared to be settling in for the duration.

"If you really want to help," Riley said without looking at him, "get me some antibiotics. He's burning up so he probably has an infection and if we don't get this under control as soon as possible he'll die." She tightened her grip and closed her eyes. The faster she got going the better. Her head was spinning a bit and it was harder to concentrate than usual.

"How's it work?"

"Shhh," she hissed. She did not need an audience. "And some acetaminophen," she ordered as her previous first-aid training meandered into her brain. "A large bottle of liquid, instead of pills. So I can dump it in his mouth." She opened her eyes and gave Kerry a hard glance. "Are you still here?"

"I'm going," Kerry said. Riley felt his weight lift off

the bed and a minute later the door closed with a quiet snick. There were murmured voices in the living room but she paid no attention. Darius needed her, urgently, and she couldn't let herself get distracted, either by their newfound confidante, her swimming head, or Darius's warm skin under her fingertips.

D espite Riley's best efforts, several doses of acetaminophen, and an antibiotic with an unpronounceable name—courtesy of Kerry's sister's boyfriend's next door neighbour, who was a pharmacist—Darius had steadily worsened.

It hadn't been easy to get Darius to swallow the medication in his state. Interspersed with dosing him, she focused the power of the orb and her own natural ability towards the raging battle that was going on in his lungs. Even though it seemed the more she worried about him the more clarity she developed, her strength was woefully inadequate. Clearly it had been mostly Darius's power that had healed Alec's stab wound.

25

Anna had appeared only once in the last couple of hours. Riley had opened her eyes to find Anna staring at them with an intent look on her face that gave away nothing, but scared Riley nonetheless. Did she care at all for Darius? What had happened to the woman who had sacrificed herself in the caves underneath the island near Newfoundland so Darius could escape? Was she still on their side or had the change in time changed more than just Riley's place in the world? Or, the thought seeped into her mind, had that only appeared to be a sacrifice? Wordlessly, Anna had turned on her heels and returned to the living room leaving Riley alone with her uncomfortable thoughts and more questions than answers.

Riley shoved those concerns from her mind. She

had a task to perform and nearly falling asleep was not going to help. Castigating herself under her breath, she shifted slightly to get comfortable and carefully positioned the orb over Darius's heart. She breathed deeply. Even with a hair full of seawater he smelled wonderful.

The bedroom door opened, spilling soft light onto the bed. Riley sat up and squinted. A tall, gangly shape stood in the doorway. A hand reached out and flipped on the overhead light before Riley could shout out to stop. She clamped her eyes shut against the sudden glare.

"Crikey, mate, you don't half get on while I'm gone, do ya?"

The voice was strident and seemed to slam through Riley's already pounding skull. "Turn off the light," she snapped.

"Jeez, Normie, what are you doing here?" Kerry, sleep rumpled, appeared behind the newcomer. "Estelle's party is tonight. Did you forget?"

"Nah," Normie shrugged, "she kicked me out again. Persona non grata. Who are they?"

Riley squinted against the light. Normie, the key-forgetting roommate, was a scarecrow of a man, easily taller than Darius or Anna by a head. He had a wild Afro of light brown frizzy curls and heavy tortoise-framed glasses that had slid halfway down his beaky nose. His jeans ended several inches higher than his hairy ankles. Whoever Estelle was, she had good taste if she'd dumped him, Riley thought.

"Guests of mine." Kerry took hold of Normie's arm and none too gently pulled him out of the bedroom. "I'll explain it in the morning."

"No way." Normie pulled his arm out of Kerry's grasp and came to stand at the foot of the bed like a human Q-tip. "Whatever's going on, I want in. She's kinda cute." 169

Kerry sighed. "The guy is sick. Riley's his nurse."

"Yeah, right." Normie gave a short laugh as he stared at Riley.

Another goon who kept his brain outside his skull, Riley groused silently. "Turn around and heave your skinny butt out of here," she said, raising the orb off Darius's chest for a second and levelling it at Normie's stomach. The faintest yellow flash leapt from the orb to Normie, all but invisible in the bright overhead light.

"Whoa," Kerry hissed.

Riley pushed again, none too subtly. "*Leave.*"

Normie began to back out of the bedroom, wide-eyed with interest, when Anna appeared behind him and halted his retreat.

"Who is this person?" Anna asked, her sharp gaze travelling from Kerry to his roommate and back again.

"Normie Weinstein. Roommate and astrophysics major. We've known each other for years," Kerry said by way of introduction. He turned to Normie. "Anna's the leader of this little tour. Wait till you hear what she has to say about gravitational slingshot effects. It's totally mind blowing."

"A beautiful woman who knows something about galactic expansion and dark matter behaviour?" Normie turned to peer down at Anna from his great height. Her hard look didn't appear to faze him at all. "No way. Count me as impressed."

"Riley has important work to do, and we are disturbing her," Anna said curtly. "Come into the lounge and we'll talk."

"I'm yours to command."

Riley could barely suppress the grin. Someone was in for a very nasty surprise.

Kerry still stood in the doorway. "How're you getting on?"

Riley shrugged. "Fever comes and goes but his breathing's a bit worse."

"Normie's not as big a jerk as he first seems."

"Really? Coulda fooled me." Riley tilted her head to try and ease a slight kink.

"He's a brilliant scientist. Almost finished his Ph.D. and he's only twenty-two." Kerry scratched an ankle with the toes of his other foot while leaning against the doorjamb. "He's a huge Trekker. Meeting you guys will be the highlight of his entire life."

"Yeah, terrific." Riley yawned. She hoped Normie enjoyed the moment because the second Anna was capable of transporting them somewhere else Riley knew she'd wipe Kerry's and Normie's memories.

There was a shout from the living room and a bright flash of yellow light that seared the picture of Kerry leaning on the doorjamb into Riley's retinas.

"Ahh," Riley cried, covering her eyes with her free hand.

From the doorway, Kerry yelled, "What was that?" He spun around. Riley scrambled in front of Darius's helpless form and aimed her orb at the doorway. She held her breath, her heart hammering somewhere in the vicinity of her throat. Who was using orbs to attack them?

"That was unfortunately necessary." Anna's cool voice could be heard from the other room.

"Good grief, woman," Kerry exclaimed. "What did you do to him?"

Riley jumped off the bed and went to the doorway. For a moment she couldn't see what was wrong. The living room appeared entirely normal. Perhaps a bit messier with a throw blanket tossed to the floor beside the sofa and several empty glasses on the coffee table. It wasn't until she realized Kerry was craning his head upward that Riley knew where to look.

Normie was on the vaulted ceiling spread-eagled and looking absolutely thrilled. Anna's arms were crossed tightly in front of her body and she was staring at Normie as if he was a slug she'd just found in her sandwich.

Kerry breathed a low, "Whoa," and held onto the doorframe in disbelief.

"And just how long are you planning to keep him there?" Riley asked.

Anna gave her a brief, scathing look. "This Terran cannot keep his hands to himself."

"A quick mind wipe would have worked just as well," Riley offered.

"Like the ones you attempted on the bridge?" Anna pursed her lips. "We have spent most of the evening dealing with the entire tour company, all of whom apparently saw you leave and attack two employees. I have had to deal with the director, six employees, one spouse, and a pair of armed officials of the local policing establishment. I have wiped enough minds today."

Riley sucked in her breath. She'd totally forgotten Kerry's workmates.

"No worries," Kerry shrugged beside her, his eyes glued to his friend on the ceiling. "I can get a new job."

"And him?" Riley raised an eyebrow at Normie, who was now trying to push himself off the ceiling with no success.

"He stays there until we are able to leave." Anna crossed the few steps to Riley's side and brushed past her into the dark bedroom. She stopped at the side of the bed and reached down, touching Darius's brow in a movement that was both too intimate and coldly clinical for Riley to watch.

"He's worse," Riley said.

"Agreed," Anna replied.

"He needs a doctor. Probably IV fluids. Round the clock monitoring."

"I concur."

"Are you strong enough to transport him back to Home Base?" Riley asked quietly. The last place she wanted Darius was in the hands of the Tyon Collective but if that was the only place he'd get the care he needed, then, so be it.

"I should be able to transport them," Anna replied quietly. "However I cannot manage three."

"I'll stay here," Riley offered, carefully keeping any thoughts of escape out of her head. "Kerry won't try anything stupid. I think he's learned the power of the orb and respects it. And besides, when you come back you can wipe his memory."

Anna was silent for a minute. "We cannot inform Logan of this situation," she said slowly, almost as if she were thinking out loud. "We would not be able to keep the knowledge of your companion's gift forever. Someone would eventually let an errant thought slip and the Collective would know about Alec and what he can do."

Maintaining a blank expression, Riley stayed quiet.

"I cannot bring anyone from the Collective here for the same reason."

Riley crossed her fingers behind her back and kept her thoughts away from Peter and the possibility he might blab about his brother when he woke up. Anna was smart. She'd think of that and take steps to prevent it. Darius tossed his head and coughed weakly. A moan escaped his lips, hanging on the air like an entreaty. It seemed to help make up Anna's mind.

"You will stay here," Anna said. "Keep your orb on you at all costs. Do not permit the two Terran males to touch it. You can defend yourself with it, can you not? Darius has taught you?"

Riley nodded. "I can take care of myself."

"I will return as soon as possible. To leave Darius at the Base in this state would encourage suspicion. I will have to stay until he is well."

Riley was about to ask how long, but Anna answered before the words could leave her lips. "Two days, maximum. Our medical technology is vastly superior and despite the seriousness of his illness, it will not take long to heal him." Anna turned and faced Riley. In the dim light her eyes appeared silver. "Under no circumstances should you leave this apartment. I will use my orb to create a mild repellant force to encircle the perimeter, which will minimize any danger. Leave the apartment and the force field is negated."

Riley shrugged a shoulder. She'd do what she wanted the second her regal frostiness left the building. "Sure," she replied. "Got it."

"Remain vigilant, Riley," Anna warned. "The Council is on their way to Earth and will arrive shortly. Hope that they don't find you."

Alec spun around so quickly he stumbled backwards and fell against Dean. Strong arms gripped him from behind and he was lifted up, his arms pinned to his sides. He nearly bit his tongue stopping the vitriol that threatened to spill from his lips and worsen his situation tenfold.

"Do not move," Dean warned quietly into his left ear.

Alec willed himself not fight but the surge of fury was rising inside. He wouldn't win. His five years of kickboxing hadn't a hope against Dean's advanced level of alien martial arts. His only hope was to talk his way out of the situation, which was pretty hopeless—he was much more used to using his fists.

"Bring him to Central Command," Logan ordered sharply as he stared down his long nose with an air of deep satisfaction. He turned and strode quickly away.

26

"Yes, sir," Dean said to Logan's back. His voice dropped as he murmured into Alec's ear. "I do not know what you have done or who you are, but I would say that you are in trouble."

"He's always hated me," Alec began. Realizing his mistake the second the words left his mouth he urgently backpedalled. "I mean, since the second he saw me in the hotel. I don't know why."

"This way." Dean pointed towards the corridor Logan had disappeared down and gave Alec a slight shove between his shoulder blades.

"What's he gonna do to me?" Alec reverted to the scared and guileless tone he'd used with Dean an hour ago. "Why's the guy so mad at me? I didn't do nothing."

"Commander Logan is quick to make judgments," Dean said, his voice barely audible above their footsteps. He was staring straight ahead, walking at Alec's side, his face curiously blank of any emotion. But his words held dynamite. "If he decides something, no matter what evidence is brought forward, he will not change his mind. Some consider it a vital skill of command." Dean's pause left no doubt as to his personal feelings on the subject. "Appeal is perhaps better made to those currently in charge."

"Commander Kholar seems like a reasonable man," Alec replied just as quietly. Several Tyon operatives passed them going in the other direction. Alec held his tongue until they were out of sight. "He won't let Logan kill me, will he?"

They turned a corner, then another. Ahead, the column of central command reached towards the roof. They were almost there. Dean slowed his steps. "Kholar is merely inspecting. He'll be gone in a few hours. Logan is in charge of this venture and makes all decisions regarding this mission. We are not in the habit of killing Potentials. Why do you fear this?"

"He thinks I know something I don't," Alec said with desperation. He had to get someone on his side right away. "I don't know how to use one of these marble things. But I found one, in London, and I discovered that when I used a bank machine and held the orb at the same time, money came flying out of it. I thought I'd won the lottery or something. But Logan doesn't believe me." Dean stared straight ahead but his jaw was clenched. "You saw Logan. You felt his hate same as I did. He isn't going to listen to reason. You just said he doesn't once he's made up his mind."

Too late. They rounded the last corner and entered the circular enclosure of central command, stopping at a respectful distance. There were only two people there. Kellin and Logan, wearing identical expressions and deep in conversation.

"Keep searching," Logan was saying in a low and barely discernible voice. "He is being untruthful and I will discover why."

"Anna is close to him," Kellin remarked. "Have you asked her?"

"No," Logan gave a sharp shake of his head. "I cannot."

"Why not?" Kellin began. He immediately clamped his lips shut as he caught sight of Alec and Dean.

Logan noted the change in expression and turned around. "Leave him with us," he barked.

"Yes, sir," Dean responded. Without a glance at Alec, he turned and left.

Alec's stomach dropped to his knees. How could Riley have liked a spineless creep who jumped the second Logan barked? Alec forced himself to think quickly despite the churning in his guts. He had to play this smart. Make them believe he was pathetic and of no consequence. He whimpered, "Why do you hate me? We just met. I haven't done anything."

"There are several questions you will answer." Logan ignored Alec's words. "Kellin will witness this interrogation and verify the sentence."

"Sentence?" Alec squawked. "What sentence? I didn't do anything. Why won't you believe me?"

"You were in possession of an orb," Logan continued.

"You mean the glass ball? Yeah, sure. I told you." Alec turned to face Kellin in appeal. "I found it. But it's just a marble. It doesn't have any special powers. I had a bag of these when I was a little kid. So did my brother. Everyone has marbles when they're a kid on earth."

"You were aware of the rip and the danger it posed."

Logan interrupted the second Alec paused for breath.

"What rip? What are you talking about? The cloud of dust?" Alec's mouth was so dry he could barely get the words out. "Hey, man, if you aren't scared of some weird cloud of sparkles coming at you, then you know something I don't."

"You are guilty of collusion with the Others." Logan took a step towards him.

"I don't know who you're talking about." Alec retreated. His back was drenched with sweat.

"The Others know you. You work for them."

"No, no I don't."

Kellin gave Logan a sharp look but said nothing as the bigger man took another menacing step towards Alec. Then another. There was nowhere to go. The solid wall of a divider was now firmly against Alec's back. There was no way Alec could out-maneuver Kellin and make it into the main room in the same way he'd never get past Logan. Both were grown men, strong and exceptionally fit. Both had orbs and knew how to use them in ways Alec hadn't a clue. Teleporting out of the compound wasn't an option without an orb and Logan had taken his. He had no other choice; drop the feigned cowardice and stand and fight. Well, he'd faced death before. Alec straightened up and gritted his jaw.

"See, the child is preparing to fight, Kellin. He knows I will not permit this traitorous game to go any further."

Kellin's lips twisted into a half smile.

"So, boy. Any last words before I pass sentence and carry out your execution?"

178   *What?*

"I don't deserve to die for something I didn't do," Alec said angrily. "Even the Tyon Collective doesn't sanction the murder of innocents. You know it. So do I."

"I am in charge on this planet. My first priority is to protect the Collective from any and all danger. Collusion with our enemy sanctions immediate action."

"You're making a mistake," Alec argued. "I'm just a kid. I didn't know anything about you guys until you grabbed me and took me to Ireland. I swear." That much was true. He'd met Darius and learned his destiny in July. It was still only June. "I don't have any special powers. I don't know anything about these Others you're talking about. I only saw the sparkles for the first time with you. I'm innocent."

"You are found guilty of being a traitor to the Tyon Collective," Logan intoned gravely.

"You're doing just what someone wants you to. You're someone's puppet," Alec shouted.

Logan didn't seem to hear him. "You will be summarily executed and your body returned to your family for whatever burial process is customary."

R iley was too worried to sleep. What if the Tyon medical team couldn't reverse the damage done by inhaling seawater? What would Darius think when he woke up surrounded by Tyons, including the loathsome commander Logan? What if Kerry's sister, Kithrey, returned and found Normie on the ceiling? There was also the nebulous threat about the Council. What were they planning to do? Darius had warned about the Council too. A shadowy organization that essentially ran the galaxy and made the rules, he'd said. Heaven only knew what kind of power they had at their fingertips (did they even have fingertips?) and what they'd do to Alec once they discovered his ability to move in time.

27

Riley swung her legs off the sofa and padded over to the stainless-steel refrigerator and opened the door. She pulled out a container of pineapple juice and went searching for a glass.

She was licking the center icing out of a cookie when Kerry wandered out of the bedroom. He was on his cellphone and talking quietly. He looked up, gave her a roll of his eyes and carried on. "Of course Normie is here, Estelle. He's asleep and pining for you as we speak." Riley heard the strident tones across the living room as Kerry held the phone away from his head until the high-pitched yakking paused. "No, Ashley isn't here tonight. The only person who's here is my...," Kerry gave Riley a quick grin, "my new girlfriend." His grin widened with

Riley's outraged snort. "You have to stop worrying. He's practically on the ceiling with despair that you've dumped him. And besides, who else would be interested in him?" Another pause. "Come by after work tomorrow and tell him yourself." He turned off the phone and tossed it onto the kitchen table.

"Who's Ashley?" Riley heard herself ask.

Kerry leaned over and picked up a framed photo on the side table. A sunburned, smiling, arm-entwined couple stared back; the gorgeous Ashley and equally gorgeous Kerry.

"So, you date beautiful girls." The words were out of her mouth before she realized she'd said them. She tried not to cringe.

Kerry laughed. "All women are beautiful to me," he said cheerily. "Estelle thinks every female on the planet is in competition with her. And besides, you are beautiful, when you're not scowling at everyone and acting so tough."

"I don't—" she began to say but never got any further. Kerry's hands had cupped her face and his mouth lowered to hers. His lips were surprisingly soft and pleasantly warm. The kiss was really nice, as kisses went. Who ever said that science geeks couldn't kiss?

He stepped back and gave her a lopsided look. "You're really crazy for the guy Anna took with her, aren't you?"

There was no point in lying. "And he doesn't know I'm alive." Riley stared at his chin. "He's in love with Anna, the idiot. How could anyone compete with that?" She turned away and walked over to the kitchen table. She pulled out a chair and sat down. Above her, Normie was still flailing about but whatever Anna had done to his voice still held firm.

"It's classic." Kerry took the seat opposite her. "Typical love triangle. They happen all the time."

"Easy for you to say," she muttered.

"Happens to everyone, mate. Trust me, I know." Kerry's

face broke into a lopsided grin. "Bet there's someone who likes you and you don't return the affection. Isn't there?"

Riley shrugged a shoulder. This was a stupid subject and she wasn't going to discuss it.

"The state of human existence," Kerry continued. Eagerness practically oozed from him. "We always want what we cannot have. Me, I'll give up anything to go with you guys, see the universe, learn all the stuff I've always wanted to. But your Anna says, no, we don't take civilians along for the ride."

"I'm sorry," Riley sighed. "I'd do anything to go home again, have this whole thing never happen."

"Would you really?"

Riley paused. If she could move back in time, like Alec did, would she really want this entire experience to have never happened? No weird women after her in Halifax? No Darius Finn grinning at her in the train station and offering coffee? No hug from Alec in the pizza store when she'd really, really needed one? Home Base, the rip, Kerry's apartment—all never seen or known?

"It was worth it to me," Kerry continued. "Even knowing that I can't follow you any further or see the things I've always wanted to see, it was worth meeting you. Ignorance is not bliss. Don't believe it."

Riley felt her lips curl into the beginnings of a smile.

"See, that's my girl. You get rid of the raccoon eyes and the piercings and the Estelle's of the world will spit in your general direction."

Riley tried to smother her laugh. Kerry was right. It had been worth it, just to meet him. And Alec. And Darius. Anna and Peter she could well have done without, but these three were definitely worth the effort.

The sudden flash of brilliant light hit all of them with the force of a barrelling transport truck. Riley might have screamed, she didn't know. One second she was reaching for another cookie, the next, she was on the floor, her left hand grabbing at her eyes and her right, scrambling for her orb. She distantly heard Kerry's grunt of pain and the sound of a chair toppling to the ground. Blinded, she tugged furiously at her pocket but the button refused to pass through the hole.

Two hands grabbed her upper arms from behind. She was hauled upright to her feet. Waves of nausea and a searing pain threatened to cut her head in two. She didn't know where her legs were. She couldn't reach her orb. She was pulled backwards, against the firm chest of whoever held her arms. Sickened, she couldn't even manage to struggle.

A man's voice harshly spoke behind her. Riley had no idea what he said. The words were garbled and strange and didn't sound like any language she'd ever heard before. She still couldn't see. Tears streamed down her face and dripped off her chin. She blinked furiously. Who had broken in? What did they want? If only she could see.

There was a resounding crash and a painful cry as someone fell to the ground. More shouts, still in the unknown language. The pain was easing. Everything had gone from brilliant white to grey in front of her. She shook her head, willing her eyes to start working again but it only made the nausea worse.

"Hey, leave us alone!"

That was Kerry, Riley realized as her gut clenched. He sounded in terrible pain. There was another scream, this time male and close by. More shouting. The sickening sound of flesh pummelling flesh. Kerry's groans.

"Stop!" Riley yelled at the top of her lungs.

One of the hands that held her arms let go for a second and slapped across her mouth, preventing further sound. The skin was dry and wrinkled against her lips. The other arm wrapped around her, pulling her directly off the ground, pinning both arms to her side.

Riley could almost see now. The room was taking on definition. There were several dark shapes, tall and imposing, interspersed around the kitchen. The table had been knocked over. Normie lay spread-eagled on the floor by the stairway. There was a huge dark mound on the floor at her feet. It took a moment for her to discern that the mound was in fact several people. Two figures swathed in dark fabric were hitting Kerry, who was curled into a ball, his hands clasping his head in feeble protection. Riley kicked backwards. Her heel came in contact with something hard but her attacker didn't flinch. Kerry stopped moving and his attackers straightened up.

One stepped over Kerry and came towards Riley. He was unnaturally tall, wearing what seemed to be a winding bandage of dark material all over his body. His head was draped with fabric, like a hood, leaving only a dark, shadowed space where the face was hidden. Riley didn't see any weapons. She stopped struggling. There was no point. Terrified and furiously angry she stared at the dark spot under the cowl, willing the idiot who'd beaten Kerry to a pulp to show his face. If it was Logan she was gonna kick him so hard he'd be a soprano forever.

The hooded figure stepped closer. It leaned over her. A peculiar sickening smell drifted closer. She froze.

The shadowed face was the most horrible thing she'd ever seen. It had grey mottled skin and features that were only the barest semblance of humanoid. No lips, just a slash where a mouth would be and three large and protuberant eyeballs dangling on the end of short fleshy stalks. It smelled like something sweet that had been in the sun for way too long.

She jerked her face away from the hand that covered her mouth. Just the thought of that grey, disgusting skin touching hers gave her the serious willies. "Breathe on someone else, jerk face," she hissed.

The alien didn't respond. It merely stood far too close and stared at her. Behind it, one of its companions was picking Kerry up under the arms and hoisting him to his feet. Kerry groaned but his eyes didn't open. Another was pulling Normie upright. Blood trickled from Normie's nose and from his left ear. His eyes were partly open but Riley had the impression he wasn't seeing anything. He was deathly pale.

There was another, less bright flash of light.

Riley jerked her head away to shield her eyes but wasn't quite fast enough. For the second time in minutes she was temporarily blinded. When her sight cleared she realized someone else had joined the group.

A small man, not much taller than herself, stood by the stairs, surveying the situation with the type of nonchalance that made her think instantly of hidden guns. He had wispy, greying hair combed over his high forehead and sad, monkey eyes that cut like lasers when he directed his gaze in her direction. The man cocked his head to one side and stared at her for a long moment. Riley resisted the urge to make a scathing comment. He spoke directly to her but the words were gibberish. He paused then tried again, this time in what must be another language altogether.

"Might help if you spoke English," she said.

"Ah," the man nodded slowly. The smile did not reach his eyes. "No translator," he replied in accent-less English, similar in cadence to Anna and the Tyons. He tapped his head with one finger, just behind his right ear.

"Nope," Riley answered.

"I will speak to you in your native tongue," the man continued, "as it is important you understand me. Who are your companions?"

"Normie's over there. I forget his last name." Riley nodded towards Kerry. "This one is Kerry Darling. He owns this apartment."

As if on cue, Kerry groaned and raised his head. Blood dripped from his nose and his left eye was swelling but other than that he didn't look too bad. His one good eye opened a fraction and glanced around. He frowned, closed both tightly and gave his head a short shake.

"Tell your zombie friend here to let go of me," Riley said. "I'm not going anywhere."

"True," the man replied. "You are not."

"Who are you?" Kerry had twisted his head and was squinting at the small man. "How'd you get into my place?"

"I can go wherever I wish, young Terran. Your paltry defenses do not apply to me."

Kerry swallowed. He turned back to Riley, incredulity in his slurring voice, accompanying the pain. "Is he..?"

"Yep," Riley said. "An alien."

"Whoa," Kerry breathed.

The grey-haired commander raised three fingers and made a complicated gesture. Instantly, the hooded figure holding her released his pressure and she was able to shrug free of the tight embrace. She moved away, trying not to shiver with revulsion. Kerry, she noted, was staring under the fabric layers of her former captor in a mixture of horror and amazement. She watched his Adam's apple bob.

The man took several slow and deliberate steps towards them. Riley began to back up then stopped herself. She was not going to give the creepy alien the satisfaction of showing just how unnerved he made her. She crossed her arms. "So, who are you?"

"My name would be unpronounceable. You may use the term Councilor. It is an approximation of my function, but one you would understand."

"Okay," Riley began slowly. "What's with the rough stuff?"

It took a moment before the Councilor's face cleared with comprehension. "Your colloquial speech is amusing but delays information transfer. Please continue any conversation with the most direct references," he instructed.

"Why did you hit us?"

"The use of force is required in the initial meeting in order to set the tone of further interactions."

"We'll behave if you whip our ass the first time we meet," Riley paraphrased.

The councilor inclined his head. "We prefer rapid capitulation of the inferior species rather than protracted negotiations and pointless altercations."

"I don't know who you guys are or what you want with us," Riley said. She gave a quick glance at Kerry to see if he was taking any of this in. Kerry's one open eye was darting back and forth from her to the Councilor. She could only hope he was ready to help her the minute she thought of a plan.

"I belong to the Enforcement division of the Intergalactic Council. I see from your reaction that you have heard of us."

"Only rumours. I have no idea what you guys actually do," Riley said.

The Councilor didn't look overly pleased. "Even in this little backwater of the Galaxy our mandate and mission should be fully understood by your population. However, if it is not, that can be rectified. The Council is charged with intergalactic control, if you will. We make the rules and you and your fellow inhabitants of this quadrant follow them. My companions are Thktas, warriors of a planet much closer to the center of this galaxy. They provide a policing function."

"They're good at it," Riley said. "Had us captured in seconds. Mind you, we were totally off guard."

"The element of surprise is often the key to a short battle," the Councilor concurred. He turned to his left and raised his right hand towards Normie. There was a slight flash of light from the center of his palm. He shrugged as he dropped his hand to his side and faced Riley. "This Terran male is severely injured."

"What?" Riley took a step forward but was immediately grabbed by the Thkta closest to her. "Let me go," she struggled. "He's hurt."

The Councilor gave a brief shrug. "Internal bleeding in the brain. Multiple skull fractures. Generally untreatable."

"Let me call an ambulance." Riley spoke in her most reasonable tone. Intracranial bleeding was really bad and needed attention immediately. "They'll come and take him to the hospital, you know, the place where we treat sick people. The rest of us will wait out of sight until they've come and gone. No one will see you."

The councilor's facial expression didn't change. He stared at her implacably as if her concerns were totally beneath his interest.

"Please," Riley pleaded. "I don't want him to die."

"We are wasting time. This Terran is of no use to us," the Councilor said. He made a brief movement with one hand to the closest Thkta. The swathed figure didn't hesitate. He bent over, grasped Normie's head with both his huge long-fingered hands and rapidly twisted. There was a horrible cracking *pop*. The Thkta dropped Normie to the floor. His face now pointed completely the wrong way.

Riley couldn't help it. She screamed.

Alec held his breath. Waited. Prayed.

Logan raised his orb. Kellin didn't move.

"What are you doing with this Potential, Logan?"

Alec's knees nearly buckled with Kholar's words. He turned to the source of the voice. Kholar and Dean stood side by side, expressions of polite interest across their faces. Alec didn't hesitate. Stumbling, he launched himself at Dean, reaching his side with three strides. Logan would have to pry him away.

Logan's fist dropped back to his side. The flame in his eyes dialed down to a flicker. "As Commander of this base it is my duty to protect the members of my unit from dangers without and within. I am doing so."

28

"Did I hear you state that this Terran boy is to be terminated?" Kholar asked. He could have been inquiring about the weather.

"He has been interrogated. There was a witness."

Kholar glanced from Logan to Kellin and back again. His face was impassive. "What were the charges?"

"Treason," Logan replied

Kholar raised one eyebrow. "Evidence?"

"The boy had an orb and had been trained to use it. He is in collusion with the Others." Logan faced his superior with the same cold demeanor he had used with Alec.

"I found the marble in the subway station," Alec interjected before Logan could stop him. "I had no idea it was useful. I told him that. I only realized later that it was somehow helping me get money out of the ATMs. I didn't use it on purpose."

Kholar stared at Alec for a moment then transferred his implacable gaze at Logan. "Are you a traitor, boy?" Kholar reached out and grabbed Alec's upper arm as he spoke the words. He was holding his orb in his free hand.

Alec felt the probe but it wasn't painful. His answer was too quick and reflexive to be a lie. "No. I'm not."

Kholar gave him a long interested look before turning his attention back to Logan. As he spoke, his free hand reached up to absently stroke a small crystal on a chain around his neck. "He is telling the truth. I sensed it. I also sensed a deep fear of you, Logan, and true worry that you will kill him for personal reasons. We do not kill innocents unless there is no other choice."

Logan's jaw tightened. "I observed the Others contacting this Terran. They spoke directly to him and knew who he was. There is only one explanation. The Others have formed a link with this boy and will employ his Tyon abilities against us."

Kholar frowned. "The Others have no history of utilizing local inhabitants to resist the Tyon Collective."

"There have been possibilities. You received my report on this some time ago."

"Just so," Kholar replied. His face was expressionless but something about his eyes made Alec feel that the contents of that report had angered him. Regardless, he kept all emotion from his voice. "However, there was no corroborating evidence to prove your conjecture. Until there is, I cannot act on the belief that the Others are employing more sophisticated campaigns than they have in the past."

"This boy is working with the Others," Logan said more

forcefully. "Interrogate him yourself and determine the truth."

"You just hate me," Alec interjected. He turned to Kholar. "He won't listen to anything I have to say."

"Do you have a personal vendetta against this Terran, Logan?" The words were said politely but the steel underneath was obvious. There was no love lost between these two. And of the two of them, Alec knew whom he'd rather take his chances with.

"The minute you leave, he's going to find an excuse to kill me," Alec exclaimed into the tense silence. He felt Dean's sharp intake of breath beside him but went on recklessly, knowing he had only one chance to save his skin. "He never gave me a chance to explain anything, just made assumptions. I tried over and over and he wouldn't listen. And you know that Logan never changes his mind, regardless of the facts."

Logan spoke with a slight curl to his lip. "See how he manipulates you, Kholar? Splitting the Tyons within their ranks is the plan of a traitor. The Others have clearly twisted his mind to do their bidding."

Alec turned to face Kholar. He looked him straight in the eye. "I have never planned any treason against the Tyon Collective. I didn't do anything Logan says I did. He'll kill me if you leave me here with him." Alec tried to swallow, but his mouth was completely dry. "Please, take me with you."

Kholar looked from Alec to Logan. His face remained entirely impassive and his grip on Alec's arm never wavered. Dean was staring straight ahead at something off in the distance and for all intents and purposes appeared entirely disinterested in the proceedings. Logan was breathing more heavily than usual and the faintest tinge of pink blotted each cheek but his lips had blanched free of colour as they pressed tightly together. He was staring at Alec and, if looks could kill, Alec would have been dead and buried.

Alec's heart was beating a tattoo against his ribs as if it was a wild animal trying to escape. Had he signed his own death warrant the minute he spoke those words?

"I see that the boy is right, Logan. A fine commander of seasoned officers, there is no question, but impertinent fresh recruits, unfamiliar with our ways and filled with their wild, untamed emotions require a more adaptable, sympathetic hand," Kholar said slowly.

"Potentials serve the Tyon Collective. They all must learn."

"True. But these are valuable resources. I do not wish to waste them," Kholar said with deceptive softness as he again stroked the pendant around his neck. A strange tingling crawled over Alec's skin with his next words. It wasn't the typical Tyon *persuasion*, but something less distinct yet perhaps more powerful. He was too worried about his own safety to think about it or to wonder if Logan was the intended target or even why one Tyon officer would use his power on another. Anxiously he watched Logan's face as Kholar continued. "I believe there is no coercive endeavor. There is no traitor within the ranks. This boy will be my concern. He will travel with me to our next destination and train under my leadership." He turned to Alec. "Prepare to leave. Gather any belongings you might have and meet me at the Control center in two hours." He let Alec go.

Kholar turned back to Logan but Alec wasn't interested in any further conversation. Darting behind Dean, Alec fairly flew down the corridor behind them with no actual plan in mind other than putting distance between himself and the commander.

Two hours and he was leaving Earth. Unbelievable. How would he get back? What Kholar's offer actually meant hadn't entered into his mind while Logan and Kholar argued but now that he thought about it, a sickening feeling crept down his back. He was going into outer space and might never get home. He'd be totally on his own with this cold, order-obsessed crowd and he wasn't going to fit in for a minute.

Crap. Had he made things worse? He shook his head as he turned a corner and nearly barrelled into an oncoming Operative. Muttering a "sorry" out of the side of his mouth, he lengthened his stride, needing the soothing expenditure of energy. Logan was going to kill him. There was nothing worse than that. Darius would come and find him, eventually. He just had to wait and keep his nose clean until then. Annoying Kholar would be a stupid thing to do, no matter how idiotic he found this quasi-military regime. Keep your fists to yourself and your mouth shut, he advised himself. It wasn't going to be easy, but it was sure better than being dead.

There was nothing like waking up from a faint to make you feel like a real idiot, Riley groaned. She slowly sat up, keeping her eyes closed for the moment until the world around her settled down.

They weren't in the kitchen anymore and she knew she wasn't alone. The air smelled unusual: cold, metallic, and something indefinably strange. The acoustics were different too. The sound of someone's breathing was much more audible now than it had been in Kerry's loft and there was almost an echo, as if the space were larger and emptier. It was also cold. Not freezing, but reach-for-a-sweater type cool. She shivered and her teeth chattered together, not wholly from the ambient temperature.

29

The huge room was made of metal. Brownish, dull and unfurnished, it stretched across the same amount of space as a soccer pitch and roughly the same shape. There were neither windows nor doors. The walls were slightly curved, as was the ceiling. There were no rivets or seams: the material had been grown, not fitted together like back home.

Tyon construction.

Riley shivered again. If the purpose of the chamber was to make captives feel insignificant and vulnerable, it was a great success. She looked around for the source of the breathing. Kerry was huddled in a fetal position about halfway down the room and facing away. There was no sign of Peter.

She felt sore all over, as if she'd run a marathon

or had the flu. The back of her head ached, especially behind her right ear. She rubbed the sore spot. Funny she didn't remember hitting her head, but then she'd never fainted before. Maybe you don't remember anything? Getting to her feet, she headed towards Kerry. She squatted down beside him and touched his shoulder. He startled.

"I didn't mean to freak you out," Riley said.

Kerry only swallowed convulsively. He looked like he wanted to talk but the words wouldn't come. His eyes were wide with fright and something else Riley wasn't sure of. She gave his shoulder a slight squeeze.

"You said you wanted to see alien stuff," she said, waving her free hand around expansively. "Well, here you go. It's totally lame. I haven't met an alien yet with one iota of style."

Kerry swallowed again. He licked his lips as his eyes darted around the room. He settled on her face for a moment. "This is an alien ship?" he croaked.

A ship hadn't occurred to her, but why not? Just because she couldn't feel any movement didn't mean they weren't going somewhere. "I dunno. Might be, might not. I thought it was another one of their bunkers, but you know, you could be right." She straightened up and a shiver of fear mixed with excitement slithered down her spine. How cool would it be to travel on an alien spacecraft?

"Are they going to kill us?"

Riley shrugged. "I doubt it. Not right away anyway." She answered his puzzled look before he could give voice to the question. "What would be the purpose of transporting us here just to kill us? They could've done that at your place."

"They killed Normie."

Riley took a deep shuddering breath. She doubted that the image of Normie's blank expression facing his shoulder blades would ever leave her brain for as long as she lived.

"What'll they do to us?"

"I don't know," Riley answered truthfully. Who knew

what aliens thought? But there were several suspicious ideas darting through Riley's mind, none of them pleasant.

"But you know these people," Kerry said. His voice had taken on a distinct whining tone. Riley's lip curled. Where was the unflappable Aussie she'd met on the Sydney Bridge?

"Look, just because I know a few aliens doesn't mean I fraternize with the whole universe," she answered sharply. She stood up and looked around at the walls. "We need to check this place out. See if there's a door or something. Get up."

Without waiting to see if Kerry followed her directive, Riley headed towards the closest wall. She stopped when the wall was within touching distance. Tentatively she reached out a finger and felt the cold, almost slippery material. A slight hum travelled up her hand to her shoulder. She quickly pulled her finger away. Nothing had the same, creepy feeling as the Tyon metal. This stuff was actually alive—not breathing alive, but not inert either. Riley remembered Dean telling her about it and demonstrating the creation of a chair, back at Home Base. She'd felt both fascinated and repelled by the machine oozing brown metal and the final product. Why, she couldn't say.

She bit her lip. So, was this a spaceship or another bunker? If the former, where were they going? If the latter, where exactly was it located? If the former, could they get off and get back home? If they were underground somewhere then same question, slightly different parameters. Either way it boiled down to escape. Riley blew out a heavy breath and brushed her bangs off her forehead while Kerry shuffled up behind her.

He tapped her on the shoulder. "Have you figured out where we are?"

"Nope."

"Any idea how we can go home?"

"Nope."

"We're in trouble, right?"

"Yup." Riley turned and faced Kerry. There was better colour in his cheeks and his eyes didn't have the haunted, I-am-so-screwed look they had a few minutes ago. Good. "'Kay, here's the deal. We're being held by aliens. Not the ones I know and hang with, but other ones. I have no idea if they're the enemy or on our side but I'm guessing enemies. I don't know if we're orbiting Earth or heading out into the universe at the speed of light or if we're still on Earth but hidden somewhere in one of their secret bases. If we're on a spaceship, we're screwed, because I have no idea how to pilot a ship back. So start praying that we're only underground somewhere and will be able to find the exit."

Kerry nodded. "I can navigate celestially but have no idea about warp drive."

Riley resisted the urge to roll her eyes. "This is not TV. It's real. I know this is difficult to get your head around. Trust me, it took me a few minutes to get with the program the first time too."

"Any interstellar vessel will have some type of light-speed drive," Kerry said as if he hadn't really heard her. "It stands to reason. Galactic distances are huge. Travel has to occur at light speed or higher to make it viable."

"Yeah, whatever." Riley turned back to the wall. "Main thing for now is figuring out where we are. Then, how to get out."

"Okay," Kerry agreed.

There was an awkward silence. Riley tapped her foot. "So you want me to puzzle this out," she said. "You're just along for the ride."

She felt his shrug. "You're the one who knows aliens. I just watch TV. I'll watch and learn."

197

"Yeah, you do that." Mildly annoyed, Riley began to walk along the wall, peering closely for any sign of a seam. Darius would wave his orb at the wall and doors would appear, she remembered. She pulled her new orb from her pocket with relief. For a second she'd worried that the Councilor and his cronies had taken it away from her, but strangely they hadn't. Either they didn't care she had one, because it wouldn't work against them, or they hadn't noticed. But how would aliens who could diagnose brain hemorrhage with the palm of their hands miss an orb if it were important? She gave her head a shake. Too many questions.

She searched the entire room without finding a sign of a door, with Kerry trailing behind her like a hulking wraith. He was now humming off key and drumming his fingers on his leg as he stood at her side as she came to a halt. Ignoring him, Riley reviewed her findings. No entrance or exit. No air vents. No bathroom—which was shortly going to be a serious worry—and no food or water. Waving her orb had not made a bit of difference. Standing still and concentrating, difficult with an aching head, hadn't accomplished anything either. Riley hadn't been able to sense anyone's thoughts or emotions and there would have been *something* if there were other captives or aliens outside the walls.

Yelling wasn't going to do any good either. If there was a way of monitoring them inside the room, Riley hadn't seen it. Her only conclusion was that the room was a storage facility, currently only storing them, and their captors would eventually come to either let them out or gloat over their imprisonment. Hopefully. Being left to die alone and of starvation didn't even warrant thinking about.

Pursing her lips with annoyance, Riley leaned against the wall and slid down until she was in a sitting position. Kerry squatted down beside her.

"Well?"

"We're trapped," Riley sighed.

"No exit?"

"None. No intercom either. I doubt anyone will hear us if we start yelling, but if you want to, go ahead."

"And your orb thingy. Can you send a message to Blondie?" Kerry asked.

Riley scowled. "It's not a phone."

"Yeah, right. But you did before. On the bridge. Remember?"

Riley was about to give a scathing reply but she bit her tongue. Kerry was right. Sure, the orb wasn't a phone per se, but she could use it to communicate if someone was waiting for her signal and could reply. Would a signal get through the Tyon defense system at Home Base? Were orbs limited by distance?

Riley sucked her teeth. She pulled out her orb and held it in front of her eyes. There was only one way to know for sure. Closing her eyes, she tried to concentrate on sending a message to Anna without feeling like a complete idiot. *Anna, help us.* She pushed all the other thoughts out of her head, one by one: the coolness of the chamber, the fear they were in enemy hands, the worry about their future. The orb seemed heavier than normal and a distinct warmth was flowing upwards from her palm into her arm and shoulder. She tightened her fingers around it. *Anna, talk to me.* She felt as if she was falling slowly into herself, that the orb was tugging her ever so gently. She resisted the pull. She'd never felt that before. The orb pulled more strongly. Riley resisted. With a sudden panic she cut off the connection, dropping her orb back into her pocket and standing up so quickly she nearly barrelled into Kerry.

"I can't do it," she muttered.

"Why not?"

"Just can't, okay?" Riley snapped. Her face was flushed and an odd prickling along her skin had started.

"Why not?" Kerry asked.

"Cause someone's watching me," she said. Only with the words out did she realize that was exactly the feeling she'd had. She gave a slight shiver.

Kerry turned and looked around at their huge metallic prison and rubbed his hand over his face as if he was just waking up from an unpleasant dream. "We're screwed then."

"Looks like," Riley replied with a sigh.

"Usually the good guys have an ace up their sleeve."

"Yeah. Usually. On TV." Riley gave a ghost of a grin. "In case you haven't noticed, this is real life which tends to suck."

"What do we do?"

"Wait." Riley shrugged. What else was there to do? "Hope they remember we're human and need food and water and bathrooms and stuff." Suddenly she wished she hadn't mentioned bathrooms.

"Wish I had a towel," said Kerry. "You know, for travelling through the universe." He gave her a sly look.

Riley couldn't help but grin back. That book had been a favourite of hers too. "If anyone threatens to read poetry at us, run."

They both laughed weakly for a moment until the weight of their situation smothered all good feelings.

"You know," Kerry said slowly, "I've read about this sort of thing."

"What?"

"Being captured by aliens."

"Kerry, I hate to break it to you, but anything you read was speculative fiction, not a how-to manual. Not too many people have actually been captured by aliens. And those claiming they've been probed are probably all off their medications."

"Yeah, right. I know that," Kerry continued, a gleam in his eyes flickering into life, "but lots of stories have been written about hypothetical situations. At least one of those should reflect what's happening to us, fairly closely."

Enthusiasm was flooding his expression. Riley nearly snorted out loud with the ridiculousness of it. But, and this was the sobering thought, they had nothing else to fall back on and it was a lot better for both of them if Kerry was in fighting form, not the stunned zombie of half an hour ago.

"Okay, spill," said Riley, smothering the need to roll her

eyes. She knew very well when the crunch came, she'd be in charge, making the decisions. "What's your plan?"

"Well, we fake an injury, call for help and overpower the guards when they come in," Kerry said. "Or, we manufacture a weapon out of your orb thingy and overpower the guards when they come in. Or," his eyes were starting to gleam, "you make a play for one of them and I overpower them when they're totally distracted."

He could use a slap across the face, Riley thought as she turned away.

"Or we negotiate," he said.

Riley turned back. "Negotiate for what?"

"Dunno. What've we got?"

Riley frowned. Good question. "Intimate knowledge of how Earth is run. How to blend in, where the power resides, that sort of stuff."

"Great," Kerry enthused. He rubbed his hands together. "Plus you know stuff about the other aliens. Maybe these guys don't know anything about them. We could trade knowledge for freedom."

Riley was already shaking her head. "Darius told me the Intergalactic Council actually created the Tyon Collective to do their secret work. Darius and Anna work for the Collective. I'm just along for the ride." Her forehead creased as she thought out loud. "But maybe the Council doesn't know very much about the Others. We do. We might just be able to sell that info if we're smart."

"Who are these Others?"

"Pan-dimensional bad asses with no sense of humour," Riley replied. "The main one we dealt with was called Rhozan. A seriously scary dude who can possess people like that." She snapped her fingers. "He's out for the usual world domination and destruction. Alec kicked his metaphorical butt."

"Cool," Kerry said. "Who's Alec?"

Riley looked down at her shoes and scuffed the toe along

201

the metallic floor. "Just this guy who was travelling with me and Darius."

"The one who's crazy about you but you don't feel the same way?"

Riley pulled a face. Someday she was going to have to learn not to blush. "No."

"So how'd Alec do it? Kick Rhozan's butt, I mean."

"That's the thing," Riley sighed. "We don't know how he did it. He doesn't know how he did it. Alec just...," Riley floundered for a moment, "he just, I mean he's, like, I don't know. Super powerful with this Tyon power stuff. Using the orb. He can do it better than anyone."

"Better than Blondie?"

"She's trained. Alec isn't. But yeah, Darius figures that Alec is the strongest Potential ever. Stronger than him, and Darius was the strongest the Collective had ever found."

"Which makes him dangerous to someone, right?"

From stunned to super acute, Kerry made some pretty astounding leaps and was remarkably dead-on where he landed. "Yep, exactly. So right now, Alec is hidden where hopefully no one can find him."

"Do you know where he is?" Kerry leaned up against the wall. He immediately backed away and gave it an odd sideways look.

"Nope. No one does. That's the point. Oh, and the metal is alive."

Kerry grimaced. "Really?"

Before Riley could answer, a familiar voice spoke loudly beside them. "You are prisoners of the Intergalactic Council. Prepare to transfer."

R iley whirled around and stopped the instant the Thtka was in her sight. With a strangled gasp she leapt away from the guard's outstretched arm. No way would that creepy grey skin touch her again. She fell backwards into Kerry, who caught and steadied her.

The Thtka's raised arm pointed to the side of the chamber. Riley stole a glance in the direction indicated and ruefully noted the appearance of a doorway. At the same instant, the Councilor's voice echoed through the room.

"Exit the holding station and follow."

The Thtka turned and headed to the doorway without turning its head to see if they followed. Riley gave Kerry a sharp glance. He shrugged his shoulders and gave her a slight nudge.

30

"Be ready," she whispered to him. He squeezed her shoulder slightly in response.

The door didn't open as usual but rather pulled upwards into the wall above it, as the Thtka approached. The alien passed through and turned left. The doorway was too narrow for them to walk through at the same time. Riley went first, her orb gripped tightly in her right hand, her left clasping Kerry's. Heaven only knew what they might find on the other side of the door and she didn't want to take the chance of being separated. The hallway beyond the door stretched out into what seemed like infinity. Made of the Tyon brown metal, it ran both right and left in a straight line. Riley couldn't see any doorways or occupants. The thought of running as fast as she could in the opposite direction crossed her mind but she quickly discounted it as a reasonable option. The Thtka had very long legs and would likely be able to overtake both of them, even if they had a head start. The Councilor had already sanctioned violence against them and Riley fully expected an attempt at escape would only result in more bruises.

"Where do you think he's taking us?" Kerry leaned over and said quietly, his eyes never leaving the back of the Thtka's swathed head, as they walked side by side after the alien guard.

"No idea," Riley muttered back. That wasn't entirely true, though. She did have an idea what was coming next and it was highly doubtful it was going to be something good. While they walked, her mind raced ahead. What could the Council want with both of them? She was a Potential and therefore of some use, if only for the latent Tyon power they might exploit. But Kerry didn't have the gift, at least as far as she knew, and her imagination was working overtime considering what might be in store for him. Kerry didn't seem to be overly worried though. She was still holding his hand and his emotions were overwhelming curiosity and excitement.

The corridor echoed with the sounds of their footsteps. Otherwise it was very quiet and not a little creepy. The dim lighting didn't help the ambiance either. After what seemed to be an inordinately long time, but in reality was probably only minutes, the corridor abruptly turned to the left and stopped in what seemed like a dead end. The Thtka stood still, facing the wall. Riley and Kerry stopped as well, keeping a healthy distance between themselves and the guard.

They didn't have long to wait. Another door appeared in the wall and slid silently upwards. A blinding white light from beyond the doorway flooded the hall and both Riley and Kerry flung a hand over their eyes and turned away.

"Enter," boomed the Councilor's voice.

Riley couldn't open her eyes to see where she was going. The brightness was far too painful. Tears streaming down her cheeks, she thrust an arm out in front of her and took a tentative step. Kerry must have done the same. His arm lightly smacked hers as he moved forward. She took another step. Suddenly her wrist was gripped by a fleshy vice and she was yanked unceremoniously forward with enough force that she lost her balance.

"Hey," she yelled. "Let go."

"Leave her alone," Kerry shouted from her left side.

The light dimmed around them and Riley was able to drop her hand from her eyes. She had to blink several times before she was able to see clearly. They were in a much smaller room than the holding cell. Riley could have walked from one side to the other in ten steps or less. The ceiling, however, was so far away she couldn't see it. There were two hexagonal light panels hanging in the air above them providing the light. The Thtka was gone. In its place, the Councilor stood quietly less than an arm's length away.

It was a holographic projection. It had to be. Riley squinted at the Councilor. He was definitely see-through. She quickly scanned the room but there was no sign where the projection was coming from. She heard Kerry's sharp intake of breath.

"Pay attention." It was the Councilor's voice but the sound emanated from all around them. The holograph's mouth didn't move, which was distinctly odd.

Riley exchanged a look with Kerry but said nothing.

"You will be transferred to the interstellar craft in one hour. You will be interrogated later. There is no escape from this facility. Food, water, and cleansing units will be available once transfer is complete. Do not injure yourselves or each other." With that he disappeared.

"Great. We're totally screwed," Riley muttered. "Guess your wish is coming true."

"What wish?" Kerry was frowning. He'd walked over to the spot where the projection had manifest and was waving his hand through the now vacant air with a look of awe.

"The let's-go-on-a-spaceship wish."

"Holy cow," Kerry breathed.

"That's an understatement."

"No, I mean you can understand him. That's totally cool."

The penny dropped. "He was speaking a different language?" Riley breathed. Her hand rose unbidden to the back of her head and she touched the skin tenderly. It still hurt. "Whoa, they gave me one."

"Who gave you what?" Kerry asked.

"The translator." Riley grinned. "They gave Alec one, when he was at Home Base, and I was like, totally jealous, but now they've given one to me, which is way better."

"But I didn't get one?"

"They only give them to Potentials. People like Alec and me," she said when the scowl crossed his face. "People with an inborn ability to use an orb. It's rare." She wasn't going to say anything about the Tyons interfering with human genetics in order to breed the trait into the population. "They must mean to keep me alive. At least for a while, otherwise they wouldn't have bothered."

"I must be expendable then," Kerry said.

Riley swallowed. Another one of Kerry's leaps of logic and likely true. "I'll do my best to keep you breathing. Don't worry. They want me for something. I'll just tell them you have it too."

"Sure, great." Kerry was giving the room an appraising look as if he was now deeply interested. "So we're not on a ship right now." He said it slowly as if thinking out loud. "So that means we're in a building. And that means we can leave it."

"I thought you were keen on seeing the universe?" said Riley.

"Honoured guest, sign me up. Likely for the chop, uh uh." Kerry smiled. "That orb of yours. Blondie used it to beam your friend Darius and herself away. So can't we use it too? For the same thing?"

Riley bit the inside of her lip. "Technically, yes. But there's a catch."

"Thought there might be."

"Yeah, well, you have to be really strong to move people around with one of these things. I can steer but I don't have enough push."

"I'll help," Kerry offered. "You just tell me what to do and I'll do it. I'm a fast learner."

"I wish it was that simple," Riley said. "You aren't a Potential. You don't have the right power. It isn't physical."

"I'm smart. Got a four-point-oh average."

"It isn't brains either," Riley sighed. "It's something else, something I don't think you have and that I can't test you for. Sorry."

"Can you get us out by yourself?"

Riley shook her head. "Even if I had the strength, they're probably blocking me. But the clincher is that I don't think orbs can transport people without the Tyon gene."

"The thing that gives you the power. "

She nodded.

"So, even if you could get out, you'd leave me behind."

"I might."

"I'm not in favour of that."

"For what it's worth, neither am I."

"Guess you're stuck with me."

"Guess I am."

They both smiled.

"Then, if we can't use that orb of yours to beam out of here, we're back to unlocking the door and making a dash for it." Kerry crossed the short space to the wall where the door had been and began to run his fingertips over the smooth metal. Riley watched him shudder and couldn't suppress one herself. Something about that metal gave her the heebie-jeebies.

"Let me try," Riley offered as she came to stand beside him. She pulled out her orb and clasping it tightly waved it in the general direction of the door. Nothing happened. Riley took a deep breath and focused her will. *Open.*

Still nothing.

Kerry made a fist and hit the wall. His hand bounced off with a dull clang and he grabbed his hand to nurse it as he swore underneath his breath. Riley rolled her eyes. A second later the door seams appeared and the door itself slid upwards. Riley was too shocked to speak. She peered out into the hallway. It was completely empty.

"Did I do that?" Kerry asked as he leaned over her shoulder.

"I dunno," Riley murmured. This was either a trap or Kerry's blow had released some inner mechanism. Either way, she wasn't going to waste the possible chance. She pocketed her orb. "C'mon."

She ran out of the room. Kerry dashed immediately on her heels. They headed down the long corridor as fast as they could. Hearts pounding, they headed for the far end. No alarm bells rang. The overhead lighting didn't change. No one appeared. Riley kept an eye out for other doors. Nothing.

Ahead of her, Kerry's feet thudded on the metallic floor.

Several minutes later she was starting to get a bit short of breath. But the urgency of escaping their captors forced her to ignore it. Kerry glanced behind them. He waved her onwards. It was no use. Riley grasped his arm and pulled him to a halt. The corridor ahead seemed just as long as it had when they'd started. She rubbed her forehead. Were they actually going anywhere?

"What?" he asked.

"Are we actually covering any distance or is this an optical illusion?" she panted. She looked behind her then forward. "I mean, I know we're running somewhere, but I don't get the feeling we've actually travelled."

"Don't be silly," Kerry frowned. "We've run at least five kilometers. I do that daily and I know how it feels."

"Yeah, but—" Riley stopped. It sounded ridiculous to say it out loud. "Guess you're right. Keep going."

They both began to run again. Several minutes passed. A stitch started in her side and refused to work itself out. The weird feeling someone was yanking her chain continued and grew in strength. Finally she called a halt again.

"What now?" Kerry complained as he looked around anxiously. "We're not going to get out of here if you keep stopping."

"I know," Riley gasped as she rubbed her side angrily. "It's just that this corridor is far too long. It doesn't go anywhere."

"Sure it does," Kerry argued. "We've covered about twice my daily run."

"Kerry, I just have a strange feeling about this." Riley shivered. "I can't explain it." She pulled out her orb and wrapped her fingers tightly around it. The normal soothing sensation instantly travelled up her arm but seemed to stop at her shoulders. "This doesn't feel right."

"Figure it out while we get out of here," Kerry demanded. He was flushed from the exercise and a frown was furrowing between his brows. "This might be our only chance."

"I think it's some kind of game they're playing with us," Riley said slowly. "It's all too easy. The door unlocking when you hit it. No guards on duty in the hall. No one shouting, 'Stop, come back.' It's weird."

"Well done," said a voice from behind them.

They whirled around. The Councilor stood about a meter away. He was fully solid this time and flanked by two

Thtka's, one on either side. The guards moved quickly. Before Riley could shout a warning, the Thtka's had lunged forward and grabbed Kerry by his arms, pulling them behind his back so sharply he cried out in pain.

"Hey," she shouted. She grabbed a hold of the Thtka closest to her and tried to pull his long grey fingers away from Kerry's wrist but it was next to impossible.

"My guards are implacable," the Councilor said. "They cannot be reasoned with. Desist your efforts lest you be injured."

Riley slowly let her hands release the Thtka's arm and took a step backward.

"Who trained you to use the orb?" the Councilor asked.

"Why'd you want to know?" Riley countered cautiously.

"He is to be congratulated," the Councilor replied. "You have acquired significant skills. Despite my compatriots assurance you are useless, I believe I can use you."

Riley bit the inside of her cheek to prevent herself from answering. Being used by the Councilor did not sound like a great way to pass her time.

"Just what is it you want from us?" she asked.

The Councilor gave a slight incline of his head. "You do not question the Council." His hand gave an imperious wave. Instantly the Thtka's went into overdrive. Riley saw the blow to Kerry's head out of the corner of her eye. There was no time to shout.

Kerry dropped instantly to the ground like a marionette whose strings had been cut. She cried out and whirled away but the Thktas were too fast for her. Both her arms were grabbed and pulled back into painful submission. A grey hand slapped over her mouth immediately cutting off her shout of rage. She struggled but the pain in her shoulders blossomed into agony and she had no choice but to desist.

The Councilor stepped closer, coming so close she could see each individual whisker in his chin and the cluster of crinkles around his eyes. She raised her eyes to his and gasped in shock. The slits of his pupils were vertical.

"The Council controls the galaxy, Terran female," he said, more terrifying for his lack of emotion than for any villainous position he might express. "You have no rights, no argument, and no resistance."

Riley jerked her face away from the hand. She managed to get the words out. "You can't tell me what to do."

The Councilor cocked his head like a bird interested in the worm but not quite ready to pounce. "You have no choice."

"I have free will," Riley sputtered. "You can't make me."

The Councilor leaned back on his heels. He clasped his hands behind his back and an expression of comprehension crossed his face. "The implant inside your head translates so that you understand me," he said. "Consider that a gift. However, it provides several other functions. It allows us access to your emotions. It issues our commands. And it provides punishment should you refuse to obey us."

Alec wandered randomly down yet another corridor, lost in his increasingly worried thoughts. He knew he didn't have any choice; he couldn't see any option other than the one he'd chosen. He felt distinctly uncomfortable and why, exactly, he couldn't decipher. The actual argument between Logan and Kholar was now a foggy memory. Obviously he'd been more upset at the time than he'd thought. His brain was usually a lot sharper than this. Two voices cut through his worries, abruptly focusing his attention.

"If he dies, the plan is finished."

Alec stopped. His feet had unconsciously brought him to one of the places in the base that was familiar: the medical facility. The voice was familiar too. He peered around the edge of the divider wall that separated the corridor from where the beds were located. Martje, the chief medic, was standing next to one of the raised medical beds and waving a large reddish lump of glistening crystal over a sheet covered figure. Alec could only see the patient's pale bare feet. On the other side of the bed, Anna stood with her arms crossed and an expression of cold detachment etched across her features.

"There will be another opportunity. Darius has discovered a stronger one."

Martje glanced up briefly. "Stronger than himself?" She sounded impressed but skeptical.

"I have not run a thorough scan. When we find him and transport him here, you will have ample

31

opportunity to evaluate his potential. I am assured it will more than suffice for our purpose."

Alec bit his lower lip as an uncomfortable shiver ran down his spine. Was it possible they were talking about him? And what purpose were they talking about? Defeating the Others or, he wondered with a sinking feeling, something else? He silently straightened up and took a step backwards. For reasons he couldn't explain to himself, he suddenly didn't want Anna to see him.

He turned and started to walk away, keeping his head down so it wouldn't be seen over the top of the divider wall. Two Operatives passed him as they headed towards Med Ops. Both gave him a curious look but said nothing. He avoided their eyes and kept going. He couldn't risk confirming who was lying on that bed.

"Potential, what are you doing here?"

Alec stumbled to a halt. The Operative looked vaguely familiar, although Alec couldn't put a name to his face. He was imposingly tall, with granite features, pale grey eyes and a demeanor that brooked no arguments. Alec had a chemistry teacher just like him in grade ten. Best class he'd ever taken.

"I'm waiting for Commander Kholar," Alec responded, remembering just in time to add Kholar's rank in a deferential tone. "He's taking me with him."

"Why are you near Med Ops?" the man demanded. "Are you ill?"

"No," Alec shook his head. "I was just wandering around."

"Tyrell, accompany this Potential to Med Ops." Anna's sharp voice cut across the distance. Alec turned. She was standing at the entrance to Med Ops and staring directly at him. She must have heard his voice.

Tyrell's hand came down on Alec's shoulder with the weight of the world behind it. There was no choice but to turn around with the man's slight push and retrace his steps. Tyrell shadowed behind him. Anna didn't take her eyes off him as he passed her and entered the small area designated for medical care. The minute he was within arm's length of Anna, Tyrell turned and left. Alec's eyes were immediately drawn to the figure laying on one of the raised medical beds.

Darius's skin was deathly white and his eyes were closed. Only the rapid rise and fall of his chest and a rattling grunt with each breath indicated he was still living. Two medical personnel approached from behind a divider wall and after a nod of Martje's head, held out their orbs over his forehead. Both closed their eyes in concentration.

"Is it true he's going to die?" the female on Darius's right asked Martje.

The older woman was peering at a monitor screen and didn't turn around. "Likely but not certain."

Alec found himself gripping the edge of the bed. What had Darius been doing?

"And the Potential he saved?" the woman continued.

"In a state of dis-derridement." Anna responded. She caught Alec's eye for a moment but nothing in her expression gave away that she already knew him. "I have sent an officer to retrieve him."

"Dis-derridement is very nasty," Martje murmured. She seemed mildly distracted with something that had just rolled across the screen.

At that moment another Operative entered behind Alec. He jumped slightly at her voice. "There was a message from the Council," she said to Anna. "Kholar instructed me to hold it until you returned."

Anna focused her attention on the woman, who took a nervous step backwards and clasped her hands behind her back. "What was the content of the message, Bryn?"

"Location of time shift verified and coordinates attached," Bryn stated as if reading aloud. "Tyon signature confirmed but no previous match reported. Investigation to focus on new Operatives and Potentials. The coordinates are encrypted and in your personal file."

Martje straightened and gave Anna a sharp look. Anna nodded towards the messenger and refocused her attention to Darius. Bryn ducked her head and backed out. Alec watched her leave.

"A time shifter?" the medic with the strident voice spoke up. "Here? On this miserable planet? Are they sure?"

Martje spoke when Anna didn't respond. "It seems so, Leezl. The Council is on the hunt for him or her. All of us should review the skills of our companions and the newest among us. The shifter must be found and stopped."

Leezl wrinkled her nose. "How much damage have they done? Does anyone know?"

Anna shook her head. "There is little information as to the results and influences this particular individual has made. We have no data that multiple shifts have taken place or that the current shift was significant."

"They are all significant." Even with the limited emotional responses, the air crackled between the two women. Leezl continued, "Even the smallest change can have wide-ranging consequences. That's the reason shifters are banned. Everyone knows this."

Alec chewed the inside of his lip. It wasn't going to take long before they figured it out. Despite his sudden concern for Darius, there was no way he could stay. Any second someone was going to notice him, realize he was very new, and put two and two together and come up with five. If they forced themselves into his head, they'd know.

He inched himself backwards, keeping his face expressionless, almost willing himself to take up less room and be unnoticeable. Anna was staring into the depths of her orb and Martje had resumed staring at her screens. Both medics had their eyes closed in concentration again. Alec took another two steps and turned around.

"Potential," Martje barked from the head of the bed. All eyes turned towards him. Alec froze. "Return to the bedside."

Riley's stomach dropped in terror as the Councilor's words penetrated her mind. The Council had access to everything she thought. How would she keep her mind off Alec's gift? One errant memory or thought would sign his death warrant. Worse still was the threat that they could make her do what they wanted. How would they? And perhaps more importantly, what exactly did they want her to *do*?

"I didn't ask for this and you have no right to force me. Take it out. *Now*," she cried.

The Councilor's expression didn't change. "You have no say."

"I didn't give you permission to touch my brain," Riley said angrily. "I'm telling you now, *take it out*."

32

"We of the Council have determined that the Tyon Collective has been infiltrated by enemies intent on subverting its purpose," the Councilor began, seemingly oblivious to her retort. "This cannot happen. While the Collective is a secretive agency, created by the Council some time ago, it has gained strength and has outgrown its initial confines. To destroy it would lead to awareness and consequently our duplicity. However, a series of counterstrikes within the Collective will return it to our control. My partner suggests that you become an agent of my plan."

Nervously Riley bit the inside of her lip. What partner?

"You will return to the Collective and be assimilated into their training program. They will have no idea that you will, upon our signal, perform the cleansing so required."

"What do you mean by cleansing?" Riley found her voice but was disturbed to hear it sound so wobbly. She cleared her throat. "Just what is it you think I'm going to do for you?"

"Cleansing of the Collective can be interpreted as removal of the infective agents," the Councilor said.

Riley frowned. This wasn't making much sense. "What infective agents?" she asked again.

"This," said the Councilor. He raised his hand. A brilliant flash of light travelled from his palm to Riley's face. She recoiled as it hit her. For a moment nothing seemed to happen. Then a series of images and thoughts crowded through her mind with the speed of a locomotive. They moved too quickly to fully grasp but the gist became increasingly clear. She stepped back in horror.

"You want me to track down the traitors," she gasped. "Find them and turn them in."

"No," replied the Councilor. "Find them and destroy them."

For a moment Riley reeled as his words sunk in. "I can't kill someone," she cried. "You've got to be kidding."

"I do not jest, nor request a thing and merely hope it will be done to my specifications. This is an order. You have no choice."

Riley backed away. There was no way. "Why me?"

"The best enemy is the one no one suspects."

She shook her head. "I can't."

"My partner suggests that Terrans often require motivation," the Councilor said. "Let me be clear as to the consequences of your refusal." He waved his left hand in a curt gesture. The ground to the left of Riley's feet rippled in a most unpleasant way. She felt a surge of warmth, as if the air itself was boiling. The heat cleared and the rippling stopped. As it did, Kerry appeared on the floor. He didn't move.

"Your Terran companion was quite correct. He is of use to us. His value lies in your feelings towards him and your wish to spare him from harm."

A queasy feeling rose in the back of Riley's throat. She knew why they'd transported Kerry with her now and she didn't like it one bit.

"Wake," the Councilor said. The light flashed from his palm to envelope Kerry in a sickly bluish hue.

Kerry's eyes fluttered open. He raised his head off the ground and peered around but his eyes were unfocused and the frown marring his even features indicated that he wasn't fully aware of what was going on around him. "Riley," he croaked when he finally caught sight of her. "What's happening? Are you okay?"

"Your companion has a caring soul," the Councilor pointed out unnecessarily. "For his sake, I hope you are as endowed."

Riley clenched her jaw. They knew damn well what would get to her and what wouldn't, courtesy of their listening device inside her head, the creepy alien thugs. To pretend she didn't care at all would likely result in Kerry's immediate death but to indicate she cared for him made him a temporary hostage and tied her hands when it came to obeying the Council's directives. The best she could hope for was that if she complied and carried out their plans, the Council would let Kerry go when it was all over. Or better yet, he'd escape. Though that seemed pretty unlikely.

"I'm fine, Kerry," she said slowly. "Don't worry about me."

"Yeah, okay." Kerry was slurring his words and slightly weaving, even though he hadn't made it to his feet. He slumped at her response and stopped the effort to stand.

"To ensure your compliance, we will employ further incentives," the Councilor said. He waved his hand again. Instantly, Kerry's face screwed up in distress and he doubled over, clutching his abdomen. He cried out with pain, the sound echoing over and over in the massive chamber.

"Leave him alone," Riley shouted. "I'm going to do it. Stop hurting him."

The Councilor smiled. "I see we have chosen well." With that, he raised his hand, palm outward, in Riley's direction. There was a very bright flash of light, which momentarily blinded her. She heard Kerry's pain laden cry. Without warning, the unpleasant sensation of teleportation began and Kerry's voice was cut off.

R un or turn around? One second under Martje's scanner and the secret in his head would be out. Alec turned slowly and caught Anna's eye.

"Potential, you are scheduled to leave with Kholar, are you not?" Anna's expression didn't give anything away.

"Yeah," he answered. He avoided Martje's gaze.

"Kholar has specific plans for this Terran." Anna addressed her comments to the chief medic. "I will ensure that he is processed on board Kholar's vessel."

"Commander Kholar said to be ready to leave any minute," Alec added.

"Kholar will wait while I scan you." Martje's stern expression allowed no refusal. She locked eyes with Anna. "Leezl, inform Kholar that his Potential is here."

33

Leezl left with the Tyon equivalent of a flounce. Anna's lips tightened slightly and her hand rose to clasp something at her neck. "A full scan and insertion of the translation device will take hours. It is not reasonable to delay Kholar in this manner, when the same procedure can be performed during travel."

Martje was obviously not in the habit of having her orders countermanded and while her expression didn't change to any great degree, Alec felt her annoyance building. Who had the final say in the Tyon hierarchy? Anna or the chief medic? Alec kept his gaze on Darius, unwilling to let either woman see the worry in his eyes.

"Martje, respirations increasing." One of the junior colleagues had raised her orb off Darius's forehead and was frowning. "Core temperature rising."

"All medical personal to Med Ops," Martje said into her orb as she crossed to Darius's side and peered closely at him. The words broadcast themselves across the wide expanse of cavern, echoing slightly. Alec startled with the loudness of the sound. He caught Anna's eye. She gave a curt nod indicating that he should leave while Martje's interest was focused elsewhere. He didn't need any encouragement. As he turned to leave, several Operatives, orbs already in hand, ran into the area, quickly moving to Darius's side. They held their orbs out over his chest. The orbs began to glow in synchrony.

"The infection is advancing. He weakens," Martje said to no one in particular.

Kholar strode in. He surveyed the group and his gaze lingered for a moment on Alec's face. "Report," he ordered.

"Guardian Finn is seriously ill," Martje barely gave Kholar a glance. "Despite our treatment the lung infection continues to advance."

"Will he survive?" Kholar stepped closer to the bed and leaned over Darius's feet for a better view.

Martje gave a slight shrug. "Unknown. We shall continue our treatments until we determine futility or return to health. Your Potential is unscanned and has not been processed. This is advised before any interstellar travel. He could harbor contagion."

"Noted," Kholar gave her a sharp incline of his head. He turned to Anna. "I am leaving immediately for our next assignment. I have no one in my company who has knowledge or experience with Terran Potentials. You have trained Finn highly successfully. You will accompany me to train this new one."

Anna nodded and her face remained impassive, but Alec had the distinct impression that Kholar was speaking more for the other Tyons' benefit than Anna's.

Kholar glanced in his direction. "Report to transport immediately. Anna will show you the location."

Alec gave a nod and avoided Anna's eyes, aware she might pick up on his annoyance. The last time she had been in charge of him hadn't worked out so well for either of them. The only good thing was that she'd promised Darius not to reveal Alec's status as a time shifter. But could she be trusted? Obviously Kholar wielded a great deal of power over her. If he demanded that she tell everything she knew, would she lie?

Darius might not live, Anna was coming with them, and Alec was under the thumb of Kholar, a man he knew almost nothing about but already feared. He should have taken his chance with Riley, he decided ruefully. She was probably having the time of her life somewhere.

Riley woke up sluggishly. The first thing she noticed was the smell. A potpourri of cement, garbage, and ammonia. *Eww.* The air was cool and laced with cigarette smoke. She grimaced and slapped a hand over her nose and mouth. She was lying on the cold hard ground and something wet was soaking into her left knee. She forced herself to open her eyes.

She was in an alley between two large, rusting dumpsters. If she raised her head she could make out the street at the end of the alley and the pedestrians walking past the entrance. Groggily she sat up, pulling her leg out of the oily puddle. For several minutes she did nothing but allow the vertigo to settle. This teleportation stuff was getting worse each time she moved.

34

For a moment it was difficult to remember why she was there and what had happened. Then it came back in a rush. The Council had kidnapped her. They were forcing her to do their dirty work and had inserted a device into her head so they could monitor her success. Kerry was still in their clutches and Heaven only knew what they might do to him.

She forced the panic away. If she was going to get Kerry out of this predicament she had to have a clear mind and a plan. She dragged herself to her feet and looked around closely. Why had the Councilor sent her here? There must be a reason.

She pulled her orb into her hand and tightened her fingers around it. Instantly the soothing sensation calmed her. The alley could have been anywhere in the world but the proliferation of English on the various pieces of garbage indicated she was likely in one of the Commonwealth countries or the States. The alley wasn't very long but several business establishments had access to it, including a restaurant. Riley wrinkled her nose. The dumpster next to her was incredibly fragrant.

She carefully sidestepped a rotting clump of what likely had been food long ago and eased her way through the piles of filth. Probably when she saw the street beyond she'd have a decent idea of where she'd been sent, she reasoned. As she passed the last dumpster at the very edge of the alley, the reason she'd landed there became painfully clear.

She halted abruptly and clasped her orb tighter. A familiar and totally unpleasant sensation fluttered along her skin. She looked around for the rip. Darius had told her that the danger wasn't over, merely delayed and it looked like he'd been right. Biting her lower lip, Riley moved closer to the hovering mass of sparkles. It was small. About the size of a baseball and floating above the dumpster, almost at eye level. She gripped her orb tightly. Some poor slob was going to come out of one of the surrounding buildings, his arms filled with garbage, and touch it. She wouldn't wish that horrible sensation of nothingness on anyone.

Riley reluctantly pulled her eyes off the rip and stepped out onto the street for a quick glimpse. The shops on either side of the cobblestoned street were decidedly upmarket as were the few cars parked just to her left. An old city quarter, she decided, refurbished probably for tourists in the name of cultural preservation. She was familiar with the concept; Halifax had done a good job of reclaiming its past on the waterfront. But this wasn't Halifax. The car's steering wheels were on the right, not the left, and the accent she heard from passersby, who all spoke English, was familiar. She raised her eyes upward and caught just a corner of a familiar sight.

Sighing, she stepped back into the alley and resumed her contemplation of the rip. If she was back in Australia that meant a huge trip to Home Base and she didn't have a penny on her.

She sucked her teeth. There had to be something she could do about the rip while she figured out how the heck she was going to get back to Canada. She couldn't just leave the dratted thing unmarked, waiting for an unsuspecting victim. Maybe a box could go on top of it. Hadn't she noticed a safety cone in the street, just past the parked cars? Putting that in front of the rip would slow someone down, give them a chance to notice it. It was the least she could do.

Keeping her eye uneasily on the sparkles, she stepped backwards and straight into someone.

"Oh, sorry," she gasped as she tried to turn around. Two strong arms swung around her, clasping her against someone's chest. The air was squeezed out of her lungs. She immediately tried to kick her captor and tightened her grip on her orb, pushing mentally away at the arms that held her.

"Hold still, Potential," a sharp voice pierced her ear.

Riley nearly shouted her surprise. She glanced down at the arms that held her. Grey jumpsuit material. She stopped fighting.

"Hand over your orb and remain quiet."

"No can do, bub," Riley muttered. "The orb is mine. I'm not handing it over to you or anyone."

She was roughly pushed away and turned around, the tight grip on her upper arms never slacking for an instant. She goggled. She knew this Tyon.

"Where did you get this orb?" Tyrell's grey eyes were narrowed dangerously and held no recognition.

Riley bit down on the impulse to call him by name. "Ask Anna," she replied.

Ty's head tilted to one side. He stared down at her,

which was easy as he was at least a head taller. "She gave this to you?"

"Bring me to Home Base and I'll tell you." Riley crossed her fingers.

Tyrell didn't answer. He straightened up and pulled his own orb out, balancing it in the palm of his large hand. Riley watched as the crystal glowed for a moment then faded back to normal.

"Come with me," Tyrell ordered. His free hand reached out and grasped her upper arm in a tight grip.

"You don't have to break my arm," Riley grumbled. "I'm not running away, or have your superior Tyon powers of observation deserted you at this crucial moment?"

"Shut up," he ordered.

The Tyon Home Base was exactly as Riley remembered it. Safe, strange, and serious. She'd immediately been transferred to a holding area once they arrived. Tyrell had reverted to his usual silent self. She'd refused to hand over her orb despite several threats by other grey-uniformed personnel and at least one Tyon Operative trying to yank it out of her hands. He'd left with burned fingers. Riley hadn't actually wanted to burn him, but by then she was in a high temper and her control minimal. Besides, he was a dipstick.

Anna had not made an appearance. What was more important than checking on her, Riley wondered with annoyance? The empty space was only five paces across but short walls allowed her to peer over if she hopped up and down, which she didn't. Jumping looked so stupid. Tyrell had used his orb to create a crisscross of energy beams across the entrance and warned her that attempting to escape would be a shocking experience.

At least her first assignment had been completed, she decided. She'd made it to Home Base. But the enormity of her remaining task precluded any satisfaction. How would she get herself integrated into the company and spy on everyone to find out who was the mole without anyone suspecting? Tyons were aloof; they would hardly buddy up to her in a matter of hours.

Perhaps the only good thing about languishing in this stupid holding cell was that it had given her time to think. She already had her suspicions about a couple of people in the company. Logan topped the list. He was so bad tempered that he *had* to be the bad guy. Anna was a possibility because she was a cold and unfeeling fish. Tyrell wasn't above suspicion either. There was something secretive about him. Actually, now that she thought about it, the only Tyon she could cross off the list was Dean. He was so straightforwardly honest there was no way he could be a covert agent. Riley kicked the wall before turning to pace the other way. The mole could be someone she had never even come in contact with!

She *had* to have a plan. Time was moving forward and every minute she was stuck here not doing anything was another minute Kerry was suffering. Wandering around freely and eavesdropping on conversations just wasn't going to cut it. There was an awful lot of luck involved in being in the right place at the right time and she didn't have the time nor was she generally that lucky. The only thing that seemed to make sense was to start with the most likely suspect and work her way down the list.

But how to get close enough to Logan to figure out if he was the one the Council was looking for? What did she have to offer him that would immediately get him on her side? A sick feeling grew in her stomach. She knew *exactly* what information Logan would covet. But could she go through with it? One life for two?

"Riley, what are you doing here?"

Anna's cold voice broke into her concentration and Riley tripped over her own feet. "Jeez, nice hello."

"You were instructed to stay at the apartment."

Riley did some quick thinking. Keep it simple, she advised herself. "I went out for some air and Ty found me. He brought me here."

"You were instructed not to leave." Anna waved her orb and the lattice of red beams disappeared.

Riley quickly stepped through before Anna could change her mind. She tried to smile, aware that it didn't feel natural. "So, this is your Home Base? It's really nice. How long have you lived here?"

Anna gave her a quick sideways look before turning away and heading down a corridor. She spoke over her shoulder. "The Base has been in operation at this location for one year. We use it for monitoring for signs of the Others. As you well know."

Riley had to almost jog to keep up with Anna's long strides. "Well, yeah okay." She tried another tack. "Have you been to other planets?"

"Several."

"How long have you been a Tyon Operative?"

"All my life."

"And do you enjoy the job?"

"Yes."

"Well, that's nice." Riley ground her teeth. This was the lamest conversation she'd ever had. "How did you meet Darius?"

"I was ordered to train him."

"Hmm, I guess that wasn't easy." Riley forced the laugh. "No."

There was a long pause while Riley forcibly kept her hands at her side. Slapping Anna silly would hardly move things forward in the right direction. "How is Darius?"

"Ill."

"Can I see him?"

"No."

By the time Anna would have warmed up, hell would have frozen over. "Just where are we going anyway?"

"You will be processed and assimilated into the training program here," Anna replied curtly.

Riley's hand thoughtlessly rose to the tender spot on her scalp. If they scanned her they'd know. "Are there any other Potentials here?" she said quickly before Anna could pick up on her distress.

"Just Alec."

Riley nearly tripped again. What the heck was he doing here? He was supposed to be on the run, keeping a low profile. How had they caught him and most importantly, why?

"Alec?" Riley said. "Do they…?"

"No. I have not said anything."

Riley's heart rate dropped back to normal. At least one thing was going all right.

"Did you expect I would reveal his true nature?" Anna's tone held vague contempt.

Riley forced herself not to rise to the bait. "If Darius says we can trust you, then we can."

Anna looked over her shoulder. Her look spoke volumes. "But you don't."

The muscles in Riley's cheeks were beginning to protest. "Nonsense."

"I can feel your emotions, Riley. Distrust, wariness, worry. You cannot conceal these from me. However, Alec is safe here. I will not break my oath to Darius."

"Because you love him?" If the gloves were off, then so be it.

"Because an oath is unbreakable. Such is our training. Duty and responsibility are paramount in our society. There are no other options. I have studied Terran civilizations. You are corrupt because you care for little other than yourselves. It leads to chaos and destruction."

"Well, thanks for the vote of confidence."

"Tyon leadership would benefit your world greatly. There would be no crime. All citizens would lead productive, ordered lives. Wars and self-destruction would cease."

"Are you telling me that everyone here lives like that?" Riley scoffed. "That no one bends the rules or is out for themselves? You're human. It's in our nature to be self-serving idiots."

Anna had turned down a corridor. Riley could see her former bunk bed in the distance as Anna continued her lecture. "Tyons are selected from childhood. Our training lasts decades. We cannot defy the code of conduct that governs our actions."

"So you're telling me that all of you are as pure as the driven snow. None of you can be bought off? No one here has a secret agenda?"

"No one." Anna's reply was prompt and without a hint of subterfuge but Riley knew that it didn't mean anything. The Tyons could lie when it suited them and had such good control over their physical responses that the usual telltale signs would be missing.

"You're keeping a secret for Darius."

Anna said nothing. Score one for me, Riley thought.

They stopped at the opening of the sleeping quarters for Potentials. Only one bunk out of the line of metallic bunk beds appeared occupied. The grey blankets hung over the side and the pillow was jammed into the corner bracket of the upper bunk as if someone had forcibly kicked it there. Three guesses who.

Dean rose from the large table and crossed the short distance with a look of polite interest. Riley had to bite her tongue from yelling out, "Hi Dean," with pleasure. The last time she had seen him, he was dead.

"Another Potential for training," Anna said as introduction. "She is called Riley. She was found and began her training with Darius. She is prone to moodiness and stubbornness. Good luck with her."

Riley stuck her tongue out at Anna's swinging ponytail as she left, before turning back to Dean and gifting him with a wide smile. "She lies. I'm adorable."

Dean smiled pleasantly in return but there was none of the warmth Riley had known before. "Welcome to Home Base. We'll get you a uniform then assess your skills."

Within minutes she had donned the hated grey coveralls and was following Dean down the corridor to the center of the base where she'd previously spent so much time doing orb exercises. She looked around as she walked. There seemed to be a lot more Operatives than she remembered before. What was going on?

"How many people work at this Base?" She pretended a wide-eyed innocence.

"Currently there are forty-six Operatives here, but the First Commander and his retinue will be leaving shortly. We'll continue on with half that number until we determine whether we are needed on this planet or not."

"And if not?"

"We leave a small monitoring contingent behind and the main group will move to the next planet," Dean answered easily.

"How often have you guys done this?" Riley craned her neck to scan the huge screens that surrounded the perimeter of the base. Nothing particularly worrisome seemed to be happening but now that she knew the rips were back, it was only a matter of time.

"Personally, only once before. However, there was little we could do on that planet. The Others had decimated the civilization by the time we got there. The organization has worked on ten different worlds so far and the First Commander will be setting up the primary base on the eleventh shortly."

"And do you like this kind of work?" Riley asked.

They arrived at the training center and Dean indicated with a hand which chair was hers. She sat without argument. If she could get Dean to totally trust her he might let something slip about his colleagues that could help.

Dean seemed a bit puzzled by the question. "Why wouldn't I like it? It is my function."

"Oh you know, not everyone likes their job. I mean there must be someone here not happy?"

Dean didn't reply. He gave a funny look then turned away. Obviously Dean wasn't going to rat someone out to a complete stranger but he clearly knew what she was hinting at. A slight shiver of anticipation coursed down her back. Dean crossed to a cupboard and pulled out an orb. Riley held her hand out. If one was helpful, two could be better. She smiled as she took the orb and rolled it across her palm as if somewhat unfamiliar.

"This is an orb," Dean said. "It helps focus your power."

"I didn't know I had any power," Riley said.

"It's your power that identifies you as a Potential. Otherwise, you wouldn't be here and would not know anything about us. We don't advertise our presence to the worlds we visit."

"Why not?"

"The Tyon Collective is a secret organization. We stay out of sight and remain hidden as part of our agreement with the Galactic Council. We serve them."

"Doing what?" Riley asked.

"The Council maintains the rules of the Galaxy. Generally, each world is permitted to develop in its own fashion with minimal involvement from the Council. However, some civilizations are excessively prone to destruction and violence. The Others are such beings. The Council cannot be seen as favouring any one planet or hating another. It must remain impartial, at least publicly. Our secret society was developed to help other worlds resist the Others. The Council maintains its position but the number of worlds that are destroyed is reduced."

Riley thought this over while Dean went back to the long shelf next to the cupboard to get her something to eat. The Council knew someone in the Collective was planning to blow the whistle and shame the Council into admitting they were interfering with the natural development of different civilizations, that they were liars. No wonder this was a big deal.

Dean placed a bowl of white gelatinous goop on the table in front of her and handed over a spoon-like utensil. Riley tried to pretend to be interested. "What's this?" she asked.

"Nutritional supplement. We eat this five times per wake period. Most humans find the taste pleasant."

"No hamburgers?" she said in a hopeful tone.

Dean smiled. "This is a complex substrate of complete nutrition. I've noted that on this planet adequate nutrition is difficult to obtain and a wide variety of foods must be ingested to reach optimum quantities. Many foods have no nutritional value at all and yet are consumed at alarming rates. Why are you Terrans so determined to make yourselves ill?"

"Good question." Riley picked up the spoon and stirred the goop for a minute, remembering how boring the diet here was with profound depression. She then dropped the spoon to the side of the bowl with a clang. "Guess because it tastes good. No wonder you guys are so serious if this is all you get to eat."

Dean grinned. "You sound just like William."

"Who's William?" Riley asked.

"He is," Dean nodded to someone behind her. Riley turned around in her seat and locked eyes with Alec.

Alec nearly stumbled. He'd just thought of saying goodbye to Dean and had changed his direction towards the training center. The last person in the world he expected to see was Riley. For a second he didn't know what to do. Were they supposed to know each other?

Riley stood up and faced him. For a second he was sure she winced but then the sharp, defensive look he knew so well settled in.

"William," Riley drawled slowly. "Nice to meet ya. How's it hangin'?"

Memories of the last time he'd seen her flooded his cheeks with crimson.

"That good, huh?" Riley's smile was cutting.

"I'm leaving with Kholar," Alec said to Dean. He looked at anything else but Riley. "I was just coming to say goodbye."

"I wish you well," Dean replied.

"Yeah, well, you too." Alec shuffled from foot to foot. "And thanks. For, you know."

Dean merely gave a slight incline of his head.

"Why're you leaving?" Riley took a step towards him then stopped as if changing her mind. "They train the Potentials here."

Alec shrugged a shoulder. "Coz."

Riley looked at Dean, back at Alec, and then Dean again. Her eyes were narrowing dangerously. "Dean?"

Dean's lips may have pressed together slightly but his expression didn't change. He said nothing.

"Okay, you two have a little secret. Bet it makes you feel all manly and everything. So that's fine with me. I couldn't care less." She turned her back on both of them and picked up her bowl. She carried it over to the counter and smacked it down. The spoon leapt out of the bowl and fell with a clatter to the floor. "In fact, it's probably best that you leave, right now, coz I just don't have time to hang around with some kid, if you get my meaning."

Alec's face burned. How had he ever found her attractive?

"Riley, I don't think that was called for," Dean began firmly, but Riley didn't let him finish.

"Personally I think William should train with someone more like himself. I mean, look at him. The definition of loser."

"Riley," Dean raised his voice in warning.

The ground shuddered underneath their feet. For several long seconds the tables, counters and walls swayed back and forth. A chair toppled over. Riley grabbed the edge of the counter and her face turned white. Alec clutched at the closest divider wall.

"You know, building on a fault line is seriously stupid," Riley gasped as the shaking slowly subsided.

Before Dean could answer, the lighting turned an ominous red.

"Cripes," Riley breathed. "Not again."

All three turned towards Central command at the first sound of warning that echoed around them. "Security breech. Secure stations."

"Come with me," Dean barked.

There was no time to argue. Alec fell in behind Dean as he raced out of the eating area and down the narrow corridor. Riley was right behind him. He could hear her rapid breaths between his shoulder blades. They headed straight for the command center and reached it, along with at least ten other Operatives. Kholar and Logan stood side by side, Logan facing the arriving crowd and Kholar staring in the opposite direction at something on a small screen in front of him. Tyrell was at his side, pointing wordlessly.

Logan spoke. "We have identified a time-space anomaly beneath this Base. The tremor you just felt is the shifting of our reality with the disturbance."

"There's a rip underneath us?" someone asked from behind Alec.

Logan nodded. "Several. It is unprecedented to have so many in one area at the beginning of the invasion. Our Sensors are gathering data and will have a report shortly."

Alec stared at his shoes and tried not to let his mind churn with the worrying thoughts that Rhozan had followed him. He hardly needed anyone picking that particular nugget out of his brain. Riley was standing close behind him. He could almost feel the warmth of her skin against his arm.

Tyrell straightened. "Another two in the last thirty seconds." As if to accentuate his words there was another tremor, which rumbled along the floor of the base. Alec braced himself against Dean's shoulder and waited, heart pounding for the sickening undulation of the ground to stop.

"Our stabilizers can't manage more than this, Logan." Kholar turned to face his subordinate. "Potential for base disintegration at three point seven. Suggest withdrawal. Immediately."

Logan gave Kholar a sharp look but didn't argue. "Evacuation. Now."

Tyrell waved his orb over the console in a figure eight pattern twice and the lighting darkened to an even more disturbing hue. It began to pulse rapidly.

Instantly the Operatives around them drained away as if siphoned. Kholar reached out an arm and grabbed Alec's elbow. "Come with me, boy."

Alec turned to urge Riley to follow him, but Dean had beaten him to it. He was already tugging her away, and heading back down the corridor with rapid steps. Alec had a brief glimpse of Riley's pleading eyes before she was forced to turn away and run with Dean. Whatever she'd wanted to say would remain unspoken now.

Kholar didn't run, but his legs, shorter than Alec's, still managed to cover the ground with impressive speed. Alec found himself almost jogging to keep up.

"What's happening?" he asked.

"Objects that come in contact with time-space anomalies disappear into them. If one develops inside solid rock that rock falls into it. So does the rock around it. Until the rip seals itself closed, it's a channel between here and elsewhere."

"And if it doesn't close?" Alec gave the floor a worried look. How many rips were there under his feet, literally tunnelling into the Base's foundation?

"They always do. Eventually," Kholar said. His eyes were taking in the ordered evacuation around them as they headed directly for the main doors. "It's the increasing number of them that is causing us harm."

Around them, Tyons purposely walked in the same direction. A couple had small pieces of equipment in their hands though most carried only their orbs, which glowed eerily against the blood-red overhead lighting. No one spoke. If anyone was scared that the floor might disintegrate beneath their feet and the roof cave in, they were hiding it well. Alec hoped he didn't look like a deer in the headlights.

Several Operatives joined them, surrounding Kholar as if guards. Alec noted uneasily that all were exceptionally tall, broad-shouldered, and granite-jawed. None paid any attention to him. Encircled, he moved steadily towards the exit. Several other Tyons passed around Kholar's entourage, some giving furtive looks, none getting too close. The hair rose on Alec's arms. It wasn't just him who felt the menacing presence of this particular group of men.

The floor began to move again, this time tilting to Alec's left. A distant rumbling vibrated throughout the cavern. There was nothing to hold onto. Before he could hit the floor, two strong hands gripped his shoulders painfully, pulling him upright. The silent guard let go the instant Alec's feet could find a stable spot. The tremor stopped but the floor was slightly slanted. The stabilizers were working overtime now. He vaguely remembered standing on the island overhead. The sea had stretched for miles in all directions. A shiver coursed down his spine and ended at his ankles. They had to hurry.

"Are we going to the surface?" he asked Kholar.

The Commander didn't answer. He held his orb up to his face and was frowning. "Anna has not left Med Ops. Paran, convince her to join us."

The steel-eyed young man, who'd prevented Alec from falling, gave a curt nod and peeled off to the left, darting back into the surging crowd of Tyons and almost instantly disappearing. The rest of them continued to head for the main doors, now easily in sight over the divider walls. The doors were wide open. Alec could make out Logan and his toady, Kellin, standing on either side of the doors watching the others leave. Kellin was tapping on a small portable screen with every departing Tyon. Logan looked his usual constipated self. Kholar came to an abrupt halt and Alec barely stopped himself from walking up the back of his heels.

"Report," Kholar barked.

"Fifteen remaining. All accounted for. Six on field assignments. Tyrell has been dispatched to notify them. Med Ops is now cleared." Logan didn't look at Alec but he had the distinct impression the man was very aware of him. Alec took a slight step behind Kholar and tried to look inconspicuous.

One of Kholar's nameless guards reached out and grasped Alec's shoulder, pushing him slightly to the side. Alec turned to tell him to keep his hands to himself, but closed his mouth the moment he saw Martje and her several assistants approaching. All the assistants were holding their glowing orbs over a type of floating stretcher. They passed at a rapid jog. Alec had a glimpse of Darius's deathly pale face and his bare shoulders before the medical team passed and headed out the main door.

"Eight remain," Kellin said.

The groaning rumble of rock shifting dangerously under their feet began again. Alec grasped the closest wall and tried to stop looking scared. The floor shuddered and the walls groaned. Several chunks of stone fell from the roof not far from where they were standing. The crash as the rocks pulverized the floor reverberated over and over. It took several heartbeats for the tremor to stop.

Alec saw Anna's head over a divider wall in the distance, near where the rocks had fallen only a moment ago. She was arguing with Paran who had his back to them. Their words were not audible but then, they didn't need to be.

As if she felt Alec's gaze, Anna looked up at them. Her gaze slid past his to settle on Kholar. Her lips pursed in anger. She reached up to her neck and pulled at the chain she always wore. Alec had a glimpse of something bright between her fingers, flashing through the red haze towards him. The flash passed him and struck Kholar and dissipated into nothing. Kholar didn't react.

Another rock fell with a resounding crash, this one much closer.

Anna pulled her arm away from Paran and marched towards them, her face set and her eyes gleaming. The tremors, coming now much more frequently, didn't seem to bother her or slow her down. Within the space of a few heartbeats she was at the entranceway with the rest of them, Paran at her heel and looking implacable.

"This is the last of us," Kellin reported. He gave Anna a sharp look before waving his hand at the little screen and turning towards the outside foyer. "I'll meet you on board, sir," he said to Logan.

Logan nodded. His eyes didn't leave Anna.

"Anna has a change in her orders, as I'm sure you are aware," Kholar said smoothly.

Logan nodded stonily.

"There will be little contact. Temorilius is out of Sensor reach. Training of the Potential will take the better part of fifteen sections."

"I understand," Logan said. Alec watched his left hand curl into a fist behind his back and out of Kholar's sight.

"Your pair bond will be respected once Anna's assignment is finished, should you so wish it. Otherwise, if the training schedule for this Potential is too long, apply and I shall personally see to it you have choice in your mate."

Anna's jaw tightened.

"I will wait." Logan spoke to Anna.

Anna said nothing. She gave a slight bow of her head, turned and followed the last of the Operatives into the caves beyond the Base.

"A successful evacuation, Logan. Carry on. File regular reports." With that, Kholar turned his back on the commander and strode out the doors into the short hallway that led to the outer tunnels. Two guards on either side of him and two directly behind gave no option but to follow. Alec gave a quick glance over his shoulder. Logan was watching Anna's departure with an expression of raw anguish. The shock of it hit Alec like a punch in the guts. He'd never considered for a second that Logan could love anyone.

There was no time to think about it. Kholar had picked up speed and led them down a wide rock-hewn tunnel at a quick clip. His retinue was bunched closely to him, almost squeezing Alec into Kholar's back. It was hard to see in the tunnel. The dull red lights were spaced far apart and cast an eerie glow on the walls, almost as if they were painted in blood. Up ahead, someone shouted. Kholar stopped and held up a hand. The guards instantly came to a standstill and were silent. Several pulled out their orbs. Alec leaned over Kholar's shoulder as another shout, this time closer but still unintelligible, rang out.

"Paran." Kholar nodded forward.

The big guard said nothing. Orb drawn, he left Kholar's side and silently ran up the tunnel. He was out of sight in less than a minute. A distant tremor, slighter than those previous, rattled the walls of the tunnel. Small pebbles dropped with a clatter to the stony ground and tumbled away. Alec's heartbeat quickened. Truly horrible thoughts of being buried alive flitted across his brain and he forced them out. The power that sang in his veins strained against his control. He wondered if he could possibly fix things but quickly realized that showing Kholar just how strong he was—especially when he was supposed to be untrained and ignorant— would be a highly unintelligent move. Teleporting out crossed his mind briefly but he rejected it for the moment. The guards were too close, someone was always touching him, and if he vanished he'd likely take someone along with him. If he was desperate, and only if, he decided.

The shouting began again. This time several voices. Alec identified the sounds of several people running towards them. Kholar's orb filled with white light and lit up the entire tunnel. Alec raised a hand to shield his eyes.

Paran came first, running flat out towards them. Right behind him were several Operatives including a familiar face. Dean was near the front of the crowd.

Alec's stomach clenched. Where was Riley?

"Rip, at the ship's entrance, sir," Paran shouted when he was close enough to be heard. "Coming after us, fast."

"Retreat," Kholar shouted.

The guards immediately obeyed. Alec had no choice. Someone gripped his arm firmly and he was swung around. He was nearly pulled off his feet as they all made their way back at a run.

The Tyons were eerily silent. Only the echoing laboured breaths and the slapping of shoes against the stone made any sound. The tremors grew in strength the closer they got to Home Base. A particularly strong jolt nearly knocked Alec off balance. He recovered in time and kept running, throwing rapid glances over his shoulder. The guards who surrounded him were too bulky and tall to see past and if Riley was in the group behind, he had no way to tell.

36

Suddenly they emerged into the large cavern where the door to Home Base stood open and empty. Kholar came to a stop and the crowd behind him followed suit.

"Report," he barked.

"The rip was huge," Dean said. "It followed us. We lost Rinna."

"How quickly did it move? What was the size?"

"As tall as me and as wide," Dean replied with a quick glance over his shoulder.

"It has stopped." Paran was peering intently into his orb. He glanced up at Kholar. "Two more, section six-D-three. One advancing."

"If tunnels six and four are impassible, then we must use number two and make for your ship, Kholar." Anna's voice came from somewhere behind him. Alec twisted around but the proximity of two guards restricted his movement.

"Removal of personnel outside my contingent is not desirable," Kholar said.

"Death is not desirable either. The Base is about to be destroyed. Both the small ships are inaccessible. Logan's transport has departed. There is no other option."

"There is still a ship at dock five," Paran said. He was still staring at his orb and the slight orange glow mixed with the overhead red made his face appear to be blushing.

"Stop arguing and get us out of here."

Alec nearly burst out laughing at Riley's aggrieved shout from somewhere behind Dean. Trust her to get to the heart of the matter with no tact whatsoever.

"The Terran speaks truth," Dean said. "Time is short." Another tremor, larger than any previous, seemed to emphasize his words. Several rocks, the size of Alec's fist, fell from the roof above. Murmuring unhappily to themselves, the group clustered away from the widening crack in the ceiling.

Kholar looked as if he'd swallowed sour milk but, without any further discussion, pointed towards a wider tunnel to their far left. Wordlessly the group turned as one and headed for the opening. Several stones fell as they passed, echoing sharply among the rapid tramping of feet. The rumble of grinding rock grew louder and the vibration leeched into Alec's bones as he ran. The tunnel sloped downward and the air around them grew colder. The lights were closer together than the previous tunnel but the reddish hue had become deeper, reducing visibility. How stupid to make things harder to see in an emergency, Alec thought to himself, mostly to keep his mind off the millions of tons of water overhead, just waiting for a crack in the ceiling. Despite their advanced technology, some of the things the Tyons did made no sense.

The tunnel abruptly widened to a small room, similar to that where the main doors of the Base were located. Two smaller tunnels branched out, one to Alec's immediate right, and the other barely visible ahead and to the left, behind the shoulders of one of Kholar's guards.

A horrific cracking brought everyone to a screeching halt. A huge jagged fissure spread across the ceiling, moving like lightening from one side of the tunnel roof to the other. The sound was deafening. A second later, the fissure widened over the opening of the tunnel straight ahead and huge chunks of rock rained down. There was massive clattering of stones and pebbles as the debris rained down on the temporary orb-created force fields and onto the floor. Someone didn't get their own orb activated in time and their cry of pain was barely audible above the din.

The crowd surged back away from the rock fall instinctively. There was only one real option and Kholar didn't need to voice it. As one, the crowd turned towards the right-hand tunnel and surged forward.

Alec was thrown between Kholar and Paran. He found himself running forward, all pretext of a calm and ordered retreat abandoned. The frantic scrabbling and gasping breaths mixed with falling limestone and slate. Someone behind him shouted again, the words unintelligible but clearly laced with fear.

The swaying of the rocky floor worsened and every step was now fraught with danger. One wrong move and he'd be on the ground and trampled. He doubted anyone would stop to save him. Heart in his mouth, his hand reached into his pocket and clasped the orb. Instantly the soothing sensation filtered through him. The power in his blood began to sing.

He could stop this. He knew he could. But what would the Tyons do if they caught him?

The sky was falling around her

Riley was jolted from behind in the mad dash to the ship. She thrust out both hands to prevent herself from falling. It didn't help. She tumbled forward into Anna and for a split second her hand touched Anna's bare wrist.

Power. Control. Anger. Something locked deep inside.

Riley's eyes opened wide with shock.

Anna yanked her arm away from Riley and whirled around, her pale blue eyes sharp with crystal anger. "How dare you," she hissed.

Riley caught only the brief instant of eye contact before she hit the ground. Dean immediately grabbed her waist and pulled her up against his chest.

The crowd surged forward. Riley held onto Dean for dear life. Around them rocks were falling from the ceiling, dust was swirling around like a vortex of angry ghosts, and the red glow made everything look like it was saturated with blood. A gapping fissure cracked in the wall next to them. Riley pointed wordlessly but Dean was already aware. He aimed his orb in that direction while he pulled her away from the disintegrating wall and back into the middle of the tunnel. They ran forward as quickly as the rocking floor allowed.

37

"Transport immediately." Kholar's voice boomed throughout the tunnel as if a megaphone was directly against Riley's head. She clasped both hands to her ears and groaned. She had to warn Alec. Where was he?

"Hurry," Dean urged her as he tugged her waist. Riley couldn't stop him. He practically lifted her right off her feet. Up ahead Riley caught a glimpse of Anna's cold visage, her features carved into anger, before the heaving crowd moved between them.

"I have to get William," Riley gasped.

"He's with Kholar. He's safe." Dean didn't even turn around.

"You don't understand," she cried, gasping as a stitch caught in her side. Dean sped up, as did those around them. It was hard to see where to put her feet. If she fell, she'd be trampled.

"The island is collapsing," Dean shouted. "Run."

Galvanized by the sudden fear of millions of tons of water rushing into the tunnels in a swirling, churning wall of death, Riley sprinted forward. Her throat constricted with fear. "Where are we?" she started to gasp, but Dean's sharp tug on her wrist silenced her. The tunnel turned abruptly to the right, and up ahead, the solid metal door of the underwater craft was wide open. The bright light of the ship spilled into the tunnel like a welcome. Riley put on a burst of speed.

Behind them, a distant roaring was growing from barely perceptible to massive. No need to ask what it was.

"Go," Dean yelled.

Riley's arm was nearly pulled from her socket. The advancing roar grew louder. It drowned out Dean's next shout.

Riley couldn't help herself.

She turned around.

Several operatives passed her, shoving her into the wall in their desperation to reach the ship. Dean lost his grip on her wrist. She was slammed against the wall for a second. Her head rang.

She looked up.

A colossal wall of water, churning over itself like a moving Niagara Falls was rushing up the tunnel. Foaming death, tinged pink by the wall lights, bubbling and frothing wildly. The roar filled her ears. A lone figure was running unbelievably fast in front of the water, heading towards her and safety.

For a second, she was paralyzed with fear and awe. Whoever he was, he wasn't going to make it.

The man put on a sudden impossible burst of speed, dashing towards her into the light. It was Tyrell. He didn't slow as he grabbed Riley around her waist. She was lifted up. Thrown over his shoulder. The wind was knocked out of her lungs.

The last few jarring strides brought her into the brightness of the ship and the awaiting crowd. The small entryway to the underwater craft was dark metal and crowded with the Tyons who'd reached safety before them. She craned her neck over Tyrell's shoulder, gasping to get her breath back.

The water was almost upon them. The advancing gust of air pushed her bangs off her forehead. The spray hit her face.

The metal door slammed shut with a resounding clang, only inches away.

The water hit the door with the force of a bomb. There was a groaning, tearing sound all around them that made Riley's heart stand still. Another massive shudder of the rocks around them and the ship itself sent Tyrell towards the floor. They both fell hard. Riley's left arm ended up awkwardly underneath her, and Tyrell landed heavily across her hips. She lost her breath. She tried to suppress the cry of pain. Tears filled her eyes.

There was a hissing all around her. Someone shouted

several words from farther inside the ship. There was a massive lurch, as if they were breaking free. Several Operatives toppled to the floor.

Tyrell struggled to get to his feet. The ship continued to roll sideways. His hand reached out to hit a small reddish button on the wall next to the door. He barely depressed it before gravity tugged him downwards. He slid towards Riley, unable to stop himself. The roll continued. Several screams filled the air.

A shrill whistle echoed throughout the tiny chamber of the craft. The lights flickered. A second time. Riley scrabbled to grab onto something to stop her progressive slide onto the wall, which was now underneath her. Tyrell, unable to stop himself, hit hard as he fell.

Suddenly, the power failed and they were plunged into absolute darkness.

Alec was squished into immobility by the press of bodies around him and the unstable floor of the ship, which was tilting dangerously at a forty-five degree angle. Another few degrees and they'd all fall onto the wall to his right. At least he thought it was a wall. It was too dark to see.

He had no recollection of his previous trip in one of the Tyon's underwater ships and his surroundings didn't look at all familiar. He'd had a brief impression of the narrow hallway into the craft, the warm brown metal floor and walls, opening suddenly into a wide room also formed in metal. There were protrusions from the walls, which might be seats, but otherwise everything was strangely alien. There were no windows, no command center, and no periscope dangling from the ceiling. Everyone was crowded together in the center, except for those who arrived last and were still behind him in the entrance hall.

38

Someone just ahead of him was shouting what sounded like numbers, but Alec couldn't hear him clearly over the background hissing and the exclamations of the Tyons all around him. From the shuddering of the ship, it was clear the tunnel had collapsed. He could only hope those who were running behind him made it inside in time. Where was Riley?

He struggled for a moment, shoving the warm bodies around him away with some difficulty. The ship lurched again and the lights flickered weakly back on.

Alec reached out to brace himself as the floor inched further to the right and he lost his balance. His hand came directly in contact with Paran's broad chest, and only the desperation of trying to stay on his feet prevented him from pulling back in disgust. Paran gave him a sharp look but said nothing.

The ship lurched massively. A horrible tearing sound echoed through the walls, and Alec's hair stood on end. The floor gave way as the ship rolled onto its side. Alec fell. The lights went out again.

The Tyons shouted and grunted around him as they were all tumbled onto the sidewall of the craft and the floor shifted up. Someone fell onto Alec, his shoulder thudding against his chin painfully.

"Hold. Stabilize." Tyrell's deep voice shouted above the noise and instantly there was silence around him.

"Monitor on," someone to Alec's left called back. "Powering up."

The lights flicked, once, twice, then returned to half brightness.

Alec twisted to see what was happening. Most of the operatives around him had their orbs out and were focused on their internal work. The orbs pulsed steadily. Eyes were closed. Several operatives had managed to struggle to their feet. Underneath Alec, a growing furrow between Paran's eyes indicated his temper was near to exploding.

Alec mumbled a half-hearted "sorry," and rolled to his left and onto a narrow strip of metallic wall. He pushed with both hands and managed to get up. Beside him, Paran was already on his feet and shoving other Operatives out of his way. He bulldozed through the crowd, leaving Alec to watch in uncomfortable interest as no one reacted negatively to Paran's strong-arm techniques. Alec watched as Paran reached Kholar's side, reached down into the mass of bodies and plucked his boss from the pile. Kholar was instantly in charge, brushing at his sleeve where Paran had grabbed him.

On the other side of the room, Tyrell was also making his way through the group, although he was helping others to their feet with his free hand. His orb glowed so brightly, Alec could barely look at it.

"Righting," Tyrell called out.

The ship gave a series of hiccupping lurches. The Tyons around him shuffled along the wall towards the floor as it slowly moved into position. Only Alec fell as the ship righted itself. He scowled as he pulled himself to his feet.

Tyrell dropped into a chair in front of a panel of instruments that Alec would have sworn a moment ago did not exist. Waving his orb over the screens, which seemed to glow into life as he did so, Tyrell inched the craft forwards. Alec felt the subtle vibration of some type of power system engage beneath his feet and the slight resistance of inertia. Several Tyons were standing close to Ty, clustering behind his seat and holding their pulsing orbs close together.

Behind him, the last of the survivors limped into the main room from the entry hall. Alec caught a glimpse of Riley almost dwarfed by Dean's concerned embrace, her white face dripping with water, her body shaking with reaction. He was too far from them to hear what Dean was whispering in her ear, but whatever it was made him mad. He whirled away and watched the rest of the company.

Kholar spoke and the room hushed to an instant silence. "As many of you are aware, the tunnel to my ship collapsed before we were able to reach it. This vessel will serve temporarily until we are able to contact Logan and transfer to his unit. Our Sensors," his eyes veered towards the several Tyons holding their orbs, "have only enough power to maintain us below water. Tyrell has already begun signaling Logan's ship. We expect contact and ship to ship transfer within several hours."

Alec shifted his feet and forced himself not to look back at Riley.

"Report status." Kholar directed his query towards Tyrell.

"The island above Home Base is collapsing. The Base has fallen into the rips or has been crushed. There will be no evidence of our inhabitation."

"Casualties?"

"Four Operatives. One Terran fishing vessel with five hands aboard was scuttled with the force of wave motion secondary to underground collapse. Extreme wave action on the surrounding shore likely. Danger at seven point three."

"How high are the waves gonna be?"

Alec whirled around to face Riley. She didn't look back at him. Her eyes were locked on Tyrell and almost black against the pallor of her skin.

Tyrell gave a slight shrug of one shoulder. "Eight to eleven meters. Approximately. It is currently high tide."

"So you're saying that some monster wave is going to crash into the shoreline here, right?" Riley's jaw clenched.

"Correct."

"And have you warned anyone? This part of the world is crammed with little fishing villages, just clinging to the shoreline. Rogue waves like that could kill tons of people."

"We do not interact with the population of this planet," Tyrell replied.

Riley pulled away from Dean's arms in her anger. She didn't seem to notice Kholar or Paran who had begun to move unobtrusively through the group in her direction. "You'll just let them die. Heaven help you if you actually *help* anyone."

"The Tyon Collective stays secret. No exceptions." Tyrell wasn't even looking at her. His concentration focused on his screens.

Riley's voice rose. Alec cringed. They might not read the danger signals but he sure could. "Yes, your precious secret. We all know just how important it is not to let the secret out, don't we, Ty? You're loyal to the chief, aren't you? Never thought of letting anything slip, maybe a word in the ear of the wrong person, totally an accident—"

She didn't finish. Dean had slipped in behind her and, with his right hand, clasped Riley across the mouth. Alec saw Riley struggle for a moment while Dean whispered something in her ear. The anger faded from her face and she quieted in Dean's arms. He didn't move his hand but his body shielded her from the rest of the group as Anna stepped out of the corridor next to them. Anna gave a sharp glance at Riley then turned towards Kholar.

"I would speak to you," Kholar said.

Anna inclined her head and without another word, slipped back down the small hallway she had just come from. Kholar followed. Alec gave Riley a quick glance. She was deep in private conversation with Dean now, encircled in his arms, her head bowed. Alec caught the brief dark look Dean gave Kholar's back before the commander disappeared after Anna. Alec tried as innocuously as possible to cross the threshold and follow. He was just inching his way behind a Tyon whose eyes were closed with concentration as she powered her orb when he bumped into Paran.

The broad-shouldered bodyguard was standing directly in the middle of the hall, his bulk effectively blocking the way. Alec pretended not to care and continued past, coming to an eventual stop at Ty's shoulder. Out of the corner of his eye he noted that Paran was staring directly at him. Alec feigned curiosity in the steering of the ship and hoped Paran would lose interest.

"What kind of engines do you have?" he asked Tyrell.

"None," Tyrell responded tersely.

"How're we moving then? Magic?" Alec scoffed.

"I'm busy." Tyrell waved his orb in a complicated series of moves over the far right screen and frowned. The ship gave a sickening shudder and Alec grabbed the back of Tyrell's chair to avoid falling.

"What's wrong?" he asked. Tyrell ignored him. A second Operative, orb already glowing, dropped to the seat next to Tyrell and began to wave his orb over the instrument panel. He didn't look happy either.

"Section twenty-eight, time/space anomaly present and following," one of the Operatives spoke from behind Alec. He turned to look. The woman's eyes were still closed but her orb glowed a sickly yellow colour and was pulsing brightly.

"All Sensors, focus on rips and raise barriers. Ennis, maintain monitor on obstructions between us and Logan."

The man next to Tyrell nodded and said, "Order accepted," while the cluster of Tyons behind him raised their orbs to shoulder level and moved them closer together so the crystals were almost touching each other. The hair on Alec's arms rose and a strange sensation coursed down his spine, as if he'd touched electricity. The power being generated by the Tyons Tyrell referred to as Sensors was amazing. There was a sensation of the ship slowing somewhat but with no windows and no speed dial on the instrument panel, it was impossible for Alec to determine if it was just his imagination or not. And if rips were following them, shouldn't they speed up?

"How many are there?" Alec asked.

No one answered for a moment. Then the Sensor behind spoke again. "Second located. O-two-seven."

"Evasive maneuvers," Tyrell instructed Ennis. Both waved their orbs and the ship tilted slightly to Alec's right.

"Can you outrun them?" Alec leaned over Tyrell's shoulder.

254   "They shouldn't even be following us." Ennis's terse reply was low and Alec barely heard it.

"One followed me before," Alec said. "It moved pretty fast but I was on foot. You should be able to outrun it in a ship. How fast can we go?"

"We have only two Operatives on board that power the ship," Ennis replied. He ignored the sharp look that Tyrell gave him and continued. "Neither is experienced. Speed is unknown."

"You mean you guys power this thing?" Alec was aghast. Who in the world designed a method of propulsion that required brain power? "Can anyone do it or do you need to be trained?"

"Third rip. Seven-four-six."

Alec didn't turn at the Sensor's words. Tyrell's knuckles were whitening and that told him all he needed to know.

"Extensive training," Ennis muttered. "Hold tight."

This evasive move was anything but subtle. The ship nosed upwards at forty-five degrees and tilted to the left, jarring everyone. Two Tyons behind Alec started to fall and were grabbed by several others who were not using their orbs to sense the advancing rips. The ship rolled over whatever was in its way, steadied itself, and continued on. Tyrell's grip didn't lessen a fraction.

Kholar and Anna suddenly appeared at Alec's side. Kholar pointed at a screen.

"There."

"Yes, sir. We see it. That too." Tyrell pointed at the screen at Ennis's elbow.

Alec watched Kholar out of the corner of his eye, keen not to attract probing attention. Kholar appeared calm and focused but he clearly wasn't. Surely a commander in the Tyon Collective had dealt with rips before?

"Explain the occurrence of excessive numbers of rips," Kholar said.

"Unexplained," Tyrell answered promptly. "Unprecedented."

"This region has never experienced one one-hundredth of this activity before," a voice came from within the cluster of Tyons near the back of the room. "Our monitoring noted no such previous infiltration of rips at any place or time on this planet or any other."

"It's like they're chasing something," Ennis muttered just loud enough to be heard.

"Say that again," Kholar barked.

Ennis looked a touch embarrassed but his voice was steady. "Supposition, sir. The rips behave as if they're being brought into existence for a purpose."

"Rips are naturally occurring phenomena which the Others use to gain access to a world's vulnerable population. During an invasion the number of rips increases as the fabric of the time/space continuum deteriorates. This planet has not yet been attacked," Kholar lectured. "Rips are not capable of thought or planning, nor do they react to situations."

Alec's stomach dropped. Earth *had* been attacked. Kholar just didn't know it. He trained his eyes on the back of Tyrell's neck and gripped the chair tighter. Two people inside the little submersible knew it too.

"Logan's report indicated early contact with the Others," Tyrell interjected. The room was entirely silent as they digested those words. The ship swerved to miss something and for a second everyone concentrated on staying upright.

"Elaborate," Kholar ordered.

"File Alpha seven thirty-four. Last file updated to the main repository before the rips began underneath the base. Indicated unusual activity for a rip in Ireland." Alec's stomach hit his knees. "The rip was reported to maneuver around himself and others. The rip was unusually large and demonstrated tracking properties."

Kholar stroked his short beard. He was frowning.

"There is more, sir. Perhaps more important than stealth capabilities."

Alec held his breath. How was he going to explain this?

"Go on," Kholar said.

"Verbal contact was made with the Others." There was a suppressed gasp throughout the ship. Alec's heart stopped. Tyrell continued, unaware that every word was a nail in Alec's coffin. "Logan indicated that the Others made a request and spoke directly to a Terran. The Terran called it by name."

Riley stood inside Dean's embrace and seethed. She needed time to come up with a plan. Kholar had a hair trigger where non-Tyons were concerned and wouldn't hesitate to have her locked up, she now knew. Dean had been quite emphatic. Tyrell wasn't the problem.

The floor shifted sideways and Riley nearly fell. Dean tightened his grip. Clearly someone was having trouble steering.

Riley peeked over Dean's arms. The central room of the ship was crammed full of Tyon Operatives and most had their orbs out and working. Five were clustered together almost out of sight, their orbs touching and glowing. Several more Operatives were seated along the perimeter, wearing seat belts and grim expressions. Riley could just see Kholar's back without twisting her position. He was leaning over something. The lighting of the cabin had taken on a reddish hue and Riley didn't need to feel Dean's emanated waves of concern to know that they were still in trouble. What now?

"Calmer now?" Dean murmured close to her ear.

Riley ignored the question and whispered back. "What's happening?"

"We have entered deep water but several rips have appeared and seem to be following us. Ty is evading them as best he can but the rips are demonstrating previously unknown properties and our power is limited."

39

"What's wrong with the power?"

"Three of the Operatives who died were trained to power these crafts. Another two got separated and are likely with Logan. We now only have two for this ship."

Riley didn't bother to sort out what he meant. Bottom line: trouble. She struggled to free herself from his arms. Dean frowned but dropped his hold. She focused her attention on Kholar.

The Commander and his body guard, the hulking presence whose name Riley didn't know, were both leaning over Tyrell's shoulder and staring at something out of sight. Riley assumed it was the control panel of the ship, since Tyrell was a pilot. Alec was rigidly standing beside them, just out of touching distance. His face had the expression of pent-up frustration she knew so well.

Riley groaned silently. If he let go, grabbed his orb and used his power, all hell would break loose. Heaven knew his control was minimal. And if Kholar even had an inkling of just how strong Alec was there was no telling what they'd do to him.

She got to her feet and ignored Dean's urgent, "Riley." She carefully made her way over to where the action was, mindful not to fall into anyone as the ship bucked and twisted. No one paid any attention to her. She stepped around Kholar and sidled up beside Alec. She leaned against Tyrell's chair and watched Alec out of the side of her eye. His jaw was gritted so tightly the muscles of his neck were standing out in sharp relief. He didn't even look at her. Carefully, staring straight ahead at Tyrell's unintelligible control panel, Riley allowed herself to casually lean sideways. Her arm barely came in contact with Alec's. Practically holding her breath, she plucked her orb from her pocket and let Alec's emotions wash over her like a tidal wave.

"The report was unfinished, sir." Tyrell was speaking out of the side of his mouth. Most of his concentration was on his instruments. "The identity of the Terran was not listed. I presume Logan was interrupted before he could complete it."

Riley ignored the pilot. She was far more interested in Alec's thoughts and the danger he posed to everyone. To say Alec was on edge was like saying the Big Bang had been a nice light show. Fear, anger, impotence, boastfulness, and relief: all there, waiting for the moment to explode. He was practically humming with power.

A red hexagon on the screen to Tyrell's right blossomed into crimson brightness. The myriad lines and symbols moving both diagonally and horizontally across the screen were unintelligible but the bright scarlet needed no interpretation.

"What's that?" Riley pointed.

Tyrell brushed her hand away from in front of his face. He didn't answer. A woman behind them did.

"Another one, eight-eight-eight," the Tyon barked. She sounded worried.

Tyrell muttered something under his breath before waving his hands over the screen and what Riley assumed were the ship's controls, in a wild manner. She grabbed the back of his chair just in time.

The ship careened crazily, first to the right, then the left, pitching upwards at an angle that sent most of them falling to the floor. Alec reacted by grabbing onto the closest thing to him: her. One arm swung around her waist and the other grabbed the back of Tyrell's chair. The force yanked them backwards as the little craft strained forward. Riley's feet momentarily left the floor. The ship dropped back into position with a jarring thud. She lost her grip on the chair but luckily Alec didn't. Riley grabbed Alec to keep from being flung into Tyrell's back and onto the control panel. Her face mashed into his chest and she grunted as her nose hit his breastbone with an uncomfortable smack.

Behind them, only Kholar had managed to stay upright.

260

Riley caught a glimpse of Paran, a scowl etched across his granite features, pulling himself to his feet. His orb glowed a sickly orange between his clenched fingers.

"They're appearing more frequently, sir." Tyrell's voice was tense. His hands were still waving over the screens but the ship had settled back to normal although the speed seemed to have slowed down even further. "I believe Ennis is correct. This is purposeful."

The instant the floor levelled, Alec's hand dropped away like Riley was radioactive. In that instant she considered kicking him in the shins.

"Maintain evasive actions," Kholar said. His expression remained implacable but Riley felt the anger beneath the surface. "Sensors, focus on the source of the emanations. Calculate occurrence and relate to probability factors."

"Engaged," said one of the Tyons.

"If the Others are throwing rips at us, we haven't a chance," Ennis said so quietly to his co-pilot that Riley barely heard him.

"Why not?" Riley queried with a gasp. "You do have force fields and stuff that repel rips, don't you?"

No one replied. Ennis focused intently on his instruments.

"Don't you?" Riley raised her voice.

"What is a force field?" Kholar gave her a look that could have pickled cucumbers at twenty paces. "Do you have technology that can repel a time/space anomaly?"

"Hey, you're the ones with the advanced technology," Riley snapped back. "I'm the Earth-born kidnap victim. *You* guys are the aliens with warp drive and phasers."

"I am unfamiliar with the terms warp drive and force field, but I understand your question. We do not have the capability of repelling or eradicating a rip. Our information suggests that no civilization does. Nor does our intelligence suggest that rips purposefully attack anything." He spoke the last few words at Ennis. "Our best defense against this unprecedented incidence of rips is to monitor for their existence and evade them."

"The best defense is a good offence," Riley said.

"Explain," Anna spoke from behind her.

Riley couldn't help but jump. She'd forgotten all about Anna but it all came flooding back. She took a deep breath. One thing at a time. "Ennis is right. They are after us. Rips do that. If you don't know it, then your information is out of date." Kholar's eyes narrowed but Riley plunged on. She had no choice. "You can either run from them and hope they don't get you, or you fight back."

"There is no method of fighting a rip," Kholar stated.

"There's a third option," Riley insisted.

"Inform us, Terran," Tyrell ordered as he again tilted the ship to avoid the rips, which were now acting as depth charges and surrounding them. "We have limited time."

"Disappear." Riley waited for a moment as the silence that greeted her instructions stretched uncomfortably. "Oh, come on, you guys do it all the time." She held up her orb. "Poof. You go somewhere else. Move the target, people."

Kholar shook his head. "We cannot abandon this ship. Without transport we cannot leave this planet."

"Yeah, well, unless you can outrun the rips, which seem to be increasing in number every five seconds," Riley said as a Sensor announced the location of yet another rip, "then you've got no option. We hit one of those things and it punches a hole in the side of the ship pretty darn quick. We're under water. I don't know about you but I only breathe air."

262   "Logic dictates that we keep the ship and remove ourselves from danger. There is no evidence that the time/space anomalies are attacking us nor is there historical experience of this," Kholar stubbornly replied. "Tyrell, remove us from this area of increased rip production to somewhere safer."

"Yes, sir."

Riley stamped her foot. These people were so thick it hurt. "Ty, how many rips have we avoided?"

"Fifteen," Tyrell said as he tipped the ship to the left and quickly righted it again.

"Plot their locations."

Tyrell gave Kholar a quick look but his hands flew over the console and instantly the screen indicated with glowing red hexagons the fifteen rips and the path of the ship. It was obvious to anyone with eyes the hexagons had clustered along the path the ship took. As they watched, another hexagon winked into existence directly in front of the ship. Tyrell took evasive action while a Sensor announced the co-ordinates in the background.

"See?" Riley pointed. "Coincidence? Not likely. They're after us."

The lighting on the ship suddenly switched to a dark red. The screen in front of Tyrell was instantly ablaze with a dozen new hexagons, completely surrounding the ship. The Sensors shouted out several co-ordinates, none actually audible over Riley and Ennis's shouts of shock.

Ennis and Tyrell both made wildly complicated movements with their hands. The ship came to a shuddering, abrupt stop and everyone was pitched forward. Riley lurched into the back of Tyrell's chair and someone slammed into her from behind with enough force to knock the wind out of her. She pulled herself upright and looked around. Behind her, the Sensors were holding their orbs over their heads and the pulsing yellow glow they emitted was so bright Riley had to shield her eyes. Alec was holding onto Tyrell's chair with white knuckles. He was staring straight ahead as if seeing something the rest of them couldn't.

263

Riley gave his arm a quick shove to get his attention. Any minute now.

Kholar held up his hand and the room instantly was

silent. "The Others have us surrounded."

Tyrell pointed to the screen. "They're below and above us. There is no way to maneuver out of this. If they move towards us, they'll contact the hull of the ship. The breach will be instantaneous."

"Are they moving?" Kholar asked as he leaned over Tyrell's shoulder.

"Momentarily stationary," Tyrell responded.

There was a subdued murmuring from the occupants of the ship. Riley swallowed the lump in her throat. She inched closer to Alec, leaning over Tyrell's chair.

"Suggestions, sir?" Tyrell's eyes never left the screen in front of him. Ennis gave a covert look over his shoulder at the commander but said nothing.

The glowing hexagons ominously seemed to get larger the longer Riley looked at the screen. Was it possible the rips were growing in size? She bit her lip. There was no way she was ending up inside a rip again and she wasn't too keen on drowning with a sudden hull breach either. The ship lurched slightly again as the water surrounding them fell into the rips. There was a distant roaring of turbulence. Riley's hand slipped off the chair and she grabbed Tyrell's shoulder to prevent falling. If they didn't do something soon, they wouldn't have to worry about the rips touching the ship; it would be sucked into one.

"I think—" she began, but Kholar cut her off.

"Terrans do not give orders on my ship."

"Fine." Riley clamped her lips tightly and muttered under her breath. "Drown then." She snuck a look at Alec. He wasn't paying any attention to her. His eyes were glazed and he was almost panting. Whatever was going on in his head, Riley had to get his attention. She leaned subtly against him, then elbowed him in ribs. He didn't blink. There might be only minutes left. She nudged him again, harder this time. No response.

"The Terran is right, Kholar," Anna spoke quietly over

Riley's shoulder. "We must abandon this vessel and teleport to safety. Another craft can be obtained."

Kholar gave her a dark look. "It is inadvisable to leave this ship. The data on board cannot be replaced."

"Data transfer," Anna suggested. She pulled the crystal on the chain around her neck out from inside her coveralls. "I can store it here." Riley had only glimpsed the pendant before. It was a colourless, cylindrical crystal nearly the length and thickness of her index finger and glowed with an uncomfortable light that sent shivers down Riley's spine. It wasn't an orb crystal, she instinctively knew, but it was strong with Tyon properties and something else, even more alien. Riley noticed that Ennis quickly looked away from Anna and even Tyrell shifted slightly away.

Kholar gave a sharp shake of his head. "It is not necessary. There is another solution."

"Name it," Anna challenged.

"Tyrell, plot the path out of this cluster of rips. Immediately."

Tyrell shook his head. "Impossible. The rips occupy every possible configuration. They are moving towards us now. Slowly. Initial impact in sixty."

Even Riley could see the hexagons inching their way closer to the ship on the screen. She gulped. Sixty seconds or sixty minutes, either way it didn't matter. They were toast. Time to get out of there.

She leaned as close to Alec as she could without being obvious. She tugged on his overalls. "Get ready," she hissed. But Alec gave no indication that he had heard her or understood the message. Riley gritted her teeth in frustration. She didn't have the strength to move them, only Alec did. What was wrong with him?

She reached out and touched Alec's skin. The usual link to his thoughts was not there. Riley gripped harder and grasped at her own orb with her free hand to boost the connection. Nothing happened. Alec didn't even blink.

What was going on?

Anna pushed herself in front of Riley, standing only inches from Kholar. Without thinking about what she was doing, Riley let go of Alec and reached out and touched Anna with a finger, just enough to establish contact. It was enough. Anna's voice was low and tense and Riley doubted that anyone else heard the conversation. It was the contact and her orb that boosted the sound of Anna's words enough for Riley to hear.

"I will not jeopardize this mission," Anna hissed. "Give me the key to download the data."

"The data stays on the ship. No one has access," Kholar said.

"I must have it. This ship will be breached and we will all die."

"Teleport out," Kholar replied. "Take the Terran boy with you. Meet me at the predetermined co-ordinates."

"What will you do?" Anna glanced at the screen and frowned.

"What I must."

Anna looked back at the company of Tyons, then back at Kholar. Riley felt her anger but noted how controlled her voice was, even as her words were dynamite. "Most of the Operatives here cannot teleport. Will you leave them to die?"

Kholar's shrug said it all. "Prepare to leave with the boy. Ensure his safety at all cost."

Anna nodded once. She reached out and took hold of Alec's arm. Alec didn't seem to notice. Anna pulled him off to the side of the room and he followed passively. Worriedly, Riley followed, slipping in behind Alec like a shadow, her fingers crossed that Anna wouldn't notice. Anna led the way along the wall to the first corridor, the same that she and Kholar had disappeared down only a few minutes before. She turned the corner without giving the company a glance of goodbye. Alec trundled passively behind her.

Riley looked back. Tyrell was still waving his hands over the console but even this far away she could see the hexagons indicating the dangerous rips continuing to advance. They were almost touching the ship. Dean was not in sight. Several Tyons were looking nervously at the screen and at each other. Whether they knew Kholar had signed their death warrants wasn't obvious but several were fingering their orbs with trembling fingers.

Riley gritted her teeth and ducked down the corridor behind Alec as silently as possible. She tried to clamp down on her emotions. Anna was adept at mind reading and would sense the kind of anger that was boiling under her skin a mile away. Hoping that Dean and Tyrell—he had saved her life after all—would manage to teleport out at the last minute, she focused solely on keeping quiet and out of Anna's sight, yet close enough to grab Alec the second they started to teleport to safety.

"I know you are behind us," Anna said as they turned the corner. She didn't bother to look back at Riley.

"Yeah, well, where Alec goes, I go." Riley ran the few steps and caught up with the two of them. Noting Alec's blank look, she slipped her hand into his and tightened her fingers around his. He didn't squeeze back.

"Afraid not," Anna said. She stopped. They were now out of sight of the main room. Riley's heart began a rapid tattoo inside her ribs.

"I'm not planning on dying here on this stupid ship, Anna. Take me with you."

Anna cocked her head slightly. She pulled out the crystal pendant from around her neck. It swung free for a moment, catching the red glints from the overhead lights and reflecting them towards Riley. If there was any emotion behind her eyes, Riley couldn't see it. "There is no reason for me to save your life. Alec is the one required. Your power is limited and ordinary. Potentials such as yourself are common. Your death is not significant."

"Thanks a bunch," Riley spat. If only Darius was here to see that she was right about Anna all along.

"Let go of Alec's hand, Riley."

"No."

"As you say on this planet, suit yourself." Anna grabbed the pendant with her free hand and raised it to shoulder height. There was no time to react. The blast hit Riley squarely between the eyes.

The Others spoke inside Alec's head. Rhozan and maybe others, it was hard to tell. Every time Alec thought he was hearing them clearly enough to decipher what they were muttering about, something would change, like the tone, or the words, or the level of sound. It was puzzling and frustrating. Alec knew there was something he *absolutely* had to hear, but for the life of him he couldn't quite make it out. He wished that everyone around him on the ship would shut up and let him concentrate. He was dimly aware of someone holding his hand and a tiny part of his mind was tugging at his consciousness trying to gain his attention, but the compulsion to block everything out and figure out what the Others were saying was far stronger.

40

He hadn't heard them in the Base or the tunnels below. But as the ship disengaged from the underground port and flung itself into the deep ocean in a mad scramble to escape the island's collapse, the first tentative whispers had begun. At first, he'd been too absorbed with the residual panic of escaping the tunnels and the realization that rips were following their flight to freedom, but as the minutes passed, the whispering got louder. His attention had been momentarily averted twice. Once when Tyrell dropped the bomb that a Terran had contact with the Others and his sudden fear of discovery had blocked out the sound and taken precedence. The second time occurred when he'd had to grab onto Riley to prevent her from falling. For a heartbeat or so, with her warmth in his arms, the whispering ceased. It had rebounded double in strength a second later and he'd shoved her away in an attempt to hear the voices more clearly.

Now the voices were just out of range, as if he was at the back of his old math classroom and Mr. Thompson was speaking to the board instead of the thirty students, most of whom couldn't care less about the lesson. He was getting angry. This was ridiculous. He had to hear what the Others were saying.

He slipped his hand into his pocket and gripped his orb in an unconscious gesture. The voices instantly stopped. The silence was deafening. He felt as if he'd woken up from a long sleep. He looked around.

Anna was holding his arm in a grip that was almost painful. They weren't in the main room of the ship anymore. He was leaning up against the wall in a narrow hallway of gleaming brown metal and the ambient lighting was a dull, frightening red. Riley was sprawled on the floor at his feet. Her fingers were still entwined with his but lifeless. He tugged at her but her eyes didn't open and she didn't seem to notice.

"What's the matter with—" he got no further.

"She tried to injure you," Anna interrupted. She reached over and pulled Riley's limp fingers from Alec's grip. Riley's arm dropped to the floor. "We don't have time. We must leave."

Alec frowned. He couldn't remember what had been going on but he doubted that Riley would have tried to hurt him in any way. For one thing, she was so small. Even a well-placed kick wouldn't do much more than bruise him.

"Anna, she wouldn't…," he started. "You must be mistaken."

"I am not. She tried to inform Kholar of your abilities," Anna spoke urgently. Alec's stomach dropped. "She is jealous of your skill. You must know this. I managed to stop her speaking to him in time but she followed us to this corridor and threatened to tell everyone on this ship you can shift in time. I had to silence her."

Alec couldn't believe his ears. He knew that Riley was pissed he was stronger and more capable. She hadn't actually tried to hide it. But would she go as far as to jeopardize his life?

"You do not believe me," Anna said in response to his frown. "I understand. You have feelings for this female. However, I speak the truth."

"Wake her up and I'll ask her." Alec tried to tug his arm away from Anna but her grip was stronger than he expected and he wasn't able to fully pull away. "I can't believe for a second she'd try and get me killed."

Anna glanced upwards at the ceiling. A look of fear crossed her face for a second. "There is no time. We must leave."

"Where are we going?"

"This ship is about to be destroyed. We must teleport to safety."

"Destroyed by what?" Alec gasped.

"The Others. They are searching for you. Any moment they will contact this ship and the hull breach will cause massive instantaneous collapse."

Cripes. Alec reeled. He had no idea things had gotten so bad. Why didn't he know what was going on? The last few minutes were completely blank. What had he been doing? Puzzled, he reached down towards Riley's hand. It didn't matter now. He'd sort things out later. Now, he and Riley had to get off this ship. Immediately.

Anna grabbed his wrist before he could make contact with Riley's fingers. "You must not. She cannot come with us."

"She has to. You just said the ship was going to be destroyed," Alec cried. He tugged but he couldn't break her grip on either his wrist or his other arm. He wrenched himself as hard as he could but her hold on him didn't budge.

"Anna," he began, "this is crazy. I'm not leaving her."

"I will not transport someone who risks your life. She has turned against you, Alec. Her loyalties are with the Others. Only I can protect you."

"No, Anna, don't," Alec yelled.

Too late. Before the last word was completely out of his mouth, Anna began the teleportation process. Alec's stomach dropped to his knees with horror. He didn't have time to shout a warning to Riley, kick her awake or *anything*. The ship around him slipped away and he was sucked into the uncomfortable sensations of in and out, through and around that accompanied moving in space. A horrible wrenching sensation erupted inside him, as if part of himself was being pulled out and left behind. It was a completely new and highly uncomfortable sensation. There was something completely wrong about it too. He reacted instinctively. Mentally he gathered his resources. He aimed at the source of the pull. He had to stop whatever it was that was tearing him apart and get back to Riley. He could overcome Anna, he just had to.

Anna stopped him. How she managed to connect inside his head, Alec didn't know. Suddenly, her presence was everywhere. He fought as hard as he could but he didn't know the trick to getting her out. She was too strong, too forceful. Reeling, Alec's mental defenses crumbled underneath the onslaught.

The world around them winked into existence but Alec paid no attention. He fell to his knees, hands clasping his head, ill beyond description. His forehead hit the ground. Everything tilted wildly around him. Bile rose in his throat. He retched.

Someone's cool hands stroked his forehead and pulled him against a shoulder. Alec squeezed his eyes shut from the glare of bright lights and leaned into the soothing presence next to him. He felt awful.

Slowly the illness passed. The dizziness subsided and the urge to throw up lessened. The pounding behind his eyes dropped to a dull roar. Gently, he pulled himself away from the person who was cradling him and blinked several times.

41

A blond woman, pale and regal-looking withdrew her arms. Her smile was gentle and warm. "How do you feel, Alec?" she asked.

"Kinda sick," Alec said quietly. Even moving his mouth to speak made him feel queasy. "What happened?"

"You were ill. The effects of the attack, I'm afraid." The woman stood up and looked around. Alec remained on his knees at her feet. His fingers tugged at the long grass beneath him. It was too bright to look around properly. "Fortunately, she did not cause any permanent harm."

"Who didn't?" Alec's brain was muddled. He had no real recollection of what had just happened. The blond woman looked familiar but he couldn't quite place her.

"Riley." The blond woman touched Alec's hair in a stroking fashion. "You knew her briefly. Another Terran, taken over by the Others to do their bidding. I was fortunate enough to stop her in time."

Alec struggled to remember. The name Riley was familiar. He couldn't quite picture her. The Others were familiar too. A shudder of fear coursed down his back at the mention of that name. "I'm sorry," he said, glancing up at the blond woman. "I can't remember who you are."

"I am Anna, your Guardian," the woman replied. In her right hand she was holding something on a chain. She held out her left. "Try to stand up, Alec. We have a ways to go."

A warm sense of companionship, and something more primitive and urgent, filled Alec's heart the second he clasped her hand. Now he remembered her. Trusted her. Loved her. Of course she'd saved him. She always did. He got unsteadily to his feet.

He cracked open his eyes. He was standing on a high rocky hill, overlooking the ocean. A heavy bank of grey clouds was off to his left but directly overhead the sun was high and bright. Seagulls swooped above, their plaintiff cries echoing over the age-worn cliffs. A brisk breeze, laden with sea smells tugged at his hair and overalls. There was nothing civilized in any direction: no buildings, no airplanes, no boats. Alec had no inkling of where he was, but it didn't matter. Anna was with him.

"Where are we?" he asked.

"Newfoundland," she replied. "Shortly transport will arrive and we will leave this planet."

274   The idea of leaving Earth didn't faze Alec for a moment. He felt numb and disoriented and couldn't be sure that leaving was something out of the ordinary. Everything inside his mind was so jumbled, it was hard to sort through what was memory and what was imagination. He struggled for a

moment against an unwillingness to try and think about her. "And this Riley person, what happened to her?"

"She and her accomplice, Darius Finn, were captured," Anna replied. She let go of the crystal pendant around her neck and the sun caught the prisms inside turning it to millions of microscopic rainbows. She raised a hand over her eyes and peered back down the hill towards the wind-stunted shrubs, rocks, and grass. Far below them, the valley was blanketed by the approaching clouds' shadows.

"They were working together and were a danger to you and the mission you serve. They joined forces to attack you and render you incapable of completing your mission. They managed to injure your mind, hence your memory difficulties. It was fortunate that I intervened. Now you do not have to worry any longer, Alec."

Alec frowned. The names were familiar and tugged at him somewhere deep inside his mind but the more he tried to remember them, the more uncomfortable he felt. He shuddered.

"Why not? Won't they try again?"

"I have taken care of it as I always do," Anna replied. She reached out a finger and traced a path across Alec's forehead, erasing the worries in his mind with her touch. "They cannot hurt you any longer. Both of them are dead."

ACKNOWLEDGMENTS

I'm a very fortunate person. My husband has always been very encouraging of my aspiration to be a writer and pushed me to stop dreaming about it and make it a reality. My parents fostered the belief I could do anything I wanted, and my children seem to believe it too. I'm surrounded by wonderful friends who cheer me on with every step in the journey towards getting published. Even my dogs don't mind the hours I sit typing.

I've also been lucky that my provincial writer's association (WANL) granted me a mentor, who was tough (but correct) in reviewing the first draft of the first book of this series. My editors at Breakwater (Annamarie Beckel – who nursed the first book through a second complete revision – and James Langer, editor for this second book) were both nurturing and instructive and I owe them a debt of gratitude for taking a chance on me.

Despite the fact there is a very limited number of books published every year and competition to be one of those books is fierce, I have yet to meet one author (even those in the stratosphere of success) who hasn't been encouraging and welcoming. They are too numerous to mention here, but I remember *every single one of you.*

Photo by C Kovacs

SUSAN MACDONALD's, *Edge of Time*, the first book
in *The Tyon Collective* series, won The Moonbeam Award
(US) for best young-adult science fiction. She is married,
has two children, two dogs, a fluctuating number of
goldfish, and lives in St. John's, Newfoundland.
www.susan-macdonald.com